THE LONG AND WINDING ROAD

ROAD

BUTLER, VERMONT SERIES, BOOK 9

MARIE FORCE

The Long and Winding Road
Butler, Vermont Series, Book 9
By: Marie Force

Published by HTJB, Inc.
Copyright 2023. HTJB, Inc.
Cover Design by Kristina Brinton
E-book Layout: E-book Formatting Fairies
ISBN: 978-1958035016

The Green Mountain and
Butler, Vermont Series

Join the Green Mountain/Butler, Vermont Series Reader Group
at *facebook.com/groups/GreenMountainSeries.*

PROLOGUE

*D*ear Cletus,
 Hope this finds you doing well and enjoying your daughter's cooking as much as I enjoy my daughter's. Why'd we resist moving in with them for so long anyway? I gotta say the service around the barn is pretty darned good and includes laundry that smells fresher than a spring day. My Molly dotes on me and seems to love every minute of it, so I let her do her thing. She loves to mess with Linc by waiting on me hand and foot while telling him to take care of himself. Whatever she brings to me, I ask for a second one for my buddy Linc. It's rather entertaining! I love having the dogs, Ringo and George, underfoot, too, although Molly is forever yelling at them not to trip me. They wouldn't do that to me. I'm always sneaking them treats when Molly isn't looking. They're my buddies. They're getting on in years, but they still have lots of energy, so we hope they'll be with us for a long time to come.

 I take care of the pups when Molly and Linc are off on one of their getaways, usually with Linc's siblings. I'm so glad he's spending so much time with them these days. He's all but retired and turned the reins over to Hunter, who juggles CEO and CFO roles masterfully, as only he could do. He's hired some more help in the accounting department, which has allowed him to handle both jobs. We're very proud of the direction the kids

1

have taken the family business. It's in very good hands with Hunter, Will, Ella, Charley and Wade running the show, with lots of help from Cameron, Lucy, Emma, Mia, Amanda, Dani and many others in the office, store and warehouse. The catalog has been a huge success, growing the business at a staggering rate. The kids are planning to open two more locations in Stowe and Rutland over the next couple of years. People still come to town all the time looking for the gorgeous "models" in the catalog, also known as my grandkids, most of whom are now married with children. The best was when a woman chased Will around the grocery store after she recognized him from the catalog. He didn't think that was funny, but the rest of us sure did!

I'm glad to hear you're enjoying your new home, too. I'm sure it's not the same living in Maine, which is like a foreign country to us Vermonters! Hopefully, you can come visit sometime. We've got lots of empty bedrooms here in the barn, and you're welcome to stay. Although, we've always got a little one sleeping over, or so it seems. And there are a LOT of little ones —forty-one great-grands at last count. Can you believe that? Eighteen kids had forty-one kids (although we acquired a few through marriage and other situations—they all count), and they're not done yet!

Hannah's son Henry just got engaged to a lovely young woman named Emerson, who we absolutely adore. They grew up together here in Butler but met up in Boston at a Red Sox game. The rest, as they say, is history. Jackson is engaged to Autumn, who he met when he was in Wyoming. He's living out in Jackson Hole with her, so we don't know her all that well yet, but she seems like a peach. Sarah, my youngest granddaughter, is dating a wonderful guy named Nathanial, who more than holds his own with the family, which, as you can imagine, is essential to his success.

As for the rest of them, they're married and having babies and working and making us proud every day. Molly had to make a spreadsheet with all the kids' names and their birthdays so we wouldn't forget. I've got that printed out here next to me, so I won't overlook anyone. In a funny aside, even with all the space in the barn, Linc had no choice but to add on to the dining room so we could keep having Sunday dinners during the baby boom. For now, the addition is set up with high chairs and booster seats, but it'll convert as the little people get older.

I'll start with Molly's family. Hunter and Megan have three kids, Carson, 5, Cory, 3, and Claire, 2. Megan is still running the diner, and somehow, she and Hunter make it look easy to manage the businesses while raising three kids. Hannah and Nolan have Ms. Callie (real name Caleb, for Hannah's late first husband), who is 6, and a son named Colby, who'll be 5 soon. They're both a couple of pistols like their mother and are as obsessed with moose as she is. Hannah takes care of Hunter and Megan's kids while they're at work, which has been great for both families. Hunter and Hannah are still the best of friends like they've been from day one. Hannah and Nolan finally built the gorgeous post-and-beam house he'd been dreaming of for years on the property his grandfather left him.

"Baby" Dexter the moose is now fully grown and has his own "moose house" that Nolan had built for him out of desperation when letting Dex sleep in front of the fireplace was no longer feasible. That moose is like a pet dog to their family and is best friends with their dog, Homer Junior. Fred still comes for playtime every afternoon, the highlight of their day. He's getting on in years, but that doesn't slow him down. He's still strolling through town like he owns the place, which he probably does by now. In another unbelievable development, Nolan's father, Vernon, has gotten himself sober and is actively involved in the lives of Nolan and his family—and even helps at the garage when Nolan needs him. It's done my heart good to see those two mending fences and for Vernon to get his life back. I must admit... I never thought it would happen, and I'm very happy to have been proven wrong.

Anyway, where was I? Will and Cameron have Chase, who's almost 6, and Molly, 3, and recently had a surprise baby boy they named Murphy, which is Cam's maiden name. Will said that the C names had to stop eventually, and he wanted to name his daughter after his mother and the new little guy after Cam's family. Our little Molly is as sweet as her grandma and is crazy about her brothers and their pups. Chase and Molly are thrilled about their new baby brother, as are the rest of us since Will and Cam had said they were quitting with two. You gotta love a surprise!

Speaking of surprises, you probably read about this in the paper… Cameron's dad, Patrick Murphy, married our beloved Mary Larkin in Paris about four years ago and sent us a picture with the news. Will and Cam, those sneaky devils, managed to get there with Chase to celebrate with the happy couple. We had a big reception for them back here in Butler the following summer, and we see a lot of them when they come up from the city to visit the grandkids. Cameron says her dad barely notices her when the kids are in the room, but she loves seeing him as a doting grandfather. He's cut way back on work so he and Mary can travel and enjoy life. He's shared with me before that he regrets not spending more time with Cam when she was growing up. If you ask me, he's making up for that with the time and attention he gives those babies. It's very sweet to see.

Ella and Gavin have Sarah, almost 6, the other Caleb, almost 5, as well as Cecilia aka Cici, 2. Interestingly, Caleb is a twin to his late Uncle Caleb at the same age. I think it brings Gavin some comfort to see his beloved brother in the little boy he named after him. His logging business is booming, and they're building a new house on a lot they bought outside of town a couple of years ago. Gavin's parents are still running the Capt. Caleb M. Guthrie Inn for the widowed spouses of servicemembers. Even with the country not at war, you'd be surprised how many still come through the doors seeking the solace they offer. Amelia and Bob love being grandparents to Gavin's kids as well as Hannah's.

In a sad twist of fate, Charley and Tyler took in his nieces Kendall, 7, and Maisy, 9, after their parents were killed in a helicopter accident while on vacation in the Grand Canyon. Our Charley always said that she had no desire to get married or have kids, but she sure does love Tyler, and those sweet girls have earned a place in all our hearts. She's been a wonderful support to them as they adjust to the changes in their lives and deal with unimaginable grief. We're so proud of Charley and Tyler for what they're doing for the girls, who've become such a special part of our family.

Wade and Mia have Carlee, 5, and Corbin, 3, who are just the sweetest kids. Wade is still running the health and wellness line at the store, and Mia works very part time at the warehouse, mostly during the holiday rush. They finally finished renovating their farmhouse, and it's a gem. Of course she loves having her dad, Cabot, here now that he's married to Wade's cousin Isabella, but more on them below.

Lucy and Colton installed indoor plumbing and added on to their cabin up on the mountain shortly after the arrival of Christian, 5. They're also the parents to twin boys, Camden and Cooper, age 3. All three boys are just like their father, much to Lucy's dismay. They prefer to be naked, and she's constantly chasing them around to put clothes on them, even in the dead of winter. The rest of us think it's hysterical, but she's not as amused! She's a good sport to put up with Colton and his "feral spawn," as she refers to her offspring. Colton is still running the sugaring facility on the mountain with Max's help, and they broke all our previous records for ounces of maple syrup bottled this season.

Lucas and Dani have Savannah, now 7, as well as Sawyer, 4, and Sienna, 2. Dani is still running our warehouse and juggling work and family with aplomb, while Lucas has risen to the rank of captain at the fire department and continues his wood-working business when he has time. They opened a storefront in town for the furniture he makes as well as the pieces she enjoys rehabbing into works of art. They've done very well with the new venture.

Landon has broken the record for the most kids in their family with Stella, age 17, as well as Sloane, 5, Sarah, 3, and Stefan, 2. Amanda works from home running the catalog division, while Landon is also a captain in the fire department and still managing the Christmas Tree Farm with lots of help from Max.

Speaking of Max, his son, Caden, is about to turn 7, which is so hard to believe. He's in the first grade and doing wonderfully. Reading like a champ and writing paragraphs. They moved into my place when I came to the barn—Max and I joke that we traded bedrooms. I gave him permission to make the house where I was so happy with my Sarah his own, and he's done a marvelous job updating it and turning it into a wonderful home for him and Caden. I continue to hold out hope that he's going to find someone to love and who loves him the way he deserves, but so far, it hasn't happened—not for lack of trying on the part of his father and grandfather. We tell ourselves he's still only 28 and has all the time in the world, but you and I know how fast the years go by without us even realizing it.

Now for Hannah and her family... She's happily remarried to Ray Mulvaney for four and a half years now, which makes Lucy and Colton's kids Hannah's grandchildren, too, since Ray is Lucy's dad. Lucy's sister, Emma, is married to Grayson, Hannah's eldest, and they have Simone, 16, as well as Hannah, 4, Finley, 3, and Rowan, 1, all girls. Grayson has his hands full with five ladies bossing him around, but he loves every minute of it. Emma still works in the office at the store and is, according to Hunter and the others, the nerve center of the whole place, keeping everything running smoothly. Grayson practices law from home and is Mr. Mom to the little ones. Times sure have changed from our day, haven't they? Sarah wouldn't have dared put me in charge of our kids—haha!

Noah and Brianna have his son Elliott, 8, as well as Ethan, 4, and Elias, 2. Their construction-and-renovation business is busier than ever, and the two of them work so well together after their inauspicious start while rebuilding the Butler Inn after the fire. I told you how they fought nonstop until they realized all the fighting was actually attraction, right? We'll always be thankful to Brianna for bringing our Noah back to us and making him so happy. All he does is smile these days.

Izzy and Cabot got married just about five years ago now.

He's so thrilled to be living near his daughter, Mia, who's married to Wade. Izzy and Cabot also have twins, Miles and Madelyn, 4, who are just the cutest kids. Cabot is over the moon with them and fully experiencing every moment of his second chance at fatherhood. We're so happy for them. Izzy is a wonderful mother, but I always knew she would be. Cabot is getting to do fatherhood and grandfatherhood at the same time, and he's content as he can be surrounded by kiddos. He works a little here and there but is mostly retired now.

Vanessa married Troy Kennedy, close friend to Cameron, Lucy and Emma, about four years ago. They live in New York City with three kids, Declan, 3, Bennett, 2, and Alice, six months. Vanessa is a full-time mom, but she helps with Troy's law practice. He does some incredible work in the social justice field and has a thriving business. They get home quite often, which makes her mother—and her grandfather—happy.

Our Alli surprised us when she decided not to wait around for Mr. Right, as she put it, and had two boys on her own, Kingston, 4, and Axel, 2. She still works in marketing in Boston and has a wonderful live-in nanny who helps with the boys while she's working. She seems very happy and settled with her kids. And though she still dates from time to time, she'll tell you it's not a priority. I told you about Jackson, Henry and Sarah above, so that about sums things up for all the grandkids.

It took me three days to type all this, so you'd better write back and tell me what's going on with you and your family. I sure do miss the old days of sitting around drinking coffee and playing checkers with you and Percy at the store and arguing about everything. I miss you and good old Percy since he left us. Do come visit sometime. I'd love to see you.

Sincerely,

Your friend Elmer

The Abbotts

Hunter and Megan: Carson, Cory and Claire
Hannah and Nolan: Caleb "Callie" and Colby
Will and Cameron: Chase, Molly and Murphy
Ella and Gavin: Sarah, Caleb and Cecilia "Cici"
Charley and Tyler: Took in his orphaned nieces, Maisy and
Kendall, ages 9 and 7, after their parents died in an accident
Wade and Mia: Carlee and Corbin
Colton and Lucy: Christian and twins, Camden and Cooper
Lucas and Dani: Savannah "Savvy," Sawyer and Sienna
Landon and Amanda: Stella, Sloane, Sarah, Stefan
Max: Caden

26 grandchildren for Linc and Molly

The Colemans
Grayson and Emma: Simone, Hannah, Finley and Rowan
Noah and Brianna: Elliott, Ethan and Elias
Izzy and Cabot: Mia, Miles and Madelyn
Vanessa and Troy: Declan, Bennett and Alice
Alison: Single mom to Kingston and Axel
Jackson: Engaged to marry Autumn
Henry: Engaged to marry Emerson
Sarah: Dating Nathaniel, expecting engagement any time

15 grandchildren for Hannah + Lucy's 3 for Ray = 18
Elmer Stillman: 41 great-grandchildren

CHAPTER ONE

*"Whereof what's past is prologue; what to come,
in yours and my discharge."* —Shakespeare

"What's the point of a high school reunion when I see most of my classmates on Facebook or Instagram just about every day?" Max asked as he glanced at the invitation that had come to the barn earlier in the week.

"The point," Molly said, "is to see each other *in person.* Remember what that's like?"

"Eh." Max tossed the invite in the trash. "I see who I want to see."

"What's a reunion?" Caden asked as he stuffed ice cream into his face while seated at the table with Grandpa Linc.

"It's a stupid thing that people do to see people they don't really want to see while spending a ridiculous amount of money for something they don't care about," Max told his son.

Out of the corner of his eye, Max saw Linc load another scoop into Caden's bowl. His son lit up with delight, as he usually did when Grandpa Linc spoiled him, which was all the time. Max didn't mind because Caden was a polite, well-behaved child who was the absolute light of Max's life, and if his father wanted to give his son an extra scoop of ice cream, who was Max to stand in the way of that kind of bonding?

"Sounds dumb," Caden said.

"See? Even Caden thinks it's dumb."

"I think you should go," Molly said as she finished loading the dishwasher. "You never know who you might run into."

"Why are you acting all mysterious? What do you know?"

"Nothing," Molly said, laughing. "I just have a feeling that you should go. Besides, when was the last time you had a night out with friends? It's been ages."

"I have a night in with my best friend every night."

"Max, that's lovely," his mother said, "and you know we think you're a wonderful father, but you need to take some time for yourself, too."

"I like things just the way they are. My buddy and I have everything we need, don't we, Cade?"

"Yep. We got stuff to make pizza tomorrow night, and that's my favorite."

"I can't imagine anything better on a Friday night than making pizza with my best pal," Max said.

"Your mother is right," Linc said, "and you know how it pains me to admit that."

Molly snorted with laughter. "That's because I'm right all the time."

"Yes, dear." Linc gave his wife an indulgent smile. "About the reunion, though, I think you ought to go. Your mother pushed me to go to my fiftieth reunion, and we had the best time. Remember?"

"I do remember," Max said.

"I reconnected with so many old friends, people I used to enjoy who I hadn't seen in fifty years. To be honest, I'd forgotten about most of them until they were standing right in front of me, reminding me of the good fun we used to have. It was a great night, and I think you'd enjoy yours more than you think."

"It's one night," Elmer said as he joined them, "and right here in town. If it's lame, you can leave."

Max was smart enough by now to understand when he was outmatched and outnumbered. "Fine, if you guys want me to go so badly, I'll do it, but I bet I'm home and in bed by nine."

"Care to make it interesting?" Molly asked as she began preparing for their annual Thanksgiving pie-making marathon.

"How so?"

"I'll bet you a hundred dollars you're still out at midnight." She extended her hand. "What do you say?"

Max shook her hand. "Be prepared to pay up."

"You're going to be paying me."

"I guess we'll see, won't we?"

HOW IN THE HELL HAD HE LET HIS PARENTS AND GRANDFATHER talk him into attending a reunion he didn't give two shits about? The last thing he felt like doing the day after Thanksgiving and following a ten-hour workday was attend a high school reunion.

Ten years.

Max had to admit he found that hard to believe. How in the hell had he been out of high school for *ten years*? He'd done a lot of living in that decade, completing college at UVM in Burlington, becoming a father at twenty-two and then transitioning to single fatherhood when Chloe, Caden's mother, bailed out shortly after his birth. Max's entire life was set up to accommodate his son, and he liked it that way.

Caden was amazing—a happy, sunny, funny, sweet miracle. Every day, he did or said something new, something that made Max cry laughing or want to weep from the sheer joy he brought to every minute.

He would so much rather be making pizza with him than trying to figure out what to wear to a reunion he didn't care about. And it had cost *a hundred bucks*. For a crappy buffet at the Grange. Ridiculous. He and Caden could do a lot of skiing on Butler Mountain for a hundred bucks.

In his current mood, Max would probably be better off staying home than inflicting himself on his former classmates, but there was that wager he'd made with his mom. He didn't need to be out *another* hundred bucks over this stupid event, so he put on jeans and a sweater and got into the dark green F-150 he'd bought new three years ago to head into town.

Caden was spending the night at the barn with three grand-parents who'd spoil him rotten. Knowing his son was safe and happy, Max decided to at least try to enjoy having a night to himself. That didn't happen very often, which was fine with him. Was there something wrong with preferring the company of his son over just about anyone else?

He had to admit his mother might have a point about how one-track Max's life had become since Caden was born. His days revolved around work at the sugaring facility and Christmas Tree Farm and whatever his son wanted or needed. That was about the extent of it. Having their huge family around kept things interesting. There was always a get-together or a birthday party or something going on in the family between their Sunday dinners that had gotten so big, his parents had added on to their already enormous house to make space for everyone in the dining room.

Life was good. Did he occasionally experience a pang of jealousy being around so many happily married siblings and cousins? Sure, but it wasn't like he was lonely or anything. How could anyone be lonely in his family?

It was only sometimes, after Caden had gone to bed and the rest of the evening stretched before him with nothing much to do, that Max wished for someone to share his life with. Those feelings tended to pass as quickly as they came, however. At some point over the last few years, he'd quit dating or bothering to hook up for the sake of hooking up. He just couldn't make himself care enough to bother with any of it. Which meant it'd been a long time since he'd gotten laid. So long that he couldn't remember the last time.

Caden's kindergarten teacher had asked him out on the last day of school after a year of subtle flirting. They'd had a nice dinner, great conversation and a few laughs, but at the end of the night, he'd seen her home and declined her offer to spend the night.

Jessica was a great person, a gorgeous woman who should've been everything he wanted in a partner, but again, he just hadn't felt that special something for her.

That seemed to be his lot in life, to miss out on the *thing* that everyone around him had seemed to find so effortlessly. Well, that wasn't entirely true. It'd taken effort, some starts and stops, some heartbreak here and there, but for the most part, his siblings and cousins had made love look easy compared to what'd transpired—or *not* transpired—for Max.

He'd had it once. A very long time ago. So he knew what he was looking for and what it felt like to be truly in love. Thanks to that relationship, he also knew what epic heartbreak felt like, and he wasn't looking to experience that particular hell again any time soon.

Max wondered if he'd see her at the reunion. Would she finally show her face in town after going silent on him and everyone else for most of the time they'd been out of school? And after vowing to stay in touch with him—even though they'd decided to see other people in college—that hadn't happened. When he thought about her, he felt angry and hurt at how she'd checked out of his life and disappeared.

That was the main reason he hadn't gone to his fifth reunion and why he'd resisted this one, too. *She* was the main reason. If she decided to show up, he wasn't sure what he'd say to her, especially if she came with a husband or boyfriend. He'd be hard-pressed to hide the resentment she'd left him with when she disappeared all those years ago. He didn't want to see her, but he hadn't heard any rumblings of her coming to the reunion, and he probably would have if she were planning to be there. News like that traveled fast through a town like Butler.

In addition to his concern about running into *her*, he also wondered what he would tell his classmates about his life since they were last together. That he was still working for the family business and still raising the son they all knew about thanks to social media. After that, what would he have left to say to anyone? Did they give out superlatives at the reunions like they did in high school? If so, he would win the award for most boring first decade out of high school.

He no sooner had that thought than he felt disloyal to Caden. Nothing about being his father was boring or mundane. Fatherhood was the most thrilling experience of Max's life, and he wouldn't trade it for anything, even true love. If people thought his life was boring, then it was probably because they didn't have kids.

Max had made himself good and angry by the time he pulled into the lot at the Grange, which was already packed with shiny sports cars, fancy SUVs and a couple of pickup trucks like his. After flipping down the visor, he took a quick look at his appearance and decided he looked as good as he ever did—as good as he cared to look.

"Whatever," he muttered under his breath before getting out of the truck and heading inside, prepared to cash in on the bet with his mother if it meant he could be home and in bed in two hours.

THE BUFFET WASN'T BAD. IT EVEN INCLUDED SOME OF HIS favorites, including pasta and fried chicken. Maybe he ate like a seven-year-old, but that was easier than making two dinners most nights. He added a salad to feel better about his diet and found a table with an open seat.

"Max Abbott," one of the women said. "I heard you weren't coming!" She was a heavy-set blonde who Max tried desperately to place. She was too far away for him to see her nametag. "It's me, Mary Jane Connor, or, well, it's Foster now. I married Gig Foster."

"Ah, okay. Nice to see you again."

"You look exactly the same," Mary Jane said. "I'd know you anywhere."

"Thanks, you, too."

"Now that is just not true." She cackled with laughter. "Three babies and thirty pounds later, I look nothing like I did in high school."

The others at the table joined the discussion about the childbearing and weight gain and how hard it was to lose the pounds with kids underfoot. He heard Mary Jane say she and Gig lived in Concord, New Hampshire, and rarely got back to

Butler anymore. That explained why he never saw them around town.

"You have a son, right, Max?" Mary Jane asked.

"I do. Caden will be seven this weekend."

"You got an early start," Mary Jane's husband, Gig, said. He'd lost most of his hair in the last ten years.

"I did." Max figured they had the full rundown of how he'd had a son right after he finished college and then had to raise him on his own—with a ton of help from his parents and family — after the baby's mother decided parenthood wasn't for her. He wasn't about to fill in any gaps for them.

"I'm sure you have pictures," another woman said.

Max didn't recognize her either. If he hadn't seen a few people he knew at the registration desk, he might've worried he was at the wrong event.

This was every bit as dreadful as he'd expected it to be.

He glanced at his watch. Seven twenty. No way. He should've gone with his initial impulse and skipped this stupid reunion with people he didn't care about.

"Max?"

A jolt of shock zipped down his spine. He'd know that voice anywhere. As he spun around in his seat, he tried to brace himself to see her again. But all the time in the world couldn't have prepared him for the rush of emotion that overtook him when he took in the sight of his first love.

Lexi Bradshaw.

He stood so quickly, he nearly knocked over his chair.

"Lexi." God, she looked great. Her light brown hair was curly now, but everything else about her was just as he remembered, from the warm hazel eyes to the stunning smile to the button nose and rosy cheeks.

"When Dawn said you were here," she said, "I didn't believe her since I heard you didn't come to the last one."

"I'm here."

She hugged him, and it took his brain five seconds to send the signal to his arms that he should hug her back.

Lexi.

17

"It's so good to see you," she said.

He quickly found that she smelled the same, too, like sweetness and sunshine and everything perfect. "You, too."

Max had so many questions, such as where had she been for the last ten years? He'd tried a few times to find her on social media, but she had no presence there or anywhere as far as he could tell. A Google search had come up empty, too. How did a person not exist online in this day and age? According to Max's mother, her family had moved to Texas and only returned for an occasional visit or ski weekend.

Just as he was about to ask where she'd been, a woman with a camera came at them. "Our class couple back together again! Smile, you guys!"

Max leaned into Lexi and smiled for the camera, but he wished everyone else would go away and leave them alone so he could talk to the only person from high school he'd truly missed. And yes, now that she was standing right next to him, he realized just how much he'd missed her, despite the hurt and confusion she'd caused him with her disappearance.

However, everyone else had missed her, too, so for the next hour, they were surrounded by old friends who'd missed them both.

He barely remembered some of them and had to laugh at how far removed his life was from who and what he'd been in high school. Becoming a single father at twenty-two had sent him in a whole new direction, and even though he still lived in Butler, he felt like he'd traveled a million miles from the innocence of high school in the last ten years.

They talked about things he could barely recall—teachers, classes, specific football games, ski outings and the basketball team's run for the state championship their senior year. As one of the starting forwards on the team, that he remembered. They'd come up one win short, and Max could still taste the bitter regret that had stayed with him and his teammates long after that final loss.

But that wasn't something he dwelled on the way it seemed some of his teammates had. He'd had more important things to think about, such as first-grade homework, karate classes and peanut butter and jelly sandwiches made *only* on white bread with the crusts removed.

"You're quiet," Lexi said.

Most of the group moved to the dance floor when the DJ started playing songs from their graduation year.

"I don't have much to add," Max said. "I barely remember what the school looked like, let alone what table we sat at for lunch."

She gave him a quizzical look that brought back so many memories of spending every possible minute with her once upon a time. "You really don't remember what the school looked like?"

He shook his head. "It's like a blank spot."

"You ought to have that checked."

Laughing, he said, "It's because there're so many things that've happened since then that take up the space in my brain."

"Like what?"

"Did you hear I have a son?"

Her expression conveyed shock. "What? No! When did that happen?"

He told her about Chloe getting pregnant their senior year of college. "Caden is the best thing to ever happen to me. He's… There's not a word big enough to describe him."

"That's amazing, Max. I'm so happy for you. Let me see some pictures."

Did she sound sad after learning he had a son? He pulled out the iPhone that was mostly useless to him in Butler, but it was full of photos of his blond little boy that he shared with Lexi.

"Oh, Max. He's beautiful!"

"I'm completely biased, but I agree. He's also sweet, kind, polite, funny as hell and a great athlete. We have so much fun together."

"I can see why you're madly in love with him."

"I really am. He's like the sun, blinding out everything that isn't him."

"It's very sweet to hear you talk about him. What about his mother? Are you still together?"

Max was surprised she hadn't heard about any of this. Did that mean she'd never bothered to look him up online? "Nope. She stepped out of the picture when he was a few weeks old. It's just been me and Caden ever since. I'm thankful for my huge family every day. My parents and grandfather have been an incredible support to me, and my siblings have, too. I haven't been your typical single parent. We lived with my parents until he was four, but we're on our own now. Mostly." He laughed. "He's with them now."

"I'm sure you're a wonderful father, and Caden is lucky to have you."

"I'm the lucky one. When it first happened… When I found out Chloe was pregnant… I panicked. The relationship had been rocky from the start, and I was just about to graduate from college. We were *so* not ready. Turns out she was more not ready than I was."

"Do you ever hear from her?"

He shook his head. "Not in years."

"God," she said on a long sigh. "How can she bear not to see her own child?"

"I have no idea, but I almost feel sorry for what she's missing, not that I want her back in our lives. I don't. It's just… He's so amazing. Every day is like a new adventure." Max caught himself and grimaced. "Sorry. Don't mean to gush."

"You're not. You're a proud dad and with good reason. Your little boy is adorable."

"He really is. Anyway, enough about me. What've you been up to? You disappeared off the face of the earth. No one knew where you'd gone."

She bit her lip, seeming to think about what she wanted to say. Then she looked at him with the big hazel eyes that used to wreck him back when she was his first love and he'd thought they'd be together forever. "Can we go somewhere else and talk?"

"Sure, let's get out of here."

. . .

LEXI HAD PROMISED HERSELF THAT IF SHE SAW MAX AND HE ASKED where she'd been, she'd tell him the truth. If he didn't seem to care that he hadn't heard from her or about her in years, then she would've left well enough alone. But because he'd asked, she would fill him in, even if reliving the nightmare was the last thing she wanted to do.

As they made their escape, they put up with teasing comments about rekindling their high school romance. They laughed that off and said good night and thank you to the organizers.

"Phew," Max said when they emerged into the chill of encroaching winter.

"Smells like snow," Lexi replied.

"Spoken like a native Vermonter."

"You can take the girl out of Vermont…"

"Did you drive?"

She pointed to a small white car. "That's my rental."

"Want to come with me, and then I'll bring you back to your car later?"

"Sure. That'll work."

"Right this way."

He led her to a shiny dark green pickup truck and held the passenger door for her.

"Nice ride."

"Thanks. I got it a few years ago."

As soon as he started the engine, he turned up the heat.

While they waited for the truck to warm up, Lexi burrowed deeper into the winter coat she'd bought for this trip. She was always cold these days, even when it wasn't thirty degrees outside.

"Where do you want to go?" he asked.

"Is there still nothing open after nine o'clock in Butler?"

"Pretty much."

"And it's too cold to be outside."

"We can go back to my place. Caden is spending the night at the barn."

She didn't want to be nervous about being alone with him,

but her belly was full of the butterflies that reminded her of dating him in high school. "Sure, that'd work."

"I can't recall what condition we left it in. There're probably Legos all over the place."

"That's fine," she said, laughing at the face he made.

"We usually do cleanup before bedtime, but I was in a hurry tonight to get him packed up and over to my mom's." He glanced over at her. "Sorry. You don't care about our routine."

"Sure, I do."

"Eh, it's nothing special, same thing every day, but that's my life."

"Nothing wrong with that."

"It's not what I expected when we left high school."

"You'd talked about wanting to travel."

"Still do, but that's not going to happen for a while."

He took a series of turns that led to a familiar street.

"Do you live at your grandfather's house?"

"I do. He moved in with my parents and offered me his place. Told me to make it my own, so that's what I'm doing one room at a time. It's slow going. It hadn't been updated in decades."

"I remember how cozy it was and how cute your grandparents were together."

"They were so cute. My grandmother died quite some time ago. We still miss her."

"I can't imagine your grandpa without her."

"It was rough at first, but he's found a good groove as a widower. He's not living with my parents because he needs to. My mom wanted to take care of him, and he finally decided to let her."

"That's very sweet. I'm sure she loves doting on him."

"She does, and he enjoys having her cooking for him and doing his laundry. You'd never believe he's going to be ninety-one soon. He's going strong."

"I'm so glad to hear that. I know how much you love him."

"We all love him so, so much."

After a pause in the conversation, Max said, "Where've you been, Lex, and what brought you back to Butler?"

"I live in Houston now," she said, glancing at him. "And I came back for you."

CHAPTER TWO

"Love is lovelier, the second time around." —Sammy Cahn

*M*ax had no idea what to say to that. "You came back for me."

"You were the only one I really wanted to see, and if you hadn't come to the reunion, I was going to try to find you tomorrow."

He shook his head as he tried to figure out what she was saying. "You'll have to fill in some blanks for me."

"Before I do… Could I ask you… You said Caden's mom isn't in the picture, but is there anyone else?"

"Nope."

"How's that possible? You're *Max Abbott.*"

He laughed. "Who does nothing but work and take care of his kid, with family stuff rounding out my life. Other than that, this is pretty much it." He gestured to the house where he and his son had made a home.

"I used to worry that one of the many other girls who wanted you for themselves would take off with you. That's why I was afraid to look for you online. I wouldn't have been able to bear seeing you with someone else."

"Back then, I wasn't going anywhere as long as you were an

option, which you surely knew." He was surprised to see tears in her eyes after he said that. "Come in, Lexi. Let's talk."

He got out of the truck and went around to open her door, holding out a hand to help her down and keep her from slipping on any hidden ice. It was already freezing in the mountains, with the first snow of the season forecasted for the weekend.

When they were inside the warm house, coats off, Max gestured to the sofa. "Can I get you anything? I make my mom's hot chocolate as well as she does, and I've got some Bailey's, too, I think."

"No, thank you. I'm fine."

Max sat next to her and reached for her hand like a decade hadn't passed since the last time he did that. All the anger he'd felt about her disappearing had vanished like mist the minute he set eyes on her again. "Lex... Talk to me."

She looked down at their joined hands and then up at him. "You know I went to UC Berkeley."

"Yes, and I got the emails and texts you sent that first semester. I kept responding to you, but you quit writing back after the holidays."

"I got really sick in the spring semester."

"What kind of sick?"

"The leukemia kind."

"What?" he asked on a long exhale. "You had *cancer*?"

"Have. I *have* cancer, and yes, it's taken a lot of therapy to say those words without breaking down. I've been battling it for ten years. Eighteen months ago, I had a stem cell transplant and have been in remission ever since. But until I hit the five-year mark in remission, I'm not considered cured. And even then..." She shrugged. "It can always come back. I moved to Houston to be treated at MD Anderson. My parents and grandparents moved there, too, and took care of me."

Max was astounded. "Why didn't you tell me what you were going through?"

"I didn't tell anyone, and I asked my family not to either. I didn't want everyone making a big deal of it. I just didn't have

25

the capacity to deal with all that concern while fighting to stay alive. I hope you can forgive me."

"I already have. How're you feeling now?"

"Better than I have in years, and I'm finally allowed to be back out and about, among people." She turned to face him, curling her legs under her the way she used to do. A million memories overtook him as he looked at her, so familiar and yet so different, too. "About what I said about coming for you…"

"Yeah, about that."

She smiled and took his hand again. "During the worst of my illness, I held on so tightly to the memories of us. You kept me going. So many times, when I would've given up, I'd think of you and find the strength I needed to keep going. And I promised myself that if I survived the transplant and achieved lasting remission, the first thing I would do was come see you. Then the invite for the reunion was forwarded from the post office box we keep here, and I took that as a sign. Now or never. I was surprised you were there after I heard you didn't come to the last one."

"There was no one I wanted to see that I don't see around town from time to time."

"Why'd you come this time?"

"I've become such a bore that my parents and grandfather really wanted me to go. My mom even bet me a hundred bucks that I'd have a good time and stay out until midnight."

"I love that," she said, laughing.

"I'll win the bet because I left before midnight, but I'm glad my mom made me go. Seeing you again is worth all the other awkwardness."

"That's nice to hear. I wasn't sure you'd have anything to say to me after I disappeared for so long."

"I'll always have something to say to you. I never forgot you either. I wondered all the time where you were, but no one had heard from you. I figured that's how you wanted it."

"It was necessary at the time."

"I understand that now, and I'm so sorry for what you went through."

"I really can't believe you're still single," she said with a grin. "I figured you'd be married with four kids by now."

"Nah, never came close to getting married. I haven't had an actual girlfriend since Caden's mom, and that was a disaster, other than getting him out of it."

"I still can't believe she left her child."

"I couldn't either, but with hindsight, I wasn't as surprised as I should've been. She was always a bit shallow, which didn't bother me until it affected my son."

"I'd love to meet him."

"I'd love for you to meet him. How long are you here?"

"Until Monday."

"We're having his birthday party at the barn on Sunday if you'd like to come."

"I wouldn't want to intrude on a family thing."

"They'd love to see you."

"I'll only go if you tell me something I can get for Caden."

"He loves to ski more than anything. A day pass to the mountain would thrill him."

"Then that's what I'll do."

"I can't believe you're sitting in my house talking about what to get my son for his birthday."

"It's really nice to be home."

AFTER MAX DROVE HER BACK TO HER CAR AND SHE RETURNED TO the cabin her parents had rented when they gifted her the weekend in Butler, Lexi sent a quick email—since cell service was still nonexistent in her hometown—to her parents and grandparents in Houston to let them know the reunion had been fun, she'd seen Max and had a great time catching up with him.

He invited me to his son's 7th birthday party at the barn on Sunday (he's a single dad). Looking forward to seeing all the Abbotts. It's nice to be back in Butler where nothing ever changes—except the inn! It's been completely rebuilt after a fire a few years ago. It's been modernized, but still retains the historic feel of the original. Today was a great day. Thanks for surprising me with the trip to the reunion. And yes, I feel FINE. Go to bed and quit worrying.

Love, Lex

Her illness had been such a nightmare for so long that they suffered from anxiety that required medication to control. Lexi took hers and pictured her four-person support team in Houston taking theirs. Nothing like a potentially fatal illness to mess up a perfectly lovely life. The five of them were suffering from post-traumatic stress as they transitioned from active treatment to what they hoped would be a long-term remission. Her transplant doctors had told her they had every reason to believe she would live a long and healthy life, but of course they couldn't make any promises. Recurrence was always possible, and that was the reality she and her family now had to live with.

She'd be forever thankful to her parents and grandparents, who'd packed up their lives and moved to Houston to support her through years of harrowing treatments. Her parents had rented out their home in Butler, and those tenants had given notice that they were moving out at the end of the year.

Depending on how this weekend went, Lexi was thinking about returning to her childhood home for a year or so to regroup and see if there was anything left to salvage with the only man she'd ever loved. While she was thrilled to have seen him and caught up with him, she didn't want to put pressure on him to pick up where they'd left off. A lot had changed for both of them in the ten years they'd spent apart.

She ran a brush through hair that had grown back curly, after the third time she'd lost her hair during chemo. Lexi was digging the curls and had no desire to straighten them. She was so thankful to have hair again that it could stick straight up, and she wouldn't care.

Snuggled into old flannel pajamas she'd bought years ago at Max's family's store, Lexi pulled a down comforter over herself and then added the throw blanket from across the foot of the bed. The legacy of treatment was that she was always cold, which might be a problem if she moved back to Vermont. But even that would be worth spending more time with Max.

After seeing him, she couldn't stop smiling. He was even more handsome than he'd been in high school, and that was saying something. Every girl in school had wanted to date him, but he'd shocked the hell out of her when he asked her out in tenth grade and never looked at anyone else for the rest of high school. Leaving him to go to college out West had been brutal, but she'd been determined to chase her own dreams. Getting into Berkeley had been her goal since middle school when she'd visited the campus with an older cousin, and when she'd been accepted, she'd been excited and scared and despondent over leaving Max, who'd gone to UVM.

For a time, she'd thought about declining Berkeley. UVM was a great school with an excellent psychology department, but her parents had intervened, convincing her she'd be crazy to give up the chance to go to Berkeley for any boy, even one as wonderful as Max.

He'd broken her heart into a million pieces when he gently suggested they see other people while in college. It wasn't what he wanted, he'd said, but trying to hold a relationship together with three thousand miles between them for four years didn't seem feasible. She never forgot what he said the night they made that painful decision.

"What we have is special, Lex. If it's meant to be, it'll still be there when we're ready for it."

Those were the words she'd clung to during the worst days of her life, when everything had seemed bleak and hopeless. She'd clung to him and the years of memories they'd made together while in the throes of first love.

When she left Butler the August after they graduated, she'd never imagined she wouldn't see him again for more than a decade. That first Christmas, her family had gone skiing in Aspen and then to visit her paternal grandparents in Florida, so she'd never made it home to Vermont. By January, she was fighting for her life.

Lexi wasn't sure when or why she'd decided to keep her battle private. All she recalled was asking her family not to tell people so she wouldn't have to manage an outpouring of concern. It was all she could do to deal with the worries of her parents and grandparents, who'd aged before her eyes as Lexi got sicker and sicker. Years had passed in a blur of treatments, painful bone marrow biopsies, mouth sores, unrelenting nausea and other hideous side effects. She was too sick most of the time to talk to anyone, let alone keep up with social media or anything other than the battle to stay alive.

Her life was now a decade off schedule. Her goal was to start back to school a class or two at a time, beginning in January. She was looking at online programs since she avoided crowds out of habit after having to protect her fragile immune system from germs for so long. Depending on how this weekend went, she could work on school from here or Texas or anywhere, really, while she found a job. She'd encouraged her parents and grandparents to revisit the travel plans they'd abandoned when Lexi got sick, and they were going to Spain, France and Italy in the spring.

Her mother didn't want to go. She was still in trauma mode after seeing her only child through a near-fatal illness. They'd been to family therapy to cope with the post-traumatic fallout, and everyone was better than they'd been, but her mom was still struggling.

That's why Lexi had promised to check in during this weekend away, even though she was twenty-eight. She would always check in with them after what they'd sacrificed for her. Her dad had sold his successful HVAC business in Vermont and put a big chunk of the profit from the sale into saving her life. After she aged off their insurance when she was twenty-six, he'd paid out of pocket to keep her covered. Everything had been a struggle, and they'd been right by her side through it all.

While she was in treatment, she'd befriended a young woman named Gillian, who'd had no family support. Lexi's parents and grandparents had rallied for her, too, making her part of holidays and other events. They'd mourned together when Gillian passed away two years ago. That loss had been a setback for them, a shocking reminder that even after everything they'd been through, Lexi could still die.

"But you're not going to die today or tomorrow, and you finally got to see Max Abbott," she said with a giddy feeling inside. "Today was a very good day, and tomorrow will be even better." During long weeks of isolation during her treatments, Lexi had been driven to talk to herself when she hadn't been permitted to have visitors. That habit had lasted into remission and would likely stay with her forever.

"Max has grown into a gorgeous man, as if there was any doubt about that." But could they recapture the magic of young love after all the living they had done in the last ten years?

"Only time will tell."

CHAPTER THREE

"The future for me is already a thing of the past. You were my first love and you will be my last." —Bob Dylan

The silence woke Max in the morning. Accustomed to the enthusiasm with which his son began each day, everything felt off without Caden in the house. Max got up, changed into workout clothes and hit the home gym he'd installed in the house's third bedroom, since he had no time to go to an actual gym. He was in the shower by eight and on his way to the barn by eight thirty, eager to see his son after a night apart.

He knew he ought to be thankful for the break, but he vastly preferred being with his little boy than being without him, even if he was in the best possible hands with Molly, Linc and Elmer.

In between thoughts of Caden and what they might do that day, Max relived the night with Lexi and picked over the things she'd told him as he drove toward the covered bridge that led to Hells Peak Road.

Cancer, of all things.

And he'd had no idea she was going through such a harrowing ordeal.

That was by design on her part, but he wished she would've made an exception for him. What could he have done, though?

With college and Caden to consider, it wasn't like he could've moved to Houston to be on Team Lexi. But he could've called and visited and supported her from a distance.

Knowing he would see Caden in a few minutes, Max felt a surge of excitement as he pulled into the driveway at the barn, threw his truck into Park and killed the engine. He walked into the mudroom, where the walls were covered with hooks from the original Abbott ten and now their many children. Caden loved that his hook was first on the second row and took his job as a role model to his younger cousins very seriously.

Max stopped on the way into the kitchen to listen to his son's excited chatter as he talked to Elmer about something that'd happened at school and how funny it was when the teacher found out about it.

"She was *so* mad," Caden said, giggling, "but we couldn't stop laughing."

Elmer's low chuckle made Max smile. His grandfather took endless pleasure in Caden and vice versa. "Well, it's not very nice to put something that makes fart sounds on the teacher's chair."

"I know, but it was *hilarious*," Caden said. "You should've seen her face." He lost it laughing all over again while Max desperately hoped the whoopee cushion hadn't come from his house. He assumed he would've heard from Mrs. Langtree by now if it had.

"What goes on around here?" Max asked when he stepped into the kitchen.

Caden let out a shriek followed by "Daddy" as he ran to him, nearly toppling his chair at the table in the process.

Elmer reached out to grab it.

Loving the greeting he always received when they spent time apart, Max lifted his son into the air, realizing it wouldn't be long until he was too heavy for such things.

Caden hugged him like he hadn't seen Max in weeks. "We had *so much fun*. Grandpa-Great let me stay up until *ten* so we could finish watching *The One and Only Ivan*. It was so good!" He squiggled to get free the way he often did these days, so Max put him down, and he ran off, yelling for Grandma. "Daddy's here!"

"Ten o'clock, huh?" Max asked his grandfather as he poured himself a cup of coffee.

"It was a good movie."

"I see you're still spoiling the grandkids, even the second generation of them."

"When you're good at something, it makes sense to stick with it."

Max laughed. "You could teach the master class."

"That's a lovely compliment, my friend. He's an absolute delight, but of course you know that."

"Yes, I do. I missed him so much, and yes, I realize that sounds ridiculous."

"Nah, I get it. How was the reunion?"

"Better than expected."

"Your mother will gloat."

"I come prepared for that."

"Prepared for what?" Molly asked as Caden led her into the kitchen by tugging on her hand.

"To tell you the reunion was better than expected. And I left at nine, so I win the bet."

"Oh damn," Molly said. "I was hoping you danced the night away."

"Not exactly. I left with Lexi, and we went back to my place to catch up."

"Is that right?" Molly said, her eyes going wide.

"Now you've gone and done it," Elmer said with a chuckle.

"How is she? Where's she been?"

"She's good, and she's been in Houston."

"What's there?"

"The MD Anderson Cancer Center."

"What?" Molly asked, her face going flat with shock.

"She's been battling leukemia on and off since our freshman year of college. She had a stem cell transplant a year and a half ago and is now in remission and trying to figure out what's next."

"Dear Lord," Molly said, sitting at the table.

Caden climbed into her lap, seeming concerned by her reaction. "What's loo... Look..."

"Leukemia is a kind of cancer," Max said. "My friend Lexi from high school had it, or I guess she *has* it. She said she won't be considered cured for four more years."

"I can't believe we never heard about this," Elmer said.

"She wanted it kept private. She said she didn't have the capacity to manage everyone knowing."

"I can understand that," Elmer said. "Can you?"

"I guess," Max said. "But was I just anyone? You know I wondered for years where she was and what'd become of her. If you hadn't run into her mom that one time at the grocery store, I would've thought she was dead."

"Who are we talking about?" Linc asked when he joined them in the kitchen.

"Lexi," Molly said. "Max saw her at the reunion and found out she's been battling cancer all this time."

"Oh wow. Sorry to hear that. She's okay now?"

"She is, but she's got four years until they consider her cured."

"Are you angry with her, Max?" Molly asked.

"I was," he admitted, "before I saw her and found out where she'd been. I was surprised she didn't tell me what was going on. We'd agreed to see other people in college, but that doesn't mean I didn't care about her anymore."

"She was so crushed about that," Molly said. "Remember?"

"I do, but we were going to colleges three thousand miles apart. I was trying to be realistic."

"And she had hoped you two were forever," Molly said.

"Is anyone forever at eighteen with three thousand miles between them?" Max asked.

"I suppose it can be done, but I always supported your decision. You were old enough to know that wasn't what you wanted."

"It wasn't about her. It was about the situation. Ten minutes with her last night took me right back to all the things I loved about being with her. It was always so easy."

"Hmmm," Molly said with a satisfied smile.

"Don't say too much, son," Linc said, "or you might regret it."

"You hush," Molly said to her husband. "You want the scoop as much as I do." She nudged Caden off her lap, got up and then returned to the table a minute later, handing a hundred-dollar bill to her grandson. "Take your daddy skiing this weekend."

"Can we, Dad?"

"If we get the snow that's forecast."

Caden handed Max the money. "You'd better hang on to this. I tend to lose stuff."

If Max had one frustration with his son, that was it, but they were working on him being more responsible about keeping track of his belongings. "I'll keep it safe for you, pal."

Molly took a sip of the coffee Linc had poured for her. "How long is Lexi in town?"

"Just through the weekend."

"Did you invite your friend to my party?" Caden asked.

"I did. I hope that's okay."

"Sure, that's cool." He looked up at Max, seeming uncertain. "Grammy said Chase and Molly are sleeping over tonight and I can stay if I want to. She said I'm a big help with them. Would you care if I stayed another night?"

Caden knew that Max missed him when he slept out, thus the uncertainty. "That sounds like fun." Caden adored his cousin Chase and never missed a chance to be with him. The time he had with his cousins kept Caden from being lonely for siblings, or so Max suspected. "What about Murphy?"

"He's staying home with his mom and dad," Caden reported. "He's too young to sleep over."

Thinking about his baby nephew sparked the oddest thought. Could Lexi still have children after her treatment? And honestly, what business was that of his?

"Another night off, son," Linc said without looking away from his morning copy of the *Burlington Free Press*. "Whatever will you do with yourself?"

Max had no idea.

. . .

LEXI HAD A RESPONSE FROM HER MOM IN HER INBOX THAT SHE read as she sipped from her first cup of strong Vermont coffee, another thing she'd missed about her home state.

So glad to hear the reunion was fun and you reconnected with Max. I can't believe he's a single dad to a seven-year-old. I'm sure he's a wonderful father as he has a wonderful father—and grandfather. I can't wait to hear all about it. Were there any sparks? You two were so cute together once upon a time. Dad and I have held out a secret hope that you might find your way back to each other.

"Whoa," Lexi said. "Easy, ghost rider."

Thanks for being so good about checking in and understanding how we worry about you. We promise to work on scaling that back now that you're doing so much better. We're thankful every day for your recovery, and we want to let you spread your wings and fly free. You've certainly earned that after everything you've been through. Enjoy the rest of your weekend in VT, and we'll see you Monday. Love you! Mom

Lexi appreciated the effort they were making to back off from the critical caregiver role they'd played for so many years. Untangling the complicated emotions that came with serious illness wouldn't happen overnight, and their family therapist had told them to be kind to each other as each of them worked through their trauma on their own timelines as they found a new normal.

That term, *new normal*, had come up a lot in therapy. For a time, Lexi had expected to return to the life she'd been leading when disaster struck. But then two years became four and four became six and her college friends graduated and got married and started families, while she cycled in and out of the hospital while waiting for a stem cell transplant with her mom as the donor. It had taken two more years until she was stable enough to have the procedure. Then it was postponed again while she battled a massive infection from the grueling chemo regimen that preceded the transplant.

After the transplant, she'd developed graft vs. host disease and several other life-threatening complications that had dragged out her time in the hospital by months.

The roller-coaster ride had been breathtakingly stressful, and then…

She'd lived.

The ending of the story was far less dramatic than the earlier chapters had been, which was why she and her family were still spinning as they lifted their heads up to see what'd been going on for everyone else while they were waging war against cancer. Everything else had faded to the background during those years. Once, during a particularly harrowing time in her illness, her dad had been shocked to realize a new president had been elected two weeks earlier and he hadn't noticed.

That's how all-consuming it had been. They'd lost track of everything and everyone who wasn't the doctors and nurses keeping her alive.

Lexi typed a reply to her mom. *It was great to see Max, and the same old sparks as always were still there, for me anyway, but I expected that. Not sure how he felt to see me, but he was shocked to hear where I've been and why I dropped off the map. I think he was hurt that I didn't tell him what was going on. Maybe I should have, but I would've hated for him to see me down and out like I was so often during treatment—and you know he would've wanted to come.*

I'm looking forward to seeing him again this weekend and meeting his son. He absolutely glows when he talks about Caden, which is very sweet. It's nice to be back in Butler. I forgot how beautiful it is—and how cold! It's only twenty-eight this morning, and snow is threatening. I hope it snows like crazy. I've missed snow.

Give Dad, Gram and Gramps a smooch from me and try to have a great weekend. Everything is GOOD—now go live. That's an order. Love you. Lex

After a shower, she got dressed in more of the warm clothes she'd bought for this weekend. Some of them had been acquired through the Green Mountain Country Store's catalog, which she'd looked forward to receiving every quarter while she was away. It was like getting a piece of home in the mail—and seeing Max's handsome face in the pages of the catalog was an added extra.

Lexi was eager to get out in town and see everything and

everyone who'd once made up her carefree childhood days. Her first stop was the diner, which had been vastly expanded in her absence. When she stepped inside, a million memories assailed her in one fell swoop that left her breathless. The scents of coffee, bacon and maple syrup along with the low hum of chatter and laughter took her right back to countless mornings there with her parents and grandparents.

"Come in and grab a seat at the bar," a smiling blonde said as she circulated with a pot of coffee. "I'm Megan Abbott. What brings you to Butler?"

"I'm Lexi Bradshaw. I grew up here and am visiting for the weekend."

"Welcome home."

Lexi took a seat at the bar. "Thank you."

An older man sitting next to her leaned in to whisper to her. "If you turn the mug over, Megan will fill it for you."

Lexi turned over the mug. "Thanks for the insider info." Then she did a double take. "Mr. Stillman? Is that you?"

"It is, but I'm afraid you have me at a disadvantage, young lady."

"Lexi Bradshaw. Max's friend."

His eyes widened with recognition. "Oh, so you are. I see it now. You're all grown up since the last time we saw you."

"It's been ten years since I was here, but it's a relief that it's mostly still the same. Except I'd have thought y'all would've gotten cell service by now."

"That's never gonna happen. People here like being off the grid."

"Y'all are weird."

"Where'd you pick up that Southern twang?"

"Houston. Been there awhile."

"I heard," he said, his gaze softening. "I'm really sorry for what you've been through, sweetheart."

"Thanks," she said, encouraged to realize Max had already updated his family on where she'd been and why. She wondered what else he'd told them. "I'm better now and thinking about the future for the first time in years."

Megan came by with the coffee and filled Lexi's mug. "What can I get you to eat?"

"Do you still have the best pancakes in Vermont?"

"We sure do."

"That sounds good, with a side of hash browns and fruit, please."

"Coming right up."

"Are the hash browns still to die for?" Lexi asked Mr. Stillman.

"They sure are. I only eat them once a week because I have to watch my waistline. Megan is always trying to fatten me up."

"How is she related to the Abbotts?"

"She's Hunter's wife."

Lexi smiled. "I like her for him. He was always tightly wound, as I recall."

Elmer's bark of laughter made her laugh, too. "That he was, but Megan has smoothed out his rough edges." He pulled out an iPhone. "I only use this for pictures and when I got the Wi-Fi." After scrolling through some photos, he held one up to her. "That's Hunter and Megan's family. Carson, Cory and Claire."

"I love the C names."

"A lot of Molly's grandchildren have C names."

"That's cute, and so are your great-grandchildren."

"Here's one of all the greats. Forty-one of them now. Izzy managed to get a photo of them all recently. What a circus that was."

"Wow." In the photo, forty-one children surrounded their smiling great-grandfather. "That's a mob."

"Sure is, but I wouldn't have it any other way. Seems like every day, there's a game, a practice, a recital, a birthday. I swear they're keeping me young."

While Lexi ate the delicious breakfast, Mr. Stillman kept her entertained with funny stories about his grandchildren and great-grandchildren. She was intrigued to hear that Hunter was now the CEO at the store, that Lucas and Landon had grown into mature, responsible fathers, and that Colton was still living on the mountaintop with his wife and children.

And Max… To hear Elmer tell it, he was a wonderful, doting father to his beloved son, but she'd already seen that for herself.

"He lights up when he talks about Caden," Lexi said, sipping her coffee. "I can't wait to meet him."

"I heard you're coming to the party tomorrow. You may want to take a preventative headache tablet before you venture into that madness."

She laughed. "Thank you for the advice."

"I couldn't help but note that our Max also lit up a bit earlier this morning when he talked about seeing you again."

"Did he?" She eyed him over her mug while hoping her face wasn't turning bright red. That was a post-chemo development that drove her crazy.

"He did. He was very happy to see you again. He'd wondered what'd become of you."

"And now he knows."

"Yes, he does."

"I was so hoping to see him again. I've never forgotten him."

"I think it's safe to say he never forgot you either."

"That's nice to hear. I sure as heck didn't expect to be gone so long."

"Life is funny that way, isn't it? You think you've got a plan and then, nope. That's not happening, but this is."

"That's exactly how it went for me. I may never plan anything again after this."

"It's probably safe to make some plans now, right? You're doing better?"

"I'm in remission, and the doctors tell me I have as much chance as the general population does of getting it again. I have a whole new immune system after the transplant. But I won't be considered 'cured' for four more years."

"Then you ought to spend that time doing exactly what you want. None of us ever know what's coming round the next bend. You gotta make the best of every day. That's my philosophy."

"It's a good one. Let me ask you this… Is Dude still fostering dogs and other animals?"

"She is, and she's married now to Skeeter."

Lexi gasped. "Skeeter-from-Nolan's-garage-who-had-the-dead-cat-in-his-freezer-for-ten-years Skeeter?"

Elmer cackled with laughter. "The one and only. The two of them are happier than pigs in crap."

"Wow. That's a couple I didn't see coming."

"No one did, sweetheart. But the heart wants what the heart wants, and their hearts are firmly committed to each other."

"I'm happy for them. Dude was so good to me when I was a kid and in love with all the animals. I thought I'd have at least three dogs by now."

"If you're looking for a furry friend, she's the gal to see."

"I'm not sure I'm ready for that kind of responsibility, but it's nice to dream."

"I'm heading back to the barn after this. Be glad to drop you at Dude's if you need a lift."

"That's very sweet of you, but I have a rental car, and I remember the way."

He handed her a business card with the words JUSTICE OF THE PEACE, NOTARY PUBLIC, FREE ADVICE printed on it. "My phone number is on the back. If you need anything while you're in town, especially in the free advice department, you give me a call, you hear?"

Could he be any more adorable? Lexi leaned in to kiss his cheek. "I'll do that. It was such a pleasure to see you again."

"You as well, my friend. I'll see you at the party tomorrow."

"I'll look forward to that."

He tossed some bills on the counter. "Megan, I've got Lexi's breakfast, too."

"You got it, Elmer." To Lexi, who was about to protest, Megan said, "Don't bother. He won't take no for an answer."

"Thanks, Mr. Stillman."

"Call me Elmer, honey. You're all grown up now." He left with a smile and a jaunty wave for her and Megan.

"He hasn't changed at all," Lexi said.

"He's the most delightful human being I've ever known," Megan said. "He owns the diner now, and I'm his partner in crime. I don't know what I'll ever do without him someday, hopefully in the distant future. I tell him all the time I need him to live forever."

"I can see why. So, you're married to Hunter."

"That I am. Going on six years now."

"That's awesome. Congratulations. I used to date Max in high school."

"Is that right? Were you here for the reunion?"

Lexi nodded.

"How was it? Those things can be so awkward."

"It wasn't bad. I was really hoping to see Max again, and we had a nice time."

Megan's eyes lit up when she heard that. "Will you be sticking around in Butler?"

"I'm not sure yet. I'm here for the weekend, but I may come back to stay for a while."

"If you do, you know where to come for pancakes."

"Absolutely, and truth be told, they're even better than they used to be."

"I quite agree. Butch is cranky, but he's a great cook."

"I heard that," Butch yelled from the kitchen.

Megan smiled as she walked away to tend to other customers.

Feeling as if she'd made a new friend, Lexi couldn't wait to come back to the diner for more pancakes.

CHAPTER FOUR

"It's a funny thing coming home. Nothing changes. Everything looks the same, feels the same, even smells the same. You realize what's changed is you." —F. Scott Fitzgerald

*B*ecause it was right across the street, Lexi decided to stop into the Green Mountain Country Store before taking a ride to Dude's house. Another flood of childhood memories overtook her the second she stepped inside the iconic store. If nostalgia had an aroma, the smell of the store was it for her. Lemon-scented furniture polish, potpourri, sugar and spice and a million other things that combined into a scent she'd know anywhere as this amazing place.

It looked just as she remembered. Rough-hewn wood beams and bins of products that couldn't be found anywhere else. Vintage toys, coolers full of icy-cold bottles of Coke and samples of cheese, maple syrup, smoked meats, dips and fudge. She tried a little bit of everything, each flavor bringing back memories of simpler times when she'd come here with her mom or grandmother to pick out a toy or penny candy from the colorful bins. Usually both, especially when she was with her grandmother.

A man in a flannel shirt and well-faded jeans was on a ladder restocking the maple syrup display. When he came down and turned, she recognized him as Colton Abbott. He still had the distinctive bushy beard he'd worn since he was a teenager.

He did a double take when he saw her. "Lexi?"

"Yes, it's me. Hi, Colton."

"Wow, how long has it been?"

"Ten years."

"Ah, the reunion. That's right." He gave her a quick hug. "It's so nice to see you."

"You, too. I hear you're still up on the mountain making syrup."

"You heard right, although I've got a wife and three boys keeping me entertained these days."

"I heard that, too."

He pulled out a phone and had a picture of his family up in a matter of seconds. "That's Lucy, Christian and the twins, Camden and Cooper."

They all had reddish-gold hair, blue eyes and cherubic cheeks. "They're beautiful."

"They're holy terrors, but we love them. And yes, they look exactly like their gorgeous mother, thank God."

Colton was as good-looking as his brothers, although she'd always thought Max was the best-looking one of the bunch. But she was biased.

"Congrats on the family."

"Thanks. Also got solar power and indoor plumbing these days, which keeps my Lucy happy."

"It's the little things, right?"

His grin lit up a sinfully handsome face. "You know it. Have you seen Max?"

"At the reunion. We had a great time."

"Oh, good. That boy is all work and no play. Maybe you can get him to lighten up a bit while you're here."

At the thought of how she might "lighten up" Max Abbott, she felt her face grow warm again. Ugh, freaking chemo. "We'll see. He invited me to Caden's party tomorrow. I saw your grandfather, and he suggested headache meds before I go."

Colton's bark of laughter reminded her of Elmer's. "He gives the best advice."

"And it's free."

"That it is."

"It's so good to see everyone. I'm going to visit Dude after this. I can't wait to see her."

"It's really good to see you, too, Lexi."

"Congrats on your sweet family."

"Thanks. We'll see you tomorrow?"

"I'll be there."

He handed her a bottle of Abbott's Own Light Maple Syrup. "On the house."

"Oh, thank you."

"You got it. Tell the cashier that's a gift from Colton."

"I'll do that."

After Lexi walked away, Colton used the store's Wi-Fi to send a message to Lucy. *Got to do a quick errand in town before I head back. You need anything?*

She responded with: *Diapers, wipes, paper towels, a large bottle of wine and a sedative.*

Chuckling, he typed in his reply. *Daddy will be right back. Stay strong, my queen.*

Your feral spawn are more out of control than usual today.

Yikes.

Yep.

Be there soon. Love you endlessly.

You only say that so I won't leave you with the spawn.

That's right! He added smiling and heart emojis.

He'd never known true happiness until Lucy Mulvaney had shown up and changed everything. His city girl had rolled with his life on the mountain, living without indoor plumbing, until their eldest son arrived, and she said it was time for him to build her a bathroom *in the house.* Because he was long overdue in fulfilling that promise, he'd jumped right on it and added two more bedrooms, a playroom and a main bedroom for them while he was at it.

She'd made herself at home in his life. The least he could do was ensure her comfort.

He got into his truck and headed for Max's house, looking for intel on his brother's reunion with Lexi. Colton had been surprised to hear Max was going to the reunion he'd repeatedly said he had no interest in. Had he heard Lexi might be there? And why hadn't he mentioned the reunion to him at work last week? Inquiring minds wanted to know.

Colton parked behind Max's truck in the driveway. Even after all this time, it was still weird to think of their grandparents' home as Max's house. He knocked and opened the inside door. "Hello?"

"Come in," Max called from a room down the hall. "I'm cleaning Caden's room while he's not here."

"Where is he?"

"Mom and Dad have kidnapped him for another night because Will's kids are sleeping over. They need Caden's help."

"It's good for him to have cousin time, but what the hell are you doing cleaning when you have a break from fatherhood?"

"What else am I supposed to do?"

"Hang out with your ex-girlfriend who's back in town for the weekend?"

"We might do something later."

"Your enthusiasm is overwhelming."

"What's that supposed to mean?"

"Your son is safe with Mom and Dad, a girl you were once madly in love with is back in town for three days, and you're *cleaning Caden's room?*"

"Yes, I am."

"Max." Colton approached his youngest sibling and took his face in his hands. "Sweet Max. Has it been so long since you were properly laid that you can't recognize opportunity when it's smacking you in the face?"

Max jerked free of Colton's hold. "Fuck off. I'm busy."

Colton grabbed Max's arm to stop him from returning to

Caden's room. "You're never too busy to get laid. Lexi was heading over to visit Dude. Maybe you could stop by there on the pretext of getting Caden a dog for his birthday and end up naked between the sheets with your first love by day's end."

"It's not like that with her."

Colton tipped his head to study his brother. "It's not like what?"

"She's been through a lot since I saw her last."

"A lot of what? She looked great when I saw her."

"She's had cancer for ten years."

That news shocked Colton. "Wow. Seriously?"

"Yep, so you'll pardon me if I'm not doing everything I can to get in her pants after she told me that."

"Hear me out."

Max put his hands on his hips and rolled his eyes to high heaven. "About what?"

"Is it possible that she hasn't been with anyone but you?"

"I doubt it."

"You said she's been sick for ten years. The math adds up."

Max seemed to ponder that possibility before he shrugged. "Whatever. That's not happening."

"You're a fool. Why do you think she hightailed it right back here after she was well again? I doubt it was to see Fred the moose. She came back for you, you ninny."

"She said as much last night."

Incredulous, Colton gave Max a shake. "Then why in the *ever-loving fuck* are you *cleaning Caden's room* when he's with Mom and Dad, and your ex, who you never got over, if you ask me, is back in town to see you?"

"I got over her."

"Did you, though? Your love life has been somewhat of a red-hot mess since you were with her."

"It has not!"

"Has too, and you know it. Get your head out of your ass, man, and get over to Dude's to do some dog shopping. Right now!"

"The last thing in this world I need is a dog."

"Maybe you don't need one, but Cade sure does. What is it Dad says about how kids shouldn't grow up without a dog?"

Max groaned. "Come on, Colton. I thought you were on my side."

"I am, which is why I came right here after I saw Lexi to find out where you were while she's *in town for a few days.* Imagine my surprise when I find you *cleaning* like the eunuch you've become these last few years."

"Go away."

"Nope." Colton crossed his arms. "Not going anywhere until you do."

"I want to finish this before he gets a bunch of new stuff at his party."

Colton held his ground, glaring at Max.

"Okay, fine! Whatever." Max grabbed his coat off the hook by the door and went out the front door.

"Yes," Colton whispered as he followed his brother out.

THIS WAS INSANE, MAX THOUGHT AS COLTON FOLLOWED HIM through town, all the way to Dude's place, which was half a mile past the turnoff to the road that led to Colton's mountaintop home. Colton pulled into Dude's driveway and parked behind Max's truck, leaving his engine to idle as he waited and watched.

"For fuck's sake," Max said as he got out of his truck and sent a filthy gesture to his brother.

Colton responded by making a circle of his hand and poking his index finger into the hole in the middle.

"Disgusting," Max muttered as he stormed into Dude's yard, pretending he wasn't looking for Lexi, even though her little white rental car was parked in front of his truck. "Goddamned Colton." Max couldn't deny his brother had struck a nerve, which had him on an errand he'd had no plans to make before Colton had shamed him into it.

A freaking dog, of all things. As if he had time for that.

He saw Dude from a distance, standing at a fence with Lexi, having an animated conversation. No matter the season, Dude always wore denim overalls and a big straw hat that she tied under her chin. People in town speculated that she slept in the hat. The woman known locally as Snow White was ageless. No one had any idea how old she truly was, and many suspected that she was the one who'd domesticated Fred the moose.

Max needed to put his game face on, because now that Colton had shamed him into getting a dog for Caden, he would need to convince Dude that he could give a dog a good home.

"Max Abbott!" Dude said when she saw Max walking toward them.

Max couldn't deny that Lexi seemed happy to see him or that the warm smile she directed his way brought back a million memories of the years he'd spent madly in love with her. Being the recipient of Lexi's sexy smiles had once been the most important thing to him. A lot had changed since then, but her smile still packed a punch.

Dude gave him a hug. "What brings you by?"

"Caden will be seven tomorrow, and I'm told it's time for him to have a dog."

"How's it possible that our baby Caden is already *seven?*" Dude asked.

"If you figure that out, make sure to let me know. I can't believe he's seven."

"You remember Lexi, right?" Dude asked.

"I do." Max shifted his gaze to Lexi. "We saw each other last night at the reunion."

"Ah, right. You were in high school together. Oh. Wait. You dated, didn't you?"

"We did." Max ignored the calculating look Dude gave him. "Long time ago."

"Not so long," Dude said.

"About that dog," Max said. "Do you have anyone who might make a nice best friend for my boy?"

"I have quite a few options," Dude said. "Come with me. Both of you. Lexi, you can help him decide."

"I'd love to," Lexi said, giving Max a look that could've meant any number of things.

He thought of what Colton had said about getting naked with her, and immediately squelched that lest he embarrass himself in front of her and Dude. Once upon a time, getting naked with Lexi had been his primary goal on any given day.

But like he'd said to Dude, that was a very long time ago.

CHAPTER FIVE

*"I left the light on in my heart in case you ever wanted
to come back home."* —Lennon Hodson

*I*nteresting, Lexi thought, how she'd told Colton she
was coming to see Dude, and then Max showed up
there after having never mentioned getting a dog for Caden the
night before. Was it a coincidence, or had he come to see her?

Either way, he was there now, and she intended to make the
most of the unexpected encounter. He was wearing the Vermont
winter uniform of flannel, denim and down with a knitted wool
cap on his head that looked homemade. He probably had legions
of women knitting hats for him and his little boy, a thought that
made her jealous. Foolish, she knew, to be jealous of nameless,
faceless women. It wasn't as if she had any sort of claim on him
after all this time.

Lexi had been truly shocked to learn he was still single. She
would've figured one of the many girls they'd gone to school
with would've snapped him up the minute Lexi was out of the
picture. There'd been no shortage of girls who'd envied their
relationship or wished Lexi would get hit by a bus or something
to get her out of the way.

Little did they know she *had* been hit by a metaphorical bus
in the form of leukemia. They'd probably celebrated when she

failed to return to Butler for Christmas or summer vacation or anything else for a decade. After she and Max left the reunion together last night, everyone was probably wondering if they'd picked up where they left off in high school.

Let them wonder.

Dude led them into her home, where a scurry of paws preceded a rush of animals surrounding them. There were dogs of every size and color, every breed and mixes of many breeds.

Lexi wanted all of them for herself. She sat on the kitchen floor the way she had as a teenager and let the dogs come to her. She'd wanted all of them then, too, and getting one of her own was at the top of her post-illness to-do list.

Max sat on the floor with her, smiling as several of the dogs moved from her to him.

While they petted soft heads and silky ears, Dude gave them the lowdown on each one.

"How does anyone ever choose just one?" Max asked as a brindle mixed breed with floppy ears cozied up to him.

"People often take more than one," Dude said sadly.

Lexi recalled how it broke Dude's heart to let them go, even when she knew her babies were going to good homes.

"Which one do you think would be best for an active seven-year-old?" Max asked as he petted a yellow Lab puppy.

"That one." Dude pointed to the Lab, who'd already set her sights on Max. "Daisy is great with kids. Her family had to rehome her when the dad took a job in the UK. She would've had to spend six months in quarantine, and they didn't want to put her through that. The mom was heartbroken to have to give her up. She raved about how patient she was with her four kids."

"Hi, Daisy," Max said. "It's nice to meet you."

As he shook hands with the dog, Lexi's ovaries exploded with desire. Good Lord, the man was sexy and adorable and gorgeous and all the things he'd been ten years ago, only much more so now. Seeing him in dad mode made her fall right back in love with him. Or she should say deeper into love with him because she'd never stopped loving Max Abbott.

She could admit that now that she was with him again. Max

had been an amazing person in high school and had become even more so since becoming a single dad to Caden.

His obvious love for and devotion to his son made him even more attractive than he'd been to her in the past—and that was saying something. Max Abbott had dazzled her from the first time she'd laid eyes on him in seventh grade.

After attending a private elementary school, she'd begged her parents to send her to the public middle and high schools so she could be with the friends she'd made playing soccer and lacrosse in town leagues.

She vividly remembered her first day of middle school and seeing Max Abbott for the first time. The memory made her smile even all these years later.

"Lex?"

She realized Max had been talking to her while she took a trip back to seventh grade. "Sorry. What's up?"

"I was asking if you think I can handle a kid *and* a dog or if you think I'm crazy for taking this on."

She looked at the dog, who'd already decided she belonged to Max whether he knew it or not, and then she glanced up at the golden-brown eyes she'd never forgotten. "I think you can handle anything, and that Caden and Daisy are lucky to have you."

He looked at her for a long, intense moment before he tore his gaze off her and returned his attention to Daisy. "I guess we'll take her, Dude."

"Caden is a lucky boy to have such a wonderful daddy." Dude sounded emotional, the way she always did when she found the perfect home for one of her fur babies. "And Daisy is lucky to have both of you and all the Abbotts. She'll have so many cousin puppies to play with."

"It's dog-a-palooza when we're all together at the barn," Max said. "Dogs for days."

"I've always wanted a dog," Lexi said.

"You can borrow Daisy any time you need a fix."

"I'll take you up on that."

Daisy came over to snuggle with Lexi, as if to say, *I've got you, boo. We'll be friends.*

Her emotions were all over the place from being back in Butler and with Max for the first time in years. Leave it to a sweet puppy to trigger tears.

"Are you okay?" Max asked.

"I'm good. It's just so nice to be here and to be with you again."

"I'm really glad you came to the reunion."

"I'm really glad *you* came to the reunion."

Smiling, he said, "Me, too."

DUDE LOADED HIM UP WITH ALL THE THINGS HE NEEDED TO TAKE Daisy home—a crate, plush dog bed, harness and leash and the bowls Daisy had used at Dude's house. Max and Lexi stood back as Dude said a tearful goodbye to Daisy.

"Come visit any time you'd like, and take good care of my buddy Caden and his daddy, you hear me?"

Daisy barked and licked Dude's face.

"I love you, too, sweet girl." She handed the leash to Max. "I hope Caden loves his surprise."

"Oh, he will. He's been asking me for a dog since we moved to Gramps's house. He had George and Ringo for his first four years, and he misses living with dogs. I do, too."

"Once you've had dogs, you never want to be without them," Dude said.

"Thank you again for sharing one of your precious babies with me and Caden."

"You're very welcome."

After Max loaded the dog's belongings into the back of his truck, he and Lexi walked Daisy to the driveway. "You want to come over and help me get her settled?"

"Sure, I'd love to."

"Okay, see you at my house."

"Sounds good."

As Max drove home with Daisy sitting on the front seat, he

couldn't stop thinking about the thoughts Colton had put in his head. As much as Max hated to admit it, his brother was right. Max's love life had been a red-hot mess since he ended things with Lexi—or since he suggested they see other people in college. Maybe if he hadn't done that, she might've shared what she was going through with him before now.

He was all mixed up inside where she was concerned. He'd been so angry about her "disappearance" for so long that he got to the point where he rarely thought of her anymore because it was too painful. That she'd seemingly disappeared from his life on purpose had been a bitter pill. If he was being truthful, that was one of the reasons why his relationship with Chloe had been a disaster from the start. He'd been unable to fully commit to her while Lexi was still out there somewhere.

Max wasn't sure when exactly he'd given up on hoping Lexi might come home. Probably five years ago, when it became clear that her departure from his life had been intentional and that it was time for him to move on. Except he never really had. He could chalk that up to the heavy responsibility of being a single parent and working all the time for two of the family businesses, but that wasn't it.

It was her.

It'd always been her, and after a couple of hours with her the night before, he'd begun to wonder if it always would be.

After hearing what she'd been through and why she'd been gone, it was like the door to his heart had swung open to admit her once again—or to allow him to acknowledge that she'd never left. He wasn't sure which, but there was no doubt he felt all the same things for her he had once upon a time.

He wasn't sure what to do with that realization, but he had about ten minutes to figure it out before they arrived at his house. He glanced over at Daisy. "What would you do if you were me? Would you start this back up again, not knowing where she's going to be?"

Daisy smiled at him, her mouth open and her tongue hanging out the side.

"Well, you're no help at all. You liked her. I could tell. I like her, too. I'd forgotten how much I like her." He paused before he added, "No, that's not true, and I don't want to start our relationship by lying to you, Daisy. I've always liked Lexi in a way I've never liked anyone else. I think that's why nothing else has worked out for me, you know?"

Daisy's panting was her only reply.

"I appreciate you listening to me. I needed a friend to talk to." He scratched behind her ears as she leaned into him, already trusting him in a way that touched his heart. "You're a sweet girl."

And so was Lexi.

He pulled into the driveway, cut the engine and told Daisy to stay while he went around the truck to let her out.

She didn't need his help. She bounded out of the truck with energy and enthusiasm that made him realize how old George and Ringo were getting. They had to be lifted into vehicles these days.

Daisy immediately squatted to pee in the front yard before trotting around to give her new surroundings a thorough sniffing.

"I feel like I need to have my head examined bringing a dog into my already too-busy life," he said when Lexi joined him in the yard.

"You won't regret this. She'll be a wonderful companion for Caden, and you can take her with you to work, right?"

"Yes, I suppose I can when she gets a little older. She can play with Colton's dogs on the mountain and run around the tree farm when I'm there."

"She'll have a wonderful life with you guys."

Every minute or two, Daisy ran back over to make sure Max was still there, before resuming her exploration of the yard.

"She's already decided that you're hers," Lexi said, smiling when Daisy came back yet again to make sure Max was there.

"Caden will freak out over this."

"I'm so excited to meet him."

Max glanced at her, noting her cheeks had taken on a rosy

hue in the cold air. "I told him about you, and he asked if you could come to his party."

"I'm looking forward to it. That reminds me, I need to go to the mountain to get that day pass."

"I can run you over there if you'd like."

"Do you have time?"

"Seems like I'm free all day, as my son has ditched me for his grandparents and cousins."

"Does that make you sad?"

"Sorta, but I know that's weird. He's in the best possible place if he can't be with me, but I look forward to the time with him on the weekends."

"I can see why. You're so busy during the week."

"We are. It's nonstop. The weekends are buddy time, but it's good for him to be with his cousins."

Daisy darted toward the porch, ready to check out the rest of her new digs.

As he carried the crate while Lexi took the bed and bag Dude had packed, Max stopped short at the sight of a huge box on the front porch. "Wonder what that is?"

"Did you order birthday gifts?"

"No, I got him things he wanted from the store and some new skis." He approached the box and bent to look at the shipping label. "No way."

"What?"

"It's from his mother."

"Oh."

Max stared at the box, unblinking, his mind racing with scenarios he couldn't bear to consider, until he recalled Lexi was there and forced himself to snap out of it. After he put the crate inside, he went back for the box.

Daisy ran ahead of him, running through the house and checking things out.

Max put the box on the counter.

"I take it she doesn't usually send something for his birthday?"

"She never has. Not once. No birthday or Christmas

presents."

Lexi's hand landed on his back. "You don't have to give him whatever is in that box. You can pretend it never came and go on with your lives like it didn't happen."

He glanced at her. "Can I, though? Would it be fair to him not to tell him his mother sent him a present?"

"If it'll do more harm than good for him to receive something from her, then yes, it's fair. Your only concern is for his well-being. She chose not to be in his life. It's your choice whether to let her back in."

"I don't know what to do." He continued to stare at the box as if it contained dynamite, for that's what her reappearance would be in his well-ordered life.

"Why don't you open it and see what it is before you decide anything?" While he considered her suggestion, she pulled one of the bowls Dude had given them out of the bag and filled it with water that she put down for Daisy.

The dog took a long drink of water.

"Thanks," he said.

"No problem."

"I guess I'll open it." Why did this have to have happened today, when he had the chance to spend time alone with Lexi for the first time in so long? His stomach hurt the way it had when Chloe first left him alone with Caden. He deeply resented her for taking him back to those dark days, especially when things were going so well for him and his son.

Lexi found a knife in the block on his counter and handed it to him, handle first.

Max appreciated that she seemed to anticipate his every need and quietly tended to it before the need had even registered with him. He used the knife to slice the tape holding the box closed and pulled a wrapped gift out of the box. There were two envelopes—one addressed to Caden and one to Max.

"I can take care of this later." He tried to rally for Lexi. "What do you feel like doing?"

"Please don't feel like you can't deal with this now because

I'm here. You won't think of anything else until you know what that note says or what's in that package."

Max couldn't deny the truth of that. "I'm sorry. I hate that she picked today to reappear after years of silence."

"Don't be sorry. Let's figure out what you should do."

"I'm glad you're here to help me do that."

"I am, too."

He opened the envelope and encountered Chloe's familiar handwriting, bringing back a flood of memories from when they used to pass notes in class while in college. In the classes they'd had together, cell phone use was prohibited, so they'd done it old-school.

DEAR MAX,

I hope this finds you and Caden doing well. I can't believe he's SEVEN. Where have the years gone? I'm sure you're thinking 'I know where they've gone, Chloe. They've been spent raising our child.'

MAX HAD TO LAUGH TO HIMSELF BECAUSE THAT WAS EXACTLY what he'd thought when she asked where the years have gone.

BEFORE I SAY ANYTHING ELSE, I WANT TO SAY THIS: THANK YOU FOR raising Caden, for all the sacrifices you've made for him, for all the things you couldn't do because you were a single father, for all the days, nights and years you've given to Caden. From the bottom of my heart, thank you, Max. I'm sure you don't want my thanks or anything else from me, but I want you to know that what you've done for Caden is appreciated by his mother.

The other thing I want to say is how sorry I am that I left the way I did, that I dumped everything on you, that I wasn't strong enough to handle parenthood or anything else, for that matter. I treated you badly at the end of our relationship, and for that, I'm also sorry. You did everything you could to support me during the pregnancy, during the birth and after, and what happened between us was in no way your fault.

It was my fault. All of it.

For what it's worth, I didn't walk away and never look back. My heart was broken to leave Caden—and you—and I struggled for a long time after the night I last saw you both at your parents' home. Five years ago, I was diagnosed with severe depression. I spent more than a month in-patient, during which time I worked through a lot of things that dated back to my childhood. I was prescribed medication that's helped tremendously. In many ways, I feel like I've been reborn. Light has replaced the darkness, and while I still have difficult days, I'm so much better than I was.

I've come a million miles from the place I was in when we last saw each other. The only thing that stands between me and truly moving forward is the little boy who's growing up without a mother, possibly thinking she doesn't love him, when that couldn't be further from the truth.

The last thing in the world I want to do is disrupt his—or your— happy life. I just want him to know I love him, and I think of him all the time. I always have, and I always will. The gift is a remote-controlled truck that does all kinds of cool things. I have no idea if he will like it, and it's completely up to you as to whether you give it to him or tell him who it's from.

I have no right to ask you for anything, but if there's a chance you might let me see him at some point, I'd be eternally grateful. That, too, is entirely up to you. I've included my address, phone number and email below. I hope to hear from you, but if not, I understand that some things are unforgivable. If you've made it this far, thanks for reading this and for taking such good care of Caden. I have no doubt that you're a wonderful father to him, and he's lucky to have you.

Chloe

MAX HAD NO IDEA THAT TEARS WERE RUNNING DOWN HIS FACE until he lifted his head from reading the letter and blinked Lexi back into focus. Using his sleeve, he brushed away the tears. "She wants to see him." Before reading her letter, that would've been his greatest nightmare, but now... Now he didn't know what to think. She sounded nothing like the Chloe he'd known.

"May I?" Lexi asked, gesturing to the letter.

Max handed it over to her.

After she read it, she folded it and returned it to the envelope. Then she put her arms around him.

It took him a few seconds to respond, but then he held on tightly to her and the support she offered so freely.

"I'm sorry you're so upset."

"I feel like I'm going to be sick."

Lexi took his hand and led him to the sofa, sitting right next to him and keeping a tight grip on his hand. "I can only imagine."

"It's just been me and him for so long," Max said. "My family is always around, but at the end of the day—and the beginning—it's me and him. We're a team."

"You must know that won't change if you let her see him."

"Everything will change if I let her back in."

CHAPTER SIX

"Stop being a prisoner of your past. Become the architect of your future." —Robin Sharma

*L*exi wasn't sure how best to support Max through the bombshell that had arrived in the form of a birthday gift from Caden's mother. In a way, she felt like she was intruding, but she couldn't leave him alone. Not now, anyway.

"What do you want to do?" she asked him.

"I don't know." He held his head in his hands as he sat next to her. "I really thought she was gone for good, you know?"

"That's a reasonable assumption after years of silence."

"I need to talk to my parents about this," he said, standing.

"That's a great idea, but isn't Caden there?"

He reached for his coat. "He is, but I can send him out to play with the dogs while I talk to them."

Lexi got up and put her coat on, too.

"Will you come with me?"

The vulnerability in the way he asked that and how he looked at her made her breathless. "Of course I will."

Then he seemed to think better of it and shook his head. "I'm so sorry. You're here to have fun and relax. You don't need to be sucked into my drama."

She went to him and put her hands on his chest. "What did I

tell you last night? I came to see you. I'm here for you, and I want to help."

He leaned his forehead against hers the way he used to back when they were madly in love and forced to behave in school and in front of their parents. The simple gesture brought back a million memories and made her knees go weak under her. He'd always had the power to render her speechless, and to realize nothing had changed was amazing and overwhelming.

"Let's go to the barn. Your folks will know what you should do."

"They always do." He took hold of her hands. "It helps to have you here, too. I'd be losing it if I was alone when this happened."

"I'm here, Max." Whether her rapidly beating heart could handle the influx of love and affection was certainly not guaranteed.

"How is it," he asked, "that it feels like no time has gone by since I last saw you?"

"I'm not sure, but I feel the same way."

"We'll have to discuss that after I figure out what to do about the Chloe bombshell." He released her, somewhat reluctantly—or so it seemed to her—and got Daisy settled in her crate. "We'll be back soon," he told the puppy.

She rested her head on her paws and gave him a sad face.

"She's already trying to manipulate you," Lexi said.

"She'll have me wrapped around her paw in no time."

"That's the way it should be."

Outside, Lexi moved her car to the street and then joined him in his truck for the ride to the barn. Out of habit, she reached for his hand during the ride.

When he curled his fingers around her hand, everything inside her settled. The questions that had plagued her during the long years apart were answered. She still loved Max Abbott, and if she wasn't mistaken, he still loved her, too. Under normal circumstances, she'd laugh at the direction her thoughts were taking. They hadn't seen each other in years, and she already had them back in love. But after living with the very real possibility that she might die before she ever got the chance to live, she refused to waste a single minute of her second chance.

If Max Abbott still loved her the way she still loved him, she was determined to make it work with him. Before she came to Butler, she hadn't known he had a son, but that didn't change anything for her. If anything, Caden sweetened the pot. After hearing Max talk about him, she had no doubt she would adore him.

"I'm excited to meet Caden."

"I can't wait for you to meet him. I've thought so many times that I wish you could meet him."

"Really? You did?"

"All the time. Just because I stopped hearing from you doesn't mean I stopped thinking of you."

"I'm sorry I dropped off the map, Max. I shouldn't have done that to you."

"I understand why you did it. Who am I to say how someone should handle an illness like what you went through?"

"Still… I shouldn't have left you to wonder where I was all that time. What's funny is that you were the one I most wanted to tell, but I was afraid to."

"Why?" He glanced at her when they were stopped at a four-way intersection.

"Because I knew you'd come, and I didn't want you to see me like that."

"You're right that I would've come, and I would've been thankful that you were alive. I wouldn't have cared how you looked."

"I cared. I know that sounds so stupid, but I couldn't handle seeing you when I was in that condition."

"I hate that you were worried about that."

"Without trying to sound like an insecure fool, do you remember how I used to drive myself crazy trying to figure out why you chose me when there were so many prettier girls?"

"I remember, and I'll tell you the same thing I told you then—not to me there weren't. You were the prettiest girl I ever met. Still are."

"Stop," she said, laughing. "There's no way that's true."

"It is true. You never had anything to worry about where I was concerned. And you still don't."

Lexi fanned her face. "It's getting warm in here."

"That's another thing that hasn't changed. It was always hot between us. I bet it still would be."

"You're filling me with foolish hope."

"When I got home last night, all I could think about was how good it was to be with you again. And what a relief it was to see you, when there were times I thought you had to be dead to have stayed gone so long. I used to get really upset when I worried about that."

"I'm sorry. I was young and freaked out and battling a foe so big and scary that I had no time to think about anyone else's needs. If I had it to do over again, I would've called you—and asked you not to come."

"I would've come anyway. As often as I could."

"Do things like this happen? Do people see their first loves after years apart and still feel all the same things?"

"I don't know if it happens to other people. I can only speak for myself. Being with you again feels like no time has gone by."

"Same."

They glanced at each other and then laughed, which released some of the tension that had been building in her chest.

Max Abbott still felt the same way about her.

She still felt the same way about him.

Best day in a long, *long* time.

When he pulled the truck into the driveway at the barn, the feelings of nostalgia that she'd experienced at the store came rushing back. She'd had so many good times at the Abbotts' home. Family dinners, pizza gatherings and game nights full of laughter and love. She'd adored his family and had missed them almost as much as she'd missed Max.

They were greeted by two older yellow Labs.

"This is George and Ringo," he said. "My parents' dogs. They got them my freshman year of college."

"Nice to meet you, boys," Lexi said.

"Um, they're both girls."

Lexi laughed. "Of course they are. Your dad never lost his love of the Beatles, huh?"

"Nope, and if he does, that's when we'll know it's time to send him to the nursing home."

"Haha, I'm sure he's a long way from that."

"I hope so."

Lexi followed Max inside, where she noticed the original ten hooks on the wall now had two additional rows under them. "That's so sweet, how each of the kids has a hook."

"Family tradition." Max took her coat and hung it with his on the tenth hook on the first row, just like always.

Even the scents of cinnamon and cloves were as familiar to her as anything ever had been. "I, um, I need a second."

Max turned to her, seeming startled to see tears in her eyes. "What's wrong?"

"For the first time in a very long time, nothing is wrong." She took a deep breath and let it out slowly. "Being here again is so special."

"Having you here is special for me, too." He held out a hand to her, and she took it, returning the smile he gave her. "Let's go find my son."

LEXI WAS AS SWEET AS HE REMEMBERED, AND SO APPRECIATIVE OF the little things that made up his life, such as the hooks on the mudroom wall. He vividly recalled pointing them out to Chloe the first time she came with him to the barn, and she'd said they were cute. But Lexi… She knew they were so much more than cute to his family. They were part of the tradition that made the Abbott family what it was. She got it, and he appreciated that so much.

Still holding her hand, Max followed the sound of voices to the great room, which made up the center of the barn.

Caden let out the usual cry of happiness when he saw Max and came running.

Max released Lexi's hand and lifted his son into a hug.

"What are you doing back?" Caden asked. "I don't have to go home, do I?"

Max had known there would come a day when Caden would prefer the company of others to that of his father, but he'd expected it to take a few more years. "I wouldn't think of ruining your fun."

"That's good, cuz Chase and Molly just got here, and we're going to play tag in the yard."

Which worked out well for Max's plan to speak to his parents. "This is my friend Lexi. Can you say hi?"

Caden immediately went shy, ducking partially behind Max as he looked up at her. "Hi."

"Hi, Caden. It's so nice to meet you."

Caden shook her hand. "You, too."

Max introduced her to Chase and Molly, who greeted him with hugs and kisses.

Molly and Linc came over to give Lexi hugs.

"It's so nice to see you again, honey," Molly said.

"You, too," Lexi said, tearing up again as she hugged his dad.

"I was wondering if I could talk to you guys for a minute," Max said, glancing at the kids.

"I'll go out with them," Elmer said as he got out of his recliner and came over to hug Lexi. "Nice to see you again. Twice in one day."

"We saw each other at the diner this morning," Lexi said to Max.

"Ah, I see."

"Come on, kiddos," Elmer said. "Let's go play."

The kids ran past him to the mudroom to bundle up.

"What's going on?" Linc asked after Lexi and Max sat on one of the sofas.

"Chloe sent a gift to Caden, along with this." He got up to hand the letter to his parents, before returning to sit with her.

"Oh dear," Molly said, glancing with trepidation at the letter Linc held.

While they read it, Max held Lexi's hand and tried to keep his leg from bouncing with nerves that felt like they were on fire with agitation.

"Caden is adorable," Lexi said.

"Thanks."

"Your niece and nephew are, too."

"They're all great kids. He's lucky to have so many cousins around all the time. There's always someone to play with."

"Wow," Linc said, folding the letter. "What do you think, son?"

"I don't know what to think. That's why I'm here. I wanted you guys to tell me what to do."

"We can't do that," Molly said gently. "You're Caden's dad, and you're the one who has to decide."

"I want to do the right thing for him, but I don't know what that is."

"It sounds to me as if Chloe has done a lot of work on herself since you saw her last," Molly said.

Max glanced at her. "I guess."

"What your mother is saying," Linc added, "is that she may not be the same Chloe she was seven years ago."

"Yes," Molly said. "That's what I mean."

"I get that, and I appreciate the work she seems to have done on herself, but part of me wants to say to hell with that. What if I couldn't have stepped up the way I did for Caden or hadn't had the massive family support that I did? What would've become of him? I haven't thought of her in any meaningful way in years but having her resurface this way has made me angry."

"And rightfully so, son," Linc said. "But you're angry at the Chloe from seven years ago, not the person she is today."

"So, you guys think I should let her see him?"

Lexi noticed a slightly hysterical edge to his voice that had her reaching for his hand.

"I think," Molly said carefully, "that if you don't, it might come back to haunt you with him someday."

"How so?" Max asked.

"Roll with me here," Molly said, "but what if, many years from now, Caden decides to seek her out on his own? He's

69

bound to have questions about who she is and why she made the choices she did. What if she were to say to him, 'Back when you were seven, I reached out to your dad asking to see you, but he decided not to allow that'? How do you think he'll feel about that as a twenty-year-old?"

Max used his free hand to rub his chest. "I feel like I'm having a heart attack or something."

"You're not having a heart attack," Molly said. "And I don't think you should panic about this. She's not going to come waltzing back in here like the last seven years didn't happen and undo the bond you have with your son. That cannot happen, Max. He adores you. He knows you've been there for him every day of his life. That will never change, even if she's back in his life."

"What if she wants more than an occasional visit?" Max asked.

"You should take this one step at a time, son," Linc said. "Beginning with a conversation with Caden about what he'd like to do. If he says no, thank you, then the answer is no. If he says he'd like to meet her, then you start there. You have full custody, which means you decide what, when, where and how long."

"That's a good point," Lexi said. "You're in control of the situation."

"Why do I feel like I'm not in control of anything?"

"You're reacting emotionally," Molly said. "And understandably so, but Chloe put the ball in your court. I agree with Dad that talking to Caden about it is the best plan. He's old enough to understand who she is and what she's asking for."

Max released a deep sigh. "I'll talk to him after the party. Thanks for the advice. I appreciate that and everything else you guys have done for us."

"Helping you raise your little boy has been a joyful thing for us," Molly said. "He's an absolute delight."

"Yes, he is," Max said, smiling for the first time in a while.

"You kids need to go have some fun while your little guy is with us," Linc said. "Lexi is only here for the weekend."

Max tried to pull himself out of the tailspin to focus on Lexi and the limited time they had together. "I could eat something."

"Me, too."

"Want to hit Kingdom?"

"I'd love to. I've never had pizza as good as theirs."

Elmer came in with the kids, who ran ahead of him from the mudroom into the family room, their faces red from the cold.

"Ew," Max said to Caden. "Go do something with your nose."

Grinning, Caden darted toward the bathroom while Chase and Molly attacked Max.

He caught them in a tight hug, making them squeal when he kissed their necks. When he released them, they came right back for more.

"Lexi, you might want to look out," Linc said. "This can get rough."

She moved over to give Max and the kids room to wrestle. "I see that."

When Caden returned, he jumped on the pile.

By the time Max emerged from the scrum, he was red-faced and sweating, but the sick feeling he'd arrived with was gone. His parents were right. He was in control of this situation, and he would do what was best for his son—as always.

"Now that I've gotten them all wound up, I've gotta roll," Max said to his parents.

"Thanks a lot, pal," Molly said, smiling.

"You guys be good for Grammy and Gramps and Grandpa-Great, you hear?"

"We will," Caden said. "Grandpa-Great said we can have ice cream later if we pick up all the toys."

"Then I'd get busy picking up if I were you. Give me a hug first."

Caden hurled himself into Max's arms and was squirming two seconds later, wanting to be released to go back to playing with his cousins. Max kissed his cheek and let him go, trying not to be hurt when Caden wiped off the kiss, which never would've happened only a year ago.

His little boy was growing up, whether he liked it or not.

CHAPTER SEVEN

"Love is composed of a single soul inhabiting two bodies." —Aristotle

They left the barn and headed into town as a light snow began to fall. Lexi was full of so many emotions, she could barely process them all. Her heart and soul were coming back to life after a long, dark winter of despair and certainty that her life would be cut short.

"I'm really sorry about my drama interfering with your weekend," Max said after a long silence.

"Don't be sorry. I enjoyed seeing you in protective-dad mode. It's kinda hot, actually."

Max snorted out a laugh. "Sure, it is."

"No, really. It is. You're so good with him."

"He makes it easy. He's a great kid."

"He's a great kid because of your time and attention and the example you've set for him."

"Thank you. That means a lot."

"I thought I'd have four kids by now," she said with a sigh. "With you."

Max glanced at her. "You imagined us having kids together?"

"Oh my God, all the time! I could see it so clearly. You, me and a team of kiddos." She smiled at him. "I hope you know that if cancer hadn't intervened, I would've been right back here the minute I could've to pick up where we left off."

"Ever since I found out where you'd been and why, all I can think about is what might've been for both of us. I guess things worked out the way they were meant to in some ways, because I wouldn't have had Caden if we'd stayed together."

"You were definitely meant to have him."

"But you weren't meant to have cancer," Max said.

"I think I was, though. It was something I was supposed to go through for whatever reason, and the result is a whole new appreciation for days like today when regular life happens."

"Today hasn't been regular for me in any way. I got to hang out with you, I got a dog and Caden's mother reappeared. Any one of those things would be a major headline on any other day. That's a lot for one day. My head is spinning a bit."

"Do you feel better after talking to your parents?"

"I guess. Except for the part where I need to tell Caden his mother has resurfaced and wants to see him."

"How do you think he'll respond?"

"He'll want to see her."

"You seem sure of that."

"I am sure. He's started asking more about her in the last year or so as he tunes in to the fact that his friends and cousins have mothers, and he doesn't."

"What have you said in response to his questions?"

"Just that we were both really young when we had him and she wasn't ready to be a mom, but she loves him very much. And then he asks where she is. I say I'm not sure and try to change the subject. That's getting tougher to do as he gets older."

"It's the right thing to give him the choice to see her."

"I know, but I still don't like it. Anyway, we've talked enough about her for one day."

"Don't feel like you have to change the subject on my account. I understand that her reappearance is a very big deal to you."

"It's like a nuclear bomb detonating, metaphorically speaking."

"I'm sure, but it'll be okay. You know that, right?"

"Keep telling me."

"As much as you need to hear it."

He pulled into the parking lot at Kingdom Pizza, put the truck in Park, but left it running. "It's just like I remember with you. Easy, fun, cool." He glanced over at her. "I've never had that with anyone else. Having you back has made me realize I've been looking for that. I've been looking for *you*."

Lexi fanned her face. "It's getting warm in here again."

His smile only added to the heat level. "I mean it."

"I know you do, and I'm trying to figure out what it means."

"Me, too. Maybe we can figure it out together?"

She nodded because he'd taken her breath away with everything he'd said.

"Wait for me." He shut off the engine and got out to come around and help her down.

When she expected him to release her, he didn't. Rather, he stared down at her with a dazzled look on his face. Then he leaned in and kissed her. The brief touch of his lips to hers left her electrified. As if he hadn't just rocked her world, he put his arm around her and walked her into Kingdom Pizza.

Lexi wasn't sure if she walked or floated.

Max Abbott had kissed her, and it was just like she remembered.

Inside, Kingdom Pizza was doing a robust Saturday-night business. Someone sitting at a table in the back waved to Max.

He took hold of Lexi's hand. "Come say hi to my sister Ella and her family."

The easy affection also reminded her of their previous relationship and filled her with a warm sense of homecoming.

Ella jumped up to hug Lexi. "I thought that was you! It's so nice to see you."

"You, too. Your family is beautiful."

"Thank you. Do you remember Gavin?"

"I do. Great to see you."

"Been a long time," Gavin said.

"Too long," Lexi replied.

"These are our kids, Sarah, Cici and Caleb. Guys, say hi to Uncle Max and his friend Lexi." Like their parents, the kids had dark hair and eyes.

"Do you have a *girlfriend*, Uncle Max?" Caleb asked with an impish grin.

"None of your business, mister," Max replied as he bent to kiss the kids and steal a bite of Cici's pizza, making the little girl giggle.

Was it possible to overdose on desire just from watching a sexy man interact with dogs and kids? If so, she was in serious danger.

"I take it the reunion went well?" Ella asked her brother, brow raised in inquiry.

"It was much better than expected. Are you guys excited for the party tomorrow?" Max asked the kids.

"So excited," Sarah said. "We went shopping for presents today."

Caleb gave a fist pump. "Party time!"

"We're going to grab some grub," Max said, smiling. "We'll see you tomorrow."

"Have a nice evening," Ella said with a big smile.

"Knock it off, El."

"What'd I do?"

He scowled at his sister as he guided Lexi toward the counter, where they joined the line to order. "Sorry about that."

"About what? She's great as always."

"She's being all weird about seeing us together."

"Can you blame her? We show up together after ten years apart. That's gonna get people talking."

"It doesn't have to be my own family acting like fools."

"Doesn't bother me. Don't let it bother you. And by the way, her family is adorable."

"She's so happy. It's nice to see. She was crazy about Gavin for years before they got together—years when he was in self-destructive mode after losing his brother, Caleb. It's good to know that things work out sometimes."

Some people got all the luck, Lexi thought. Some didn't. Would she be one of the lucky ones? Would Max?

"Do you still love boring old cheese pizza?" he asked.

"More than almost anything."

He rolled his eyes. "And a salad?"

"Yep."

"You got it."

He ordered for them—a small cheese for her, a medium meat lover for him and a large salad to share.

The exact same order as ten years ago, except he got himself a beer. "What do you want to drink?"

"I'll do a glass of rosé."

Max ordered her drink and then tapped his card to pay.

"Next time is my treat."

"If you insist."

"I do. I insist."

They grabbed a table vacated by another couple and took off their coats.

"This place is just as I remember it," Lexi said, eyeing the exposed brick and the wood floor.

"Not much changes around here."

"That's not true. A lot has changed."

"Like what?"

"The diner changed hands and expanded. You have a son. Your siblings are all married with kids."

"Not Charley. She and Tyler never got married, but she's living with him and helping to raise his nieces."

"You're living in your grandparents' house, and your dad is retired. I mean, Lucas and Landon are married with kids. If that's not a big change, I don't know what is."

"That's a fact," Max said with a laugh. "I guess it just seems that other than Caden, not much has changed for me."

"Caden is a major change."

"He was at the beginning. It was so big as to be overwhelming, especially after Chloe left. But now it's like he's always been part of my life."

"You're so lucky to have him," she said wistfully.

"And I know it. What about you? Do you still want a bunch of kids like you used to?"

"I do, but I'm not sure if I can. The chemo and treatments wreaked havoc with my body, but I took the doctors' advice at the beginning and harvested some eggs for later. Just in case. But it would be a long shot."

"Still... there's a chance, right?"

"I hope so, but I won't know until I try." Her heart ached when she thought about how badly she'd once wanted children. She'd expected to do four years of college, reunite with Max, start their family and live happily ever after with their houseful of kids. That was her only dream until surviving took precedence over everything. "Listen," she said softly, "it might be better for both of us not to get all caught up in the nostalgia and think we can pick right up where we left off like nothing ever came between us."

"Nothing did come between us. We weren't apart because we wanted to be."

"Right, but a lot has happened, and it would be a risk for you to get involved with me again."

"How so?"

"Well, my life is going to be a bit of a roller-coaster ride for the next four years. Every fever, cold, sore throat and bout of fatigue will be cause for panic. I'm not sure I can have babies, and you always wanted a big family as much as I did."

"My dreams have changed as I've gotten older. I've learned to be satisfied with what I have, which is an awful lot. If I had you, too, that would make everything perfect."

Before she could respond, a server brought their salad and pizzas to the table.

"Can I get you anything else?" the young woman asked.

"No, thank you," Max said after glancing at Lexi, who shook her head.

"Enjoy your dinner."

Max put slices of pizza on each of their plates as Lexi put dressing on the salad after removing the onions.

"You still forget to ask for no onions," Max said, smiling.

"Every time."

"Did I go too far with what I said before the food came?" he asked. "You looked shocked."

"You might've shocked me a little, but in a good way."

"You were saying how much has changed here, but one thing hasn't. You were it for me ten years ago, and you still are."

AFTER HE SAID THAT, LEXI COULD BARELY BREATHE, LET ALONE eat. She picked at her pizza and salad and chased every bite with a sip of water to get the food past the huge lump in her throat. *You were it for me ten years ago, and you still are.*

He'd said the only thing she'd wanted to hear during the awful ordeal of her illness, so why did she feel more upset than elated?

"What's wrong?" Max asked, tuning in to her distress.

"Nothing."

"You never could lie to me, Lex."

He knew her so well. He always had. He *saw* her the way no one else ever had. Not that she'd dated all that much other than him, but that feeling of being known was so much a part of who they'd been together, and it still was.

"Could we take the food to go?"

"Sure." He got up to get boxes and a bag and had them on their way in a matter of minutes, leaving with a wave for Ella's family.

Max helped her into the car and handed her the bag of food.

On the ride back to his place, neither of them said anything, which only added to her anxiety.

She was jolted out of her thoughts when Max slammed on the brakes, and the truck spun in a full circle. The bag of food flew off her lap and hit the dash before falling to the floor.

"Holy shit," Max said. "Are you okay?"

"Yeah, you?"

"Uh-huh, but freaking Fred strikes again."

The town moose stood defiantly in the middle of the road,

staring them down like they were bothering him rather than the other way around.

"I can't believe he hasn't been killed by a car hitting him," Lexi said.

"He's unkillable. He's demolished a few cars, though, including my sister-in-law Cameron's MINI Cooper."

"Well, that's not exactly a Vermont car."

"That's what Will said, too. He made her get an SUV that she hates."

Max lay on the horn, which only earned him a perturbed glance from the giant moose, so he put the truck in Park. "I guess we're gonna be here for a minute." He also turned on the hazard lights so they wouldn't be hit from behind. Looking over at her, he said, "You want to tell me what happened back at the restaurant?"

"I don't really know. I had this weird reaction to you saying what you did, and I don't even know why. I spent years hoping I might one day hear those exact words from you."

"What do you suppose caused that?"

"Anxiety has been a big problem, for me and my family. We're all medicated for it."

"I'm not surprised. You went through such a stressful thing."

"It's made it so even things that should be wonderful are viewed through a lens of doom. Like, how could something so amazing be real? Where will it go wrong? Because it always goes wrong."

"Maybe it won't this time."

"I want so badly to believe that, but it always does. Every time I think things have turned around, I get kicked in the teeth again. And it occurred to me that if we pick up where we left off, I'd be taking you down with me this time."

"Maybe you'd be taking me up rather than down. Has that occurred to you?"

"No, it hasn't."

"We need to reprogram you to expect the best rather than the worst."

"Good luck with that. My therapist has been trying for years to get me to see my glass as half full. I'm a work in progress."

"We all are. You know that, right?"

"Some of us more than others."

He tucked a strand of her hair behind her ear and caressed her face with his fingertip. "I want to make a believer out of you. I want to show you that the worst is behind you, and the rest… The rest is going to be why you survived."

"How can you be so sure?"

"I just have a feeling. This was how our story was meant to play out. We were meant to go our separate ways for all this time and to find our way back to each other when we were ready to."

"Did you read *Twilight* by any chance?"

"Haha, no, but my sisters made me watch the movies."

"No wonder you're talking about fated mates and such things."

Max hit the horn again, but Fred wasn't inclined to move. "All I know is that after a couple of years, I told people to stop asking me about you because I didn't have the answers. I didn't know where you were or why I'd stopped hearing from you. It was too painful to think about why you left and never came back."

"I'm sorry I hurt you."

"Don't be sorry," he said. "I know why now, and it all makes sense. When you think about it, nothing has really changed between us. Neither of us wanted to be apart for ten years, so it's like no time has passed."

While Lexi processed that, Max put the window down. "What do you think, Fred?"

"Are you really asking a moose for his opinion?"

"His free advice is almost as good as my grandfather's."

Lexi began to laugh and couldn't stop. This was the most ridiculous ten minutes of her life.

Fred let out a noise that was between a moo and a groan.

"Do you hear what he's saying?"

"I don't speak moose."

"You're in luck. Hannah has taught me a few things." Max

listened intently as Fred continued to speak. "He's saying that you fought really hard to overcome a very serious illness, and now that you've regained your health, you ought to enjoy every second of your life, starting right now by coming home with me and spending the night. He says he remembers how much we used to wish we could sleep together all night, and now we can."

"Are you in cahoots with a moose? Did you plan this?"

"Not at all, but Fred knows a good thing when he sees it, and so do I." He reached for her hand and brought it to his lips, running them over her knuckles.

She drew in a sharp deep breath.

"What do you say? Do you want to come home with me?"

"I, um, well…"

"It's just tonight, Lex. We'll let tomorrow take care of itself."

With him, it had never been that simple, but he and Fred were right. She'd fought long and hard to regain her health, and she was determined to live every minute to the fullest in this second chance she'd been given. "Okay," she said softly.

"She said yes, Fred," Max said out the window.

Fred mooed loudly and ambled off into the brush by the side of the road.

"Is he for real?" Lexi asked, incredulous.

Max shifted the truck into Drive and continued toward his house. "As real as it gets. Fred has been interfering in our lives for as long as I can remember."

"I've tried to tell people about Butler, but I could never do justice to what goes on here. How do you explain about a moose that everyone calls by name who's as much a part of the town as any of the people are?"

"You can't. You have to experience Butler to believe it."

"I've missed it here so much. I've missed everything about it, especially you."

"I missed you, too. I can admit that now that I know where you've been." He paused before he added, "People wondered about you, and I'd have to say I wasn't sure where you were."

"It never occurred to me that you'd be forced to answer questions about me."

"It was rough for a while. I won't lie to you about that. I was angry and confused and sad not to have you in my life. With hindsight that has come with being back with you again, I can see that things didn't work out with Chloe or anyone else I dated because there was so much unfinished business with you."

"That's a good way to describe it. For me, it was like this giant question mark. 'If I see Max again, will it be like it was back then, or will it be strange and awkward?'"

"We've answered that question rather definitively. It's the same as it always was."

No, it isn't, Lexi thought. *It's even better.* She wished she could get fully on board with picking up where they left off, but now that the moment was upon them, she was worried about whether it was fair to saddle him—and his precious son—with the anxiety she and her family lived with every day.

Max helped her out of the truck, something he'd done when they were dating that she'd never forgotten, and led the way inside.

Daisy let out a happy squeak, her tail wagging so hard, it banged against the wire frame of her crate.

Max let her out and scooped her up. "No! Not on me! Outside! Damn it, she peed on me."

Lexi lost it laughing. She'd laughed more today than she had in years, and it felt good.

"It's not funny!" He held the puppy away from him, revealing the massive wet stain on his torso.

Lexi bent in half laughing.

"I'll remember this," he said with a playful scowl. "I'm taking her outside before she poops on me, too."

She was still mopping up laughter tears when he returned, shivering.

"Did you know pee freezes?" He held the shirt off his skin.

"I wasn't aware, but you learn something new every day."

Daisy sat at Max's feet, looking up at him with a big dopey smile on her cute face.

"She's very sorry," Lexi said.

"I don't think she is."

"I'll feed her while you deal with that," she said, waving her hand in the direction of his soaked shirt.

"Quit laughing at me. It's not funny."

"Yes, it is."

"No, it isn't," he said from right behind her. "I have a good mind to hug you right now since you think it's so funny."

Lexi screamed and darted clear of him.

Daisy thought that meant playtime, and she jumped into the fracas as Max chased Lexi into the living room.

"If you hug me, I'm outta here."

Max stopped short. "If you're gonna be that way about it."

"I am. No pee hugs allowed. Tell him, Daisy. You pee only on him."

Daisy barked in agreement.

"I can already see whose side she's on."

"We girls have to stick together in this bachelor pad."

"I'll be right back. Make yourself at home in the bachelor pad."

"Thank you." Lexi fed Daisy and then put their takeout food on plates she found in the cabinet over the dishwasher. She located silverware in another drawer, and by the time Max emerged from the hallway in a fresh set of clothes, dinner was on the table.

"Now," he said after he opened a beer and joined her at the table, "where were we before we were so rudely interrupted by a moose and puppy?"

CHAPTER EIGHT

"What we have once enjoyed and deeply loved we can never lose, for all that we love deeply becomes a part of us." —Helen Keller

*T*his had been the best day Max could recall in a long time. Even the drama of Chloe reappearing on the scene couldn't detract from the pleasure of being with Lexi again.

He'd forgotten how easy it was with her. In three years of dating, they'd never had a fight that he could recall. Their friends had teased them about being the perfect couple, but they hadn't minded that. It'd been true.

"Remember what people used to say about us?" he asked as he took a bite of now-cold pizza.

"That we were so perfect, we made them sick?"

"Yeah, that. They were jealous of how easy we made it look."

"Did you hear that Harry and Trish got married and divorced within two years of leaving high school?"

"No! Oh my God. No way."

"They were married just long enough to have two kids that they fought over in court for five years. It got really ugly."

"Wow. That's terrible. Those poor kids."

"It was pretty bad. For a while, the kids were living with Mr. and Mrs. Donaldson. My mom is friends with Mrs. D, which is how I heard about it. They moved to California or somewhere out West after school."

Lexi pushed the second half of her salad across the table to Max, something she used to do all the time. Judging by his grin, he remembered that, too.

"It's interesting, isn't it, that the other couple everyone thought was so perfect in high school made a total mess of things in the real world," Max said.

"Do you think that would've happened to us?"

"No."

"How can you be so sure?" she asked.

"First of all, we wouldn't have gotten married when they did. We were both in college. It wouldn't have happened until after that. Hopefully, we would've been mature enough by then to handle it."

"Hopefully. It's nice to play what-if. I did a lot of that when I was isolated from everyone in the hospital. I'd pretend that I was in Vermont with you and our family, and everything had worked out the way I wanted it to."

He sat back in his chair and gave her a penetrating look. "How many kids did we have in this fantasy of yours?"

"Four. Two of each."

"What were their names?"

"Madeline, Caroline, Sawyer and Cole."

"We can't have a Caroline. I had a one-night stand with a Caroline."

"When?"

"After my brother Wade's wedding about six years ago. She was the bride's cousin."

"All right, then. No Caroline. How about Abigail? That was another of my favorites."

"I could live with that."

"Should we be talking about this stuff?"

"Why not?"

"I don't even know if I still can have kids."

Max shrugged. "If you can't, we'll adopt."

"You're pretty far down the road with this life we're going to have together twenty-four hours after we saw each other for the first time in years."

"You agreed with me that nothing has changed between us, so why not make some plans?"

"You need to really think about this, Max. My situation is anything but assured. I have four more years until I'll be considered cured of my illness, and even then, it can still come back."

"Are you planning to spend those four years doing nothing until you get the all clear?"

"Well, no, but—"

"No buts. You're going to live, so why can't you live with me and Caden? Why can't we make a life together?"

"Max," she said on a long exhale. "It doesn't work that way."

"You said last night that you came back for me. Here I am, offering you anything you want. Since last night, I realized I've been looking for what I had with you since the day I last saw you, and I'd like to think I'm smart enough to know by now that what we had doesn't come along every day. It has never come along again for me, that's for sure."

Lexi fanned her face, which felt flushed suddenly.

"I love that you blush now. It's very cute."

"It's an effect of the chemo, and I hate it."

He shook his head. "You're not allowed to hate it. I love it."

"What I said about my health is something you need to think about for longer than twenty-four hours."

"Let me ask you something."

"Okay…"

"What if I was the one who'd battled a serious illness and was facing an uncertain future? Would you shy away from me because I might have health problems again?"

"No, but this isn't your run-of-the-mill health problem."

"I fully understand what you've been through, and it doesn't matter."

"You can't fully understand it in a matter of a few hours. You'd be bringing me into your son's life. If something were to happen to me, we have to think of him."

"Something could happen to me, too. The work we do on the

mountain isn't without risks, not to mention my brothers and I are on the Search and Rescue Team, and we like to do all sorts of things that could get us killed. We've had some close calls, here and there, like when Hunter took a bad fall when we were rock climbing, and Lucas nearly died in the fire in the inn. Shit happens. Life happens. I don't live in fear of dying."

"What about Caden, though?"

"If, God forbid, something were to happen to me, Will and Cameron have agreed to be his guardians. My cousin Grayson put that in writing for me a long time ago."

"You've thought it all out."

"I had to. I'm a single parent. I needed to ensure that he'd be okay if the worst happened. I've always been very close to Will, and now I am to Cam, too. Caden is best friends with Chase, and he loves Molly and Murphy. He'd be happy with them, and he'd have the rest of my family around him, too."

As he spoke, Max got up and cleared their plates, loaded the dishwasher and wiped the table. "What?" he asked when he caught her watching him.

"You're very domestic."

"I have to be, or my house would be a disaster."

"As the youngest of ten kids, you should be completely useless."

Laughing, he said, "Sorry to disappoint you, but my mother wouldn't have tolerated a useless kid, even if he was the youngest."

"No, she wouldn't have."

He held out a hand to her. "Come with me."

"Where to?"

"It's a good night for a fire."

"Every night is a good night for a fire."

"Even in the summer?"

"In Vermont, yes. In Houston, hell no."

"Did you hate living there?"

"I didn't get to spend much time exploring. I was in the hospital a lot. But my parents and grandparents don't care for it. Too sprawling and too busy for them after living here."

"I'm sure it was a shock to their system."

"It really was. All of it was."

He leaned in and kissed her the way he used to, as if he'd been doing that all along. "Stay here. I'll get some wood."

Lexi couldn't believe the way this weekend was unfolding. When she'd arrived in Butler on Friday, she'd hoped to see Max, to have a chance to explain why she'd disappeared for so long and to hopefully leave with their friendship back on track. She'd never expected him to ask her to stay forever.

And now that he had?

She was preconditioned to expect disaster. It was hard to turn off the part of her brain that was screaming at her to proceed with caution, to take her time, to protect herself from anything that could hurt her. Her brain was in an epic battle with her heart, which wanted everything Max was offering and to hell with the consequences.

She'd spent years wishing for what he was offering her. Why in the world did she feel hesitant to take the next step? Her therapist would tell her to go for it, to live the life she'd fought so hard to have. But in trying so hard to survive, she'd forgotten how to enjoy life.

Max returned with the wood and had a fire going in a matter of minutes. "I love fire season."

"I remember that. Your mother called you her little pyromaniac."

"Yep, Noah had that title in the Coleman family, and I was the Abbott firebug. I went through a stage where I wanted to be the one to start every fire, but my dad was adamant that I was only to do it under his supervision and in fireplaces or firepits. Nowhere else. I think they were worried I'd burn down the town if they weren't super strict with me."

"You were always the one building the bonfires in high school."

"I still do them for the family a couple of times a year. Funny that my brothers are the ones who put the fires out around here." He returned to his seat next to her on the sofa, turning to face her. "Tell me what you're thinking."

"I'm all twisted up inside. You're offering me everything I ever dreamed of, and all I can think about is how it might be a disaster."

"It won't be. We'd never let that happen."

"I'm scared."

"Of what?"

"Of falling back into what we used to have and it not working out for whatever reason. I'm scared of getting sick again and breaking your heart and Caden's. I'm scared of everything in a way I never used to be."

"We need to keep you so happy and so busy that you never have time to think about being sick or to worry about a relapse."

"Busy doing what?"

"*Living*, Lex. You need to get busy living so you're not stuck in worry mode. I know it's hard to undo years of trauma, and I don't expect that to happen overnight, but the further away you get from it, the less you'll worry."

He caressed her face and held her gaze as he moved in to kiss her, lingering this time.

She reached for him and kissed him back, shocked by the jolt to her system that reminded her of the best time in her life, back when she'd kissed him every day. Like it had then, their sweet, innocent kiss evolved into hot and sexy like someone had lit a match.

It had always been like that between them. While her friends had described awkward, fumbling first times with boys who had no idea what they were doing, she and Max had gotten it right from the beginning. She'd been his first, too, but there was nothing awkward or fumbling about it.

During long, lonely months in the hospital, she'd thought about being with him this way. She'd dreamed about him on many a night, and the emotional punch of this moment filled her eyes with tears that spilled down her cheeks.

"What?" he asked, brushing away her tears. "What's wrong?"

"Nothing is wrong for the first time in so long."

"Same." He smiled as he leaned his forehead against hers. "I had no idea how much I'd missed you until you came home."

She reached up to caress the handsome face that was at once familiar and new. The beautiful boy had become a sexy man while she was gone.

"What do you say we see what it's like to sleep in a bed together?"

"I'm all for that."

Max withdrew from her and went to tend to the fire, closing the doors to keep any stray sparks contained. Then he held out a hand to help her up. Keeping a grip on her hand, he led her into his bedroom, which had a king-sized bed with a blue-and-green-plaid flannel duvet cover.

"This is nice," she said.

"It's nothing special."

"It's your home, your bed. That makes it special."

"Having you here with me makes everything special."

"Everything that's happened is beyond my wildest dreams. That you still feel the same way I do, that nothing has changed except we're twenty-eight rather than eighteen. It's amazing."

"It always was. A few years after I last saw you, I forced myself to stop thinking about you, to stop wondering where you were or why you hadn't called me. I stuffed you in a box and put you in the back corner of my mind because it was just too painful to wonder anymore. I didn't think about you or talk about you or wonder about you anymore, but even then thoughts of you would pop into my mind and I'd ache with missing you. Now I know it was always you, Lex. Always."

"For me, too."

When he kissed her, Lexi went up on tiptoes to kiss him back, wrapping her arms around his neck the way she used to do all the time. Kissing him was familiar, but sexier, hotter, needier —and that was saying something, because they'd been hot for each other back in the day.

He raised her sweater up and over her head, and then she did the same for him. Next was the long-sleeved thermal that left her in only a bra and jeans.

Lexi shivered at the loss of the warm clothing.

"Are you cold?" he asked.

"Always."

"Hurry, let's get under the covers."

They shed their jeans and got into bed, reaching for each other the way they used to do in the bed of his first pickup truck. "Remember the truck?"

"I remember everything."

"I remember being cold," Lexi said with a laugh.

"I warmed you up."

"Yes, you did."

He ran a hand over her back, setting off a burst of goose bumps that made her shiver. "The sweetest memories of my life involved you."

"Same."

Their lips came together in another greedy, tongue-twisting kiss that had them straining to get closer.

Max moved his hand to her bottom and pulled her in tight against him.

Lexi felt like she'd died and gone straight to heaven.

THIS WAS PERFECTION, MAX THOUGHT AS HE KISSED HER AND HELD her. It felt like no time had gone by as all the turmoil inside him settled. On any other day, Chloe's reappearance would have sent him into a tailspin. With Lexi there to give him much better things to think about, the concern was still present, but it wasn't all-consuming the way it would've been otherwise.

He'd figure out the best way forward for Caden, the way he always did. But tonight, he didn't have to think about any of that. Not when he had Lexi back in his arms for the first time in years, and in his bed for the first time ever.

Max was determined to make this amazing for her. He wanted her to leave here on Monday with no doubt about where she belonged and who she belonged with. He kissed her face and neck and down to her chest, where he encountered a bump under her skin.

"That's my chemo port. They want me to keep it for another year. Just in case."

MARIE FORCE

He couldn't bear to think about her being sick again, so he didn't dwell on that, not now when everything felt better than it had since he was last with her.

"Max…"

"What, honey?"

"I'm different than I was. Thinner. Bonier. Just different. And I have scars."

"You're as beautiful as I remember. Don't worry about anything. Just relax and let me love you." He reached behind her to release her bra and eased it down, revealing the breasts that had been the source of his youthful fantasies. Hers were the first ones he'd ever seen or touched. He'd been obsessed with her and would be again before this weekend was over.

The thought of her leaving on Monday made him sadder than he'd been in a long time, and it was still only Saturday. Maybe he could talk her into staying. That possibility sent his spirits soaring as he kissed her abdomen and down to the waistband of her panties. Hooking his fingers into the elastic, he eased them down her legs and tossed them aside.

"Are you warm enough?"

"I'm very warm," she said with a suggestive smile.

"Let's see if we can make you even warmer." He settled between her legs and opened her to his tongue and fingers.

"Max… What… Wait…"

"Shhh. It's okay." They hadn't done this in the past, so it was probably new to her, which was even more reason to make it as good as it could be. He set out to bring her nothing but pleasure with his tongue and fingers. He'd learned a few things in the years since they'd been together, and he put them all into practice, curling his fingers to hit the spot inside that would set her off.

"Relax," he whispered. "Let it happen."

He doubled down and had her straining toward release in a matter of seconds.

Lexi cried out when she came, her inner muscles tightening around his fingers.

Max withdrew from her. "Don't go anywhere."

Her laughter made him smile. "Couldn't move if I had to."

He went into the bathroom and found a box of condoms he'd bought a while ago but had never opened. Colton's commentary from earlier ran through his mind. As much as Max hated to admit his brother was right about anything, he'd been right to push him toward Lexi.

He washed his face and hands quickly and returned to her.

She was snuggled under the comforter where he joined her after rolling on the condom.

Her arms and legs wrapped around him felt like a homecoming of sorts, and the feeling of rightness that came with being with her was just as he remembered.

"This feels so good," he whispered against her lips. "So right."

"Yes, it does."

"You ready for more?"

"Mmm, so ready."

He rolled them so he was on top of her, gazing down at her sweet face.

She looked up at him with love and trust and so much affection.

"How did I live so long without you, Lex?"

"I don't know how I did it either. It was torture."

"It's all good now, sweetheart." He pushed into her, overwhelmed by the memories, the sweetness, the heat, the love. "We found each other twice in a lifetime. How lucky are we?"

"So, so lucky."

Max had never felt quite as lucky as he did having her back in his arms and in his bed for the first time. Caden was his greatest joy, but Lexi... She was his one true love, and now that she was back in his arms, he would do everything he could to keep her there.

CHAPTER NINE

"Immature love says: 'I love you because I need you.' Mature love says: 'I need you because I love you.'" —Erich Fromm

*W*hen Max woke early the next morning with Lexi in his arms, a feeling of peace came over him that was another indication that all this time, he'd been waiting for her without realizing it. Had he expected her to come back to find him? Not really, but she'd set the gold standard for what it meant to be in love, and he'd never again come close to having what he did with her.

And now he knew it was all still there—the love, the desire, the laughter, the easiness. Everything about being with her had always been perfect, and last night, they'd confirmed—numerous times—that it still was.

He couldn't wait to celebrate Caden and Savvy today with their joint birthday party and to spend this day with Lexi. Max wanted her and Caden to get to know each other, which couldn't happen if she went back to Texas tomorrow. Later, he would see if he could talk her into staying awhile longer.

In the seven years since the momentous day that Caden had come into his life, Max had experienced many highs and lows. Most of the highs involved the son who'd been a joy to him from the minute he arrived. The lows had included Chloe's decision to punch out of Caden's life and the loneliness that had come with single parenthood. His entire focus had shifted toward his son, which hadn't left much space for dating or anything else that didn't involve Caden.

A nagging sense of discontent had attached itself to his personal life and stayed there as he meandered through a few meaningless encounters with women over the years. Today was the first time in years he'd woken up without the discontent, and it was all because of Lexi.

He tried to disentangle himself from her, hoping she'd sleep awhile yet, but the second he moved, her eyes opened.

And then she smiled. "Hey."

"How you doing?"

"Better than I've been in a very long time."

"Same. What do we think of sleeping in a bed together?"

"We quite like it, but we knew we would."

"I could very easily get used to sleeping with you," he said, kissing her shoulder and her neck and making her shiver.

"Me, too."

"Why do you have to leave tomorrow?"

"Because that's when my flight is."

"Flights can be changed."

"Is that what you want?"

"Hell yes, that's what I want. I want you here, with me and Caden, for as long as you want to be here, which is hopefully forever."

"What if that's not what he wants?"

"He'll be fine with it. He's super easygoing and always loves to meet new people. I'm not worried about him."

"I think, maybe, we ought to slow down a bit and be a little more cautious about our next steps."

"Why?"

"You have a son to consider, and I'm still trying to figure out what's next for me."

"I want to be what's next for you. Caden and I want to be what's next."

"And I'd love that, but I want to take it slow and have the

chance to get to know him and vice versa."

Max groaned. "Haven't we lost enough time?" He turned on his side to face her, his hand on her shoulder. "All I want is a lifetime of nights like last night."

"I want that, too, but I want us to do this right."

"I thought we did it pretty damned right."

Smiling, she said, "That's not what I meant, and you know it."

"Why are you being the wiser parent?"

"One of us needs to be. Let's proceed with caution so we don't give him a reason to dislike me right out of the gate."

"He won't."

"Correct me if I'm wrong, but this would be the first time you'd be trying to bring a romantic partner into his life, right?"

"Yes."

"Then you have no idea how he's going to react. This is different, Max, and he's going to see that. We have to give him space and time to come around to accepting me. And I want to get to know him, too."

"Fine," Max said, sounding as grumpy as he felt. "We'll do it your way."

"You'll be glad we did."

"Let me ask you this… If it was just you and me, would you stay forever?"

"Yeah, I would."

"Well, that's good to know." He let strands of her hair slide through his fingers. "How soon can you come back?"

"Probably by the first of the year. Our tenants are moving out of my parents' house. I'll move into the garage apartment so they can lease out the rest."

"You could just move in here."

"Not yet."

"Ugh, adult Lexi is making me mad."

She smiled and leaned in to kiss him. "I bet I can make you happy again in five minutes."

He put his arm around her to bring her closer to him. "It won't take that long."

. . .

THIS WEEKEND WAS THE BEST THING THAT'D HAPPENED TO LEXI since the last time she'd been with Max. She'd been so in love with him that the thought of being separated for even a day had been painful. At the time, she'd thought that applying to UC Berkeley was the biggest mistake of her life when the man she loved with all her heart would be back in Vermont, "seeing other people."

When he'd suggested that, she'd wanted to die. The thought of him with anyone else was beyond unbearable to her. But he'd been so sweet and gentle suggesting they were too young to try to hold their relationship together while they were so far apart in college.

The memories of that excruciating time swirled through Lexi's mind while she showered as Max took Daisy outside.

He'd been right, of course, but no one could tell her that then. She'd been inconsolable as she'd slogged through her first semester of college with a badly broken heart. She hadn't partaken in any of the activities her suitemates had engaged in, preferring to spend time alone with her memories.

Without telling her parents, she'd applied to transfer to UVM for the following year and had been accepted. She was about to tell Max the good news when disaster struck in the form of a raging fever and rash that had sent her to the clinic on campus. Before that day was out, she was in the hospital with the diagnosis that would take over her life for the next decade.

Missing Max had suddenly become the least of her concerns. But even in the heat of battle against a relentless foe, he'd remained a larger-than-life character from her past, who'd held a very special place in her heart. She'd clung to the memories of him and them together to get her through hell. In all the time they'd spent apart, there'd been only one other man who'd captured her attention—the young oncologist who'd seen her through treatment.

Dr. Jacob Borden.

Lexi had developed a ferocious crush on Jake, as he'd told her to call him, anticipating his daily visits the way she used to look forward to dates with Max. He was always so sweet and kind to her, answering her questions and brightening her days with his wittiness.

And then he came in one day and told her he was getting married.

The devastation of that news had reminded her of Max saying they should see other people while in college.

Somehow, she'd managed to keep it together while Jake cheerfully told her about his fiancée, Devon, and how they'd met in medical school and stayed together through residencies in separate states. After the wedding, Devon was moving to live with him in Houston and would work at MD Anderson. Jake said he was looking forward to introducing his new wife to Lexi, whom he referred to as his favorite patient.

She'd had the two weeks he'd been gone for his wedding and honeymoon to pull herself together before he returned to introduce his new wife to her as promised.

Devon had been a symbol of everything Lexi no longer was and might never be again. She was beautiful, accomplished and madly in love with her handsome husband.

Their marriage had triggered a dark period for her, one that had taken multiple therapists and new medication to pull her out of months later. And when she'd resurfaced, the one thing that had remained was Max. Even though she hadn't seen him in years by then, he was still there, as much a part of her as her fingers and toes.

Memories of him had once again saved her, and now he was dangling the possibility of forever in front of her.

She turned off the water in the shower and wrapped her wet hair in one of the two towels he'd left for her. As she wrapped the other around her body, she couldn't contain the swell of joy that came with the idea of spending the rest of her life in Butler with Max and Caden.

As wonderful as that would be, she still felt it was the right thing to slow him down and make sure they were doing what was right for all of them. And who knew if the nostalgic feelings invoked this weekend would still be there in a few months?

What if they dove all in and then realized they'd made a mistake?

Lexi simply couldn't bear to go through losing him again, and she'd rather proceed with caution than risk that kind of heartbreak. Her heart had been through enough, and thus her plan to proceed with utmost caution when it came to Max and Caden even as she celebrated the giddy pleasure of being with Max again.

"I don't suppose you have a hair dryer, do you?" she asked him.

"There might be one from my grandmother's era in the back of the closet in the hallway."

Lexi found the hair dryer behind a stack of towels and hoped it still worked. She took it to the bathroom and found that not only did it still work, it worked better than her newer one ever had. The metaphor wasn't lost on her as she picked up right where she left off with her old boyfriend, as if no time had passed, as if they hadn't both been through a lot in the years they'd spent apart.

Her emotions were all over the place, but one thing was certain. She hadn't felt this good in a long time, and even as she urged caution, she couldn't wait to spend this day with Max and have the chance to get to know Caden better.

When they were both showered and dressed, they left for the barn. Max had talked to his mother, and she'd told him to bring Lexi over for breakfast and party prep. Lucas and Dani were already there with their birthday girl and were starting to set up for the party, information that Max shared with her when they were on the way with Daisy in the back seat. Lexi couldn't wait to see Caden's reaction to his dad's gift.

"It's cute that you celebrate them both together."

"They were born on the exact same day, and they love being birthday buddies." He glanced at her. "I hope you're ready for the massiveness of my family these days."

"I'm looking forward to seeing everyone and meeting all the kids."

"That's Lucas and Dani's storefront," Max said, pointing to

the left. "They added on to the barn and now they sell his furniture and her restored pieces. It's done well for them."

"It's cool that their two hobbies were so well suited."

"I know. They're great together. We honestly thought he and Landon would never find anyone who could stand them long term, and they're both happily married to women who are saints."

"They were always so funny," Lexi said, laughing.

"They still are. They love to try to confuse Dani and Amanda by acting like the other one. It's never worked, but they keep trying."

"So you and Lucas had babies on the same day. That must've been something."

"He met Dani after she had Savvy with her late fiancé. He was killed in an ATV accident before Savvy was born."

"Oh wow. That must've been so rough for her."

"It was."

"It's a reminder that everyone goes through hard times," Lexi said.

"For sure." He reached for her hand. "I want you to know… I heard what you said before about proceeding with caution, and you're right. It's just that I'm so damn happy to have you back in my life that I want everything right now."

"I want that, too."

"But we'll take it slow, because you're also right about Caden not having ever seen me seriously interested in a woman. As much as I'd like to think I can predict how that'll go, I can't. And we've got this thing with Chloe to contend with, too. I don't want to overwhelm him."

"If it's meant to be, we'll figure it out, but that doesn't have to happen today."

"I hear you, and please note how many times I've told you that you were right and it's not even ten a.m."

"Duly noted," she said, smiling at him. How could she not? He was even cuter than he'd been at eighteen, and she wouldn't have thought that was possible.

"I can't wait for him to see Daisy."

Hearing her name, the dog gave a playful bark.

"Are you ready to meet your little boy, girl?" Max asked, looking at her in the mirror.

Another excited yip.

"He's going to freak out when he realizes she's his, and it's all your fault that I now have a puppy to care for in addition to an active seven-year-old."

Lexi laughed. "That logic is twisted, but okay. I'll accept the blame if she makes Caden happy."

"He'll be thrilled, and I'll let him know it was all your idea."

"You should take credit for her, Max. It's your big surprise."

"I'll tell him you helped."

He wanted Caden to like her, and knowing how much he loved his son, that touched her deeply.

When they arrived at the barn, Daisy perked up at the sight of several other dogs running around in the yard.

Max let her out but kept a tight hold on her leash so she wouldn't run off. "George and Ringo will teach her the ropes around here."

The older dogs came over to sniff the newcomer.

Daisy's tail wagged so hard that it thumped against Max's leg.

Caden came bursting out of the mudroom door, followed by a girl around the same age as him. She had strawberry-blonde hair and was slightly taller than Caden.

"Dad! It's my birthday! And Savvy's!"

"Is it?" Max asked. "I'd forgotten."

"No way. You did not!" Caden came to a sudden stop when he saw the dog standing next to his dad. "Who's that?"

"This is Daisy. Daisy, meet Caden. Dude told me she'd be the perfect first dog for you."

"What?" Caden's cute face expressed surprise, amazement and pure joy all in the span of two seconds. "She's *mine*?"

"Only if you promise to help take care of her."

Caden dropped to his knees to hug the dog. "I'll take such good care of her. Hi, Daisy, I'm Caden, and we're gonna be best friends."

Max gave Savannah a hug. "Happy birthday, Savvy."

"Thanks, Uncle Max."

"This is my friend Lexi."

"Nice to meet you," Savannah said, shaking Lexi's hand.

"You, too. Happy birthday."

"Thank you."

"Savvy, come see Daisy," Caden said.

Savannah got down on her knees to accept happy puppy kisses from Daisy.

Caden looked up at Max with tears in his eyes. "Is she really mine, Dad? For keeps?"

"She sure is."

Caden hurled himself at his father and hugged him. "Thank you so much. Best birthday ever, and it's just getting started."

Max returned the enthusiastic hug. "I'm glad you like her."

"I *love* her. And I love you. Let's run with her, Savvy."

"You guys need coats," Max said.

"We're fine for a little bit," Caden said.

"Keep a close eye on her, Cade," Max said as he handed the leash to his son. "She doesn't know how far she's allowed to go yet."

"We won't let anything happen to her. Don't worry."

Max and Lexi stayed outside for a few minutes to make sure Caden had things under control with the dog, who was already following him as if she knew he was meant to be her person.

"That was the sweetest thing ever," Lexi said.

"I love to see him happy like that."

"I'm sure he's happy like that a lot with you as his dad."

"We have all the fun together. Come on in. I need some coffee."

"Me, too."

They hung their coats on his hook in the mudroom and went into the kitchen, where his mother was at the stove making pancakes.

"That smells amazing," Max said. "I'm starving."

"When are you not starving?" Molly asked when he kissed her cheek.

"It's me, Max, not Colton."

"You're just as bad as he is. Hi there, Lexi."

"Hi, Molly."

"Grab some plates and silverware. This batch is almost ready."

Max poured coffee into two mugs. "Cream and sugar still?"

"Just cream please."

He stirred it into her mug and handed it to her. "Have a seat. I'll bring the food."

She took his mug with her when she went to the table.

"Thanks, Mom," he said when Molly handed him plates with pancakes and sausage. "This is the best restaurant in town."

"Don't let Megan hear you say that."

Lucas came into the kitchen. "Hear him say what?"

"That this is the best restaurant in town," Molly said.

"Well, it is," Lucas said, stealing a pancake from the new stack.

Molly smacked his hand with her spatula. "You've already had six."

"I'm a growing boy, and nice of you to show up, Maxwell. They've got me hanging streamers."

"And you suck at it," Dani said when she joined them.

"I can't be good at everything, babe." All at once, he noticed Lexi sitting at the table. "What? Lexi? Is that you?" He went to hug her. "Where the heck have you been?"

"Lucas, shut up," Max said.

"It's fine," Lexi told him. "I was in Houston battling leukemia."

"Oh crap. I'm sorry."

"It's okay. I'm better now."

"That's great to hear. It's so good to see you."

"It's good to be seen."

"This is my wife, Dani. Dan, this is Max's high school girlfriend, Lexi."

The two women shook hands.

"Did you come for the reunion?" Lucas asked, as he stole sausage from Max's plate and ate it before Max noticed it was gone.

"I did. It was a good excuse to come home to Butler."

"What do you think of our boy Max? He's all grown up and a daddy."

"So I noticed," Lexi said with a warm smile for Max.

"Do I detect sparks flying anew between the class couple?" Lucas asked.

"Go away and hang some streamers, Lucas," Max said.

"It's much more interesting in here," Lucas said, reaching for a chair.

"Oh no you don't." Dani tugged on his arm. "Back to work."

"Hurry up and eat," Lucas said to Max. "This is a *joint* birthday party, which means you have to do *half* the work."

"I usually do all the setup with Dani because you conveniently have to work until five minutes before the party starts."

"I'm a dedicated public servant."

"You're a dedicated jackass."

Lexi couldn't stop laughing as she listened to them and took bites of the delicious pancakes. Some things never changed, she thought, and the Abbott siblings' comical bickering was exactly as she remembered it.

Caden and Savvy came running in with Daisy in hot pursuit.

"What have we here?" Lincoln asked as he came into the dining room.

"Gramps! Dad got me a *dog named Daisy*, and she's the cutest dog *ever*, isn't she?"

Linc got down on a knee to greet the newest member of the family. "She is the cutest ever. What a wonderful daddy you have, Caden."

"I know! He's the best."

"Happy birthday, Caden," Lexi said.

He barely glanced at her. "Thanks."

While most of the others stopped what they were doing to greet the dog, Lexi turned to Dani. "What can I do to help?"

"We need to finish the goody bags and blow up the balloons."

"Put me to work."

CHAPTER TEN

"To love and be loved is to feel the sun from both sides."
—David Viscott

*T*he party was utter madness and the most fun Lexi had had in years. There were kids everywhere—Caden and Savvy's many cousins, as well as their classmates, the kids' parents and other siblings. She got to see all of Max's siblings and to meet their spouses and children as Dani ran the party with military precision, moving the kids from snacks to games to presents to cake to goody bags.

"She's good at this," Cameron said when she sat next to Lexi in the dining room with baby Murphy in her arms.

"So good," Lexi said.

Mia sat on the other side of Lexi. "Look at us only children over here taking shelter."

"Dani is an only, too, but look at her go," Cameron said. "I want to hire her to supervise my kids' parties."

"I bet she'd love that," Mia said.

"Remind me again who you're married to," Lexi said to Mia.

"Wade. Those are our kids, Carlee and Corbin." Mia pointed out two kids with golden-brown hair and eyes like their daddy, who stood watch over them.

"They're beautiful."

"We like them. Most of the time."

Cameron hooted with laughter. "Ain't that the truth?"

Dani led the kids and adults outside to play for the final half hour of the party.

Lexi surveyed the wreckage left behind. "Wow." Wrapping and tissue paper were strewn about, new toys in boxes were stacked in two piles—one for each of the guests of honor—and cake was ground into the carpet.

Mia laughed. "This is fairly typical for an Abbott/Coleman kids' party."

"Molly is a saint for letting them take over her house," Lexi said.

"Molly is a saint for many reasons," Cameron said as she put Murphy in a high chair and got busy cleaning up. "This is the least of those reasons."

"Truth." Mia got some trash bags and handed one to Lexi. "Hope you don't mind being put to work."

"Not at all."

"So… you and Max dated in high school?" Cameron asked in a casual tone.

"Yes, for three years, until we went to college on separate coasts."

"I haven't heard him mention you," Mia said in the same casual tone.

"That's because he didn't know where I was for the last ten years, and he had no choice but to move on."

"Where were you?" Mia asked, and then seemed to think better of it. "I mean, if you want to tell us."

"I was diagnosed with leukemia during our freshman year of college. I've spent almost every minute since then fighting it. I'm now in remission thanks to a stem cell transplant eighteen months ago."

"Oh my God," Mia said. "I'm so sorry you went through that."

"Thanks. It was hell, but it's in the past now, or so I hope. It'll be four more years until they consider me cured, but my oncologist told me to go live my life. He says the worst is behind me."

"That must be such a relief," Cameron said as she added

snacks to the tray in front of Murphy in the high chair while helping with cleanup, demonstrating multitasking at its finest.

"It is, but I'm still in panic mode. It's going to take some time to stand down from that frantic struggle. Not sure if that makes sense, but that's where I'm at."

"I get what you mean," Mia said. "I went through something a few years ago that left a similar impact on me. My ex was a drug dealer, and I helped to make the case against him. After all that was over, it took me a long time to accept that I was no longer under threat."

"That's very similar," Lexi said, comforted to hear that someone else understood that sort of stress. "Does it seem like a long time ago now?"

"Like another lifetime, and someday, your illness will be like that for you, too," Mia said. "I'm sure of it."

"I hope you're right."

"We're always right," Cameron said. "Ask our husbands."

The three of them shared a laugh that made baby Murphy laugh, too. He was so cute.

"Who watches all these kids for you guys while you work?"

"Funny story," Mia said. "About four years ago, Dani's parents moved here from Kentucky to be closer to her and Lucas and their family. Her mom, Jessie, said she wasn't ready to retire, so she opened a childcare center and takes care of all our kids, with the help of five other women. Dani's dad handles the business stuff for her. Jessie says that they'll retire when the youngest of our kids goes to kindergarten, but we keep having babies, so who knows?"

"It's so cool that she did that," Lexi said.

"We say that all the time," Cameron replied. "I don't know what we'd do without her. She's like another grandma to all our kids, and she's become good friends with Molly and her sister, Hannah, and Gavin's mom, Amelia, and Tyler's mom, Vivienne."

"Was she here today?"

"Yep, Dani's parents were here," Mia said. "There were so many people. Sorry you didn't get to meet them."

"Next time hopefully," Lexi said.

"What're your plans now?" Cameron asked.

"I'm working on that. I may come back to Butler after the holidays. My parents still own a home here, and the tenants are moving out. It comes with a garage apartment that I might take over while I figure out my life."

"Does Max figure into that?" Cameron asked with a sly grin.

"I really hope so. I never got over him. Being with him again this weekend has been like a dream come true."

Cameron placed her hand over her heart. "You don't know how happy that makes me. We've all wanted him to find someone special for so long. He's such a good guy and a wonderful father to Caden."

"I'm already sold on him," Lexi said with a laugh. "I have been since I was fifteen."

"This is so awesome," Mia said with a happy-sounding squeal.

"Don't get too far ahead of us," Lexi said. "It's all still new again. We've got a lot to figure out, and of course, Caden is part of that."

"It's still very exciting," Cameron said. "We love Max very much."

"So do I. I always have."

When tears filled her eyes, Cameron fanned her face. "This is right out of a rom-com. High school sweethearts meet up at their tenth reunion and pick up where they left off."

"I knew I shouldn't have left you in here with them," Max said when he appeared in the doorway. "Knock it off, Cam."

"Knock what off? Did you or did you not reunite with your first love at your tenth reunion and rekindle the old spark?"

Max glanced at Lexi, who shrugged as she grinned.

"We might've done that," Max said, returning her smile as he gazed at her.

"This is the best thing to happen in Butler in years," Mia said. "Since my dad fell in love with Izzy!"

"I know," Cameron said. "It's been a long time since we had a good romance to sink our teeth into."

"Keep your teeth and everything else away from Lexi," Max

said, sliding his arm around her and leading her out of the dining room.

"Bring her back!" Cameron called after them.

"In your dreams," Max said over his shoulder. To Lexi, he said, "Sorry about them."

"They're great. I had the nicest time talking to them."

"They didn't pump you for details, did they?"

"Not directly, although I suspect they wouldn't have objected to details."

He huffed out a laugh. "No, they wouldn't have. Everyone was up in my grill outside, so I figured I should come rescue you. I'm used to them. You're not."

"I remember Abbott mania from years ago."

"That was before my six brothers had wives in addition to my three sisters who like to know everything that goes on. That doesn't even count the cousins. Will suggested I might want to rescue you—from his own wife, who's more in the know about us than we are about ourselves."

"That's cute."

"She's fascinated by the family dynamics, having been raised largely by nannies after her mom died having her."

"Aw, that's sad."

"It is, but she's the greatest. We love her."

"They love you, too. They want you to be happy."

He drew her into a hug. "With the exception of every minute I've spent with Caden, I'm happier than I've been since the last time I saw you."

AFTER THE PARTY, THEY SENT OUT FOR PIZZA, AND SOME OF THE family hung out to eat before parents started taking kids home for baths and bedtime.

"Did you get a final head count today, love?" Linc asked his wife.

"Thirty-six kids, forty-two parents."

"Holy smokes," Linc said. "That's a mob."

"Sure was, but it was fun."

Lexi wondered how the Abbotts handled that level of activity on a regular basis, but then again, they were probably used to it after raising ten kids.

"Are your ears ringing, Lexi?" Molly asked.

"Not at all," she said, smiling. "It was a wonderful day. So great to see everyone again."

"We loved having you here with us."

"Thank you. I loved being here."

"It's time to pack up, buddy," Max said to Caden. "We need to get Daisy home to have her dinner."

"Grammy gave her some treats," Caden said.

"It's still time to go." Max carried Caden's stack of gifts to his truck in three trips. The downside to having a huge family was that birthdays yielded far too many new toys for one kid. Every year, they cleaned out his old toys to donate them to less fortunate kids. They hadn't gotten around to doing that before the birthday party, so that was on the docket for this week.

Before they left, Lexi hugged his parents and grandfather. "It was so nice to see you all again."

"You, too, sweetheart," Elmer said. "We hope we'll see you again soon."

"I hope so, too."

Max handed Caden his coat and snapped the leash on Daisy. "Come on, girl. Let's go home."

Daisy waited until Caden was coming, too, before she headed for the door.

"Did you see that?" Max asked Lexi.

"I did. She already knows who her best friend is going to be."

He gave her shoulder a squeeze. "So do I."

On the ride back to his house, Lexi wasn't sure whether he wanted her to stay for a while or if they would say their good-byes when they arrived.

Max solved that concern for her. "Hang out for a bit?"

She nodded and followed him, Caden and the dog into the house.

Max showed Caden where the dog food was and how much to give her. "While she eats, hit the shower."

"I want to play with my toys."

"Tomorrow after school. Right now, you're heading for bed."

"I don't want to go to bed."

"Caden…"

The note of warning in Max's tone brokered no room for negotiation.

"Fine," he said, storming off toward the bathroom.

"And use soap!" To Lexi, he said, "Sorry about that. He's always a little cranky after his birthday party when he has to get back to reality."

"No need to apologize. I don't blame him. He's had a big weekend."

He put his arms around her. "So have we."

Lexi held on tight to him. "Yes, we have."

"What now?"

"Now I am going to say good night to you so you can tend to your son and head back to my rental. Tomorrow, I'm flying home to Houston."

"Are you sure you can't stay a little longer?"

"Not this time. I have a doctor's appointment on Wednesday and some other things to take care of this week."

"The doctor is nothing to worry about, right?"

"Routine checkup."

"When will I see you again?"

"Let's talk about that after I get home, okay?"

"Hey, Dad," Caden said as he came into the room, stopping short when he saw them hugging.

Lexi quickly released her hold on Max, while he kept an arm around her.

"What's up, bud?"

"Did you get more shampoo?" he asked, eyeing Lexi suspiciously.

"I did. It's in the cabinet."

"Okay."

"Hey, can you say goodbye to Lexi and thank her for the ski pass?"

"Thank you and bye," Caden said as he ran off again.

"I need to work on his manners. He's usually a lot nicer to people."

"He sees me as a threat," she said.

"What? No way."

"Max, come on. It's been the two of you for all these years. When was the last time he saw you hugging a woman?"

He thought about that for a second. "He never has."

"There you have it. It's going to take some time for him to come around to you and me being together, if that's what we're going to do."

"That's what I want."

"Then we need to ease in slowly, for all our sakes, but especially his. I don't want him to think I'm taking you away from him or something."

"He won't think that."

"Yes, he will, and you're going to have enough to manage when you talk to him about Chloe."

"I was almost able to forget that," he said with a sigh. "I'll talk to him about that tomorrow after dinner."

"And then you'll call me to tell me how it went?"

"Yeah, I'll do that." He withdrew his phone from his back pocket. "Give me your number."

Lexi recited the phone number that started with the 346-area code. "Send me a text so I'll have yours."

Max sent the text. "You'll get that when you log back onto Wi-Fi or leave Butler." He gave her a madly vulnerable look. "Promise you won't disappear on me again."

"I promise. I'm sorry again I did that the first time."

"It's okay." He hugged her again and then pulled back to kiss her. "Best weekend in a very long time."

"For me, too."

"I want more of this, as much as I can get as soon as I can get it."

"I want that, too. Give me a little time to figure things out."

"I can do that as long as you promise to come back soon."

"I will."

He held on tighter to her. "I don't want to let you go. I'm so afraid I won't see you again for another long time."

"I won't let that happen."

"Can you promise me one more thing?"

"Depends on what it is."

"If, God forbid, you get bad news at that appointment this week, I want to know. No matter what happens going forward, I want to know."

"Okay." Lexi looked up at him. "Thank you for an incredible weekend."

Max kissed her again. "Thank *you*."

He grabbed his coat to walk her out and kissed her more intently as they stood next to her car. "Please come back."

"I will. As soon as I can."

"I'll be here waiting for you."

Lexi took another long look at his ridiculously handsome face before she got into her car and drove off, leaving a huge piece of her heart with him.

CHAPTER ELEVEN

"Who so loves believes the impossible."
—Elizabeth Barrett Browning

*M*ax felt like total crap the minute Lexi's taillights disappeared from view. He had the worst feeling that he'd made a huge mistake letting her leave again, but what choice did he have? They led separate lives in cities thousands of miles apart. Yes, she'd mentioned the possibility of coming back to Butler to live, but her life was in flux as she figured out her next steps now that her treatment was hopefully over for good.

And what if it wasn't over? What if she went to the doctor on Wednesday and learned that it had come back? What then?

"Ugh," he said out loud as he carried in Caden's gifts and made a stack in the corner of the living room, next to the box Chloe had sent.

With Lexi in town and the party to contend with, it'd been easy to push the bomb Chloe had dropped into their lives into the background for a couple of days. But now that, too, had to be dealt with, and he dreaded broaching that subject with Caden.

His parents were right, though. Caden had a right to know she'd sent him something and was interested in seeing him.

He went to check on Caden, who was in bed with Daisy stretched out next to him.

"Did you have a nice birthday, pal?"

"It was awesome. Thank you for the best gift ever and the new skis and everything else."

"You're welcome. I'm glad you're happy about Daisy. Dude said she was the perfect dog for you."

"I'll tell her thanks the next time I see her."

"I'm glad you got to meet my friend Lexi."

"Uh-huh."

"Did you like her?"

He shrugged. "She's okay."

"She was my girlfriend in high school."

"Oh. Really?"

"Yep. I really liked her then, and I really like her now."

"Is she going to be your girlfriend again?"

"I don't know yet, but I sort of hope so. Would that be okay with you?"

"I guess."

"Tell me the truth."

"I don't know. Why do you need a girlfriend? We're fine the way we are."

"We're great, but you know how Uncle Will has Aunt Cameron and Uncle Colton has Aunt Lucy and all the others have someone?"

He nodded.

"Sometimes Daddy would like to have someone like that, too. It wouldn't change anything between you and me. It would just make everything better."

"I'm tired. Can I go to sleep now?"

"Sure thing, bud." Max leaned over to kiss him. "Happy seventh birthday."

"Thanks. It was fun."

"Love you best of all."

"Love you, too, and Daisy."

"I'm going to let her out to pee one more time."

"Can she come back in here after?"

"Sure." He called for Daisy to come with him.

She trotted along to the door, already in tune with what was expected of her.

Max was thankful to Dude for the work she'd done to house-train Daisy. He stood outside in the cold to wait for her, looking up at the stars that filled the sky. He withdrew the phone from his back pocket and dashed off a text to Lexi.

You just left, and I already miss you.

He was determined to do whatever it took to have a second chance with her.

AFTER WILL AND CAMERON GOT THEIR KIDS IN BED, THEY MET back in the living room for their nightly glass of wine and debrief, as they called it.

A few years ago, they'd renovated the cabin, adding three more bedrooms, two bathrooms and a vastly expanded living room and kitchen.

Will put some logs on the fire, scratched the ears of Tucker and Tanner, who were settled on their beds for the night, and plopped down next to Cam. "Another weekend in the books."

"I'm not sure which is busier—weekdays or weekends."

"They're equally crazy, but it's a good crazy, right?"

"The best kind of crazy. I got a text from my dad. They're in Bali."

"I'm so jealous of them. They're having all the fun."

"So are we. I've never had as much fun as I am raising kids with you."

Will smiled as he leaned in to kiss her. "Agreed, but the minute Murph goes to college, we're borrowing your dad's plane to go to Bali."

"You've got yourself a date, my friend, seventeen and a half years from now."

He groaned. "Why you gotta put a number on it?"

Cameron laughed. "You're the one who knocked me up with a third one. It's all your fault."

"He was worth it. He's the cutest."

"He really is. They all are. Chase and Molly had the best time today, and Mom said the sleepover went well, too."

"I love seeing all the cousins together and how much fun they have."

"That's like a dream come true for me after growing up alone," Cameron said.

"I'm so glad you have that now. I love seeing you in the thick of things with my family, always in the know about what's going on."

"I'm like a weirdo stalker. I know."

"They love you." Will stretched his legs out on the ottoman. "What'd you find out about Max and Lexi?"

"That they had a really nice time together this weekend and they're going to keep in touch. Wouldn't that be something if they ended up back together after all this time?"

"It would. If you ask me, she's the reason he's never really made it work with anyone else. He was really crushed when she disappeared without a word to him."

"It was because she was sick."

"We know that now, but at the time… It was rough on him. I was relieved when I heard he was seeing Chloe. She was the first girlfriend he'd had after Lex, and that was years later."

"I was surprised to hear Lexi was so important to him, and I'd never heard about her."

"He asked us to stop asking about her. He didn't know where she was, and he felt that was intentional on her part. It was too hard for him to have to answer questions about her. So we stopped asking."

"The poor guy," Cameron said. "That had to be so rough."

"It was. He's had a tough go of it with women in general. He seemed so happy to have her there today. I just hope she doesn't disappoint him again."

"I liked her a lot. She seemed very genuine."

"That's good to hear. You'd know if something was off with her, being the keen observer of people that you are."

Cameron put down her wineglass and snuggled up to him. "I love our kiddos more than anything, but this is my favorite part of every day."

Will put his arm around her. "Same goes, love. I count the minutes until I get Mommy all to myself."

"You want to go to bed?" she asked.

He raised his brows. "Do you have to ask?"

Cameron laughed as she tugged on his hand to bring him with her.

Will released her to close the doors on the woodstove and shut off the lights before he followed her to bed.

THE NEXT DAY, MAX COULD THINK OF LITTLE ELSE OTHER THAN the conversation he needed to have with Caden later and that Lexi hadn't responded to his text the night before. That could mean she didn't get it or that the Wi-Fi at her rental wasn't working or any number of things. Her silence worried him. After the way they'd reconnected, he'd be seriously bummed if he didn't hear from her again.

"What's with you today, man?" Colton asked toward the end of their workday as they trekked down the mountain after tending to hundreds of sap-producing trees that day. "You've barely said a word all day."

"Just got a lot on my mind."

"Including Lexi?"

"Among other things."

"What other things?"

"I could tell you to mind your own business, you know."

"I do know, but you won't, so tell me what's eating you."

"Chloe sent a gift for Caden along with a note saying she's cleaned up her life and would like to see him."

"*The fuck you say?*" Colton's expression was one of total shock.

"Yeah, so I gotta deal with that. I talked to Mom and Dad, and they said it should be up to Caden. I'm going to talk to him tonight."

"No, wait, don't talk to him about it. Just tell her to fuck off."

"As much as I'd love to do that, I can't. Mom made a good point. What if he reconnects with her when he's an adult and finds out she wanted to see him a long time ago? I don't want him to hate me for keeping her from him."

"Even if you think that's what's best for him?"

"He's old enough to know the truth, Colton, and to decide for himself. He's not a baby anymore."

They landed back in the yard just behind Colton's dogs, Sarah and Elmer, who'd spent the day with them on the mountain.

A shriek of excitement preceded Colton's three boys running to greet them, as they did every day that Colton and Max worked away from home base.

Colton grabbed the three little ones and spun them around as they screamed with delight. "How are my little redheaded monkeys this afternoon?"

"Coop got in trouble at Miss Jessie's," Christian reported. "She called Mom."

Colton put the boys down. "What'd you do this time?"

"Nothin'."

He looked to Cooper's twin, Camden. "What'd he do?"

"He brought slime to school and put it on Molly's head."

"Which means we have to call Molly and apologize," Colton said.

"Don't wanna," Cooper said.

"I don't care. You're going to call her to apologize, and that's the end of it."

"Fine," Cooper said. "Let's go, you guys."

After the boys ran off to play, Colton glanced at Max. "Quit your grinning."

"Can't help it. He's you all over again."

"Don't I know it?" Colton said with a laugh. "Lucy is going to ship us both off to live together somewhere so I can deal with him."

"I think that'd only make him worse, if you're asking my opinion."

"I wasn't but thank you anyway. About Caden... You know what's best for him, and I'm sorry about Chloe reappearing after all this time. I'm here if you need anything."

"Thanks. I'm sure it'll be fine. I knew I'd have to deal with it eventually. I'm surprised he hasn't insisted on knowing more about her already."

"Keep me posted on how it goes?"

"I will. Thanks for listening."

"I gotta go make a boy call his cousin to apologize and then smooth things over with Will and Cam. Good times."

"The best of times."

"Yeah," Colton said with a grin. "They may be feral, but they're awesome."

"I'll see you in the morning," Max said.

"See you then. Call if you need anything."

"I will."

Colton watched Max hug his nephews before he drove off down the mountain to deal with the past. As he whistled for the boys to come, Colton felt anxious for Max and Caden after hearing that Chloe had resurfaced. He ushered the boys into the house and sent them to wash up.

The smell of something cooking had his mouth watering, and the feeling he got any time he walked in the door to see her there was one that never got old. He still couldn't believe he'd been lucky enough to win the heart of Lucy Mulvaney.

"What's this I hear about slime and a cousin?" Colton asked Lucy, who was still at her computer. He leaned over to kiss her neck, making her jolt.

"Your lips are freezing."

"Your neck is nice and warm." He kissed her again, breathing in the scent of his love. "Missed you today."

"Missed you, too, especially when I got the call from Jessie."

"I heard about the slime and the cousin, and Coop is going to call to apologize."

"I already texted Cam to tell her how sorry we are. She said Molly said it was no big deal. She's used to it."

"I guess this means we need to do backpack inspections before they leave the house going forward."

"Yep, and again I'll mention that no one ever had to inspect my backpack before I left the house, so this must come from you."

"What smells so good? I'm starving."

"Nice diversion. I'll find out from your mother what you snuck to school."

"There's really no need for that."

Lucy's laughter was one of his favorite things, even when it was directed at him. "I knew you'd say that, and I knew I should've been more worried about procreating with you."

"You love our babies."

"I do. I love them very much, especially when they're sleeping."

Colton chuckled as he helped her up and out of her chair so he could hug her properly. "Thank you for putting up with me and our devils."

"It's a good thing I love you so much."

He held her tightly. "It's a very good thing. The best thing to ever happen to me."

The moment between them ended at the sound of six little feet coming toward them. Colton gave Lucy a quick kiss. "To be continued," he said. "Coop, let's call your cousin."

CHAPTER TWELVE

"You have a kid and realize what's really important. It actually takes pressure off everything. Nothing will come before fatherhood for me, ever in my life." —Austin Rivers

*A*s Max drove to the barn to pick up Caden, he was more stressed than he'd been in a long time. Having to talk to his son about Chloe was the last thing he felt like doing.

His mom picked up Caden from school and kept him on weekday afternoons, so Max didn't have to pay for after-school care. Count that as just another of the many ways his parents made his life easier. Usually, Caden's homework was done by the time Max got there, too, which was an added blessing.

Today, he was also picking up Daisy, who'd spent the day at the barn under the care of his mother, George and Ringo while Max was at work. He would take her to work with him when she got a little older.

Max stepped into the mudroom and was greeted by a rush of boy and dogs.

As always after a long day apart, Max was relieved to see his little boy, to hear about his day and to have the evening together to look forward to. Tonight, he was worried about what he had to tell him and how he would take it.

"You ready to head home, buddy?"

"Yep. I just need to get my backpack and lunch box." When he took off to do that, Daisy followed him.

"Those two are already best buddies," Molly said. "Daisy was so happy to see him when he got home."

"I'm glad it's working out. Did she behave today?"

"She was great. Dude runs a tight ship and produces well-behaved pets."

"Thank goodness for that."

"I was surprised you took the plunge with the dog. I thought you weren't ready for that."

"I wasn't until I was. Thanks for having her at Grammy Camp while I'm working."

"She's no trouble. Ringo and George like the company."

"I'm going to talk to him tonight about Chloe."

"I wondered what you'd decided to do about that," Molly said.

"I'm taking your advice and telling him the truth."

"You can never go wrong with the truth."

"I hope so."

"How'd you leave things with Lexi?"

"We're going to keep in touch and hopefully see each other again soon." Max looked around the corner to make sure that Caden wasn't coming back yet. "He was a little chilly to her."

"Was he? That's not like him."

"That's what I thought, too. Lexi says he's threatened by her because he's hardly ever seen me with a woman."

"Lexi is very wise. Caden could see right away that she means something to you."

"It worries me that he might not go along with it if Lex and I decide to give it a whirl."

"If you love her, he will, too. You just need to give him time to get used to her."

"I guess so."

"Do you still love her?"

"I think I might."

"I told your father that I haven't seen you smile like you did around her since the last time she was here."

"I haven't felt that way since her."

"Feels good, right?"

"Yeah." He rubbed the back of his neck. "Just a lot of things up in the air. She has a doctor's appointment on Wednesday that she said is routine, but is it ever routine after what she's been through?"

"Take your lead from her. If she says it's routine, it's routine." Molly paused before she added, "That sweet girl grew into a lovely woman. Your dad and I would be thrilled to see you two back together."

"That's good to know."

"Take it a day at a time. Things will work out the way they're meant to." She handed him a bag. "Dinner."

"In case I forget to tell you every day of my life, you're the best, and I love you."

Molly hugged him. "Love you, too, and your little guy, who keeps me laughing."

"I couldn't do this without you."

"I wouldn't want you to. I get as much as I give from you and your son."

"Best mom ever."

"Thanks. You know that means a lot to me."

"It's the truth, and numerous other witnesses can attest. Cade! Let's roll."

Caden came into the kitchen dragging his backpack, lunch box and coat.

Daisy was right behind him. She came over to say hi to Max.

He bent to scratch her ears. "What do you say to Grammy?"

"Thank you, Grammy. See you tomorrow at pickup."

She bent to kiss Caden. "I'll be there." To Max, she said, "Call me later, if necessary."

"Thanks. For everything."

"You got it, pal."

He drove home thinking again how lucky he was to have his mom and the rest of the family supporting him. Whatever she'd made for dinner smelled incredible, and he couldn't wait to taste it. Nine days out of ten, she had dinner ready for them when he went to pick up Caden, another thing that made life so much easier for him than it would be otherwise.

"Can we play with my new toys tonight, Dad?"

"Yep. And this week, we're making a pile to donate, okay?"

"Okay."

Years ago, he'd begun teaching him that not all boys and girls were as lucky as he was, and he needed to share the toys he didn't play with anymore with other kids. It was important to Max that Caden always know how fortunate he was and to pay it forward by giving back to others. With as many aunts and uncles as Caden had buying him gifts for every occasion, that was a lesson Max felt was important, and he knew his siblings felt the same way.

When they got home, he let Caden and Daisy run around outside for a little bit before he brought them in to wash up and eat.

Over dinner, which was rigatoni with sausage and his mom's homemade sauce, Max waited for an opportunity to talk to him about Chloe.

"Hey, Dad?"

"What's up?"

"Are you going to marry that girl Lexi who was at my party?"

"Uh, I don't know. We're just kind of talking and maybe dating a bit now. She lives in Texas."

"Oh, good."

"Why?"

Caden wrinkled his nose. "I don't like her."

Max was shocked to hear him say that. "What? Why? You like everyone."

"Not everyone. I don't like her."

"Caden... Come on. Be nice. I like her."

He shrugged. "That doesn't mean I hafta."

"It would mean a lot to me if you'd give her a chance. She's been nothing but nice to you. She hadn't even met you and she got you a birthday present."

"She did that so you would like her more."

"That's not true. She wanted to give you something you'd really like."

"I guess."

"I want you to be nice to her. I mean it. I'd be very disappointed if you were rude to any of my friends. You got me?"

"Yeah, okay."

Jeez, Max hadn't seen that coming, especially when he had something else he needed to talk to Caden about. He forced himself to press on with that, even though he was still shocked by what Caden had said about Lexi. "So there's one more gift you need to open."

Caden had sauce on his cheeks, which only made him cuter than he already was. "Who's it from?"

Here goes, Max thought. "Your mother."

Caden gave him a curious look. "I thought I didn't have a mother."

"Everyone has a mother. Yours decided a long time ago that it would be better for you if she wasn't in your life. Do you remember us talking about that before?"

He nodded. "You said it wasn't because she doesn't love me."

"Right, it was that she didn't feel like she could be a good mom to you."

"But she sent me a birthday present?"

"She did."

"Can I open it?"

"I'll get it while you clear the table."

Max brought the box to the kitchen and set it on the floor next to the table.

"Did you already open it?"

"Not the present, just the box."

"Is it okay if I open it?"

"Sure." Max helped him to wrestle the large, wrapped package out of the box it had been shipped in and put it on the table that Caden had quickly cleared.

He glanced up at his father, uncertainty etched into his cute little face.

"She sent a note with it. Let's read that first." He opened the envelope addressed to Caden and handed it to him to read out loud.

"'Dear Caden, happy seventh birthday! I can't believe you are already seven! I want you to know that I think of you every day and hope you are happy and doing well. I know I have no right to ask to see you, but I'd love to if you can find it in your heart to forgive me for not being there for you these last seven years. It's up to you and your dad, but I'd really like to see you sometime. Your dad has my number, and I hope to hear from you. In the...' What is that word?"

"Meantime."

"Oh. 'In the meantime, I hope you had a wonderful birthday. With love from your mother, Chloe.'" He looked up at Max. "She wants to see me."

"So I heard. How do you feel about that?"

Caden shrugged. "Fine, I guess." He eyed the gift.

"It's okay, buddy. You can open it."

He tore the paper off the box and gasped at the picture of the remote-controlled truck they'd seen in a store in Rutland a while back. "That's the one you said was too expensive!"

"So it is." Max silently fumed over Chloe intruding on their perfect life by sending an over-the-top gift and asking to see their son after years of silence.

"Can I play with it?" Caden asked.

"Let me see if we have the batteries we need."

"They're taped to the box. Look!"

Max tipped his head and saw the batteries. "Well, that's handy." He spent half an hour extracting the truck from the packaging and putting batteries in the truck and the remote controller, which he handed to Caden when he was finished.

The minute Caden pushed a button, the truck roared to life, which made Daisy bark and snarl at the invader.

Caden's belly laugh was the best thing Max had heard all day.

As the truck was run from one end of the house to the other and in circles in the living room, Daisy chased after it, barking like a fiend while Caden laughed his head off.

Max watched the scene unfold as bitterness churned in his gut.

"It's really cool, right, Dad?"

"Sure is."

Caden stepped into the kitchen and held out the remote controller. "You want to try it?"

"Maybe tomorrow."

"Are you okay?" Caden asked, his white-blond brows furrowed with concern.

The best thing about having a son was getting to play with him. Max always wanted to try whatever new toy Caden was excited about, and they loved playing video games together.

"Yeah, buddy, I'm good. But let's talk some more about your mom wanting to see you. Do you want me to set something up with her?"

"How do you feel about it? I mean, you know her, and I don't."

He was so smart sometimes that it took Max's breath away. "I feel conflicted."

"What does that mean?"

"I'm not sure how to feel. She wrote me a letter and told me that she's done a lot of work on herself and is in a much better place than she was when she left. I'm glad to hear that, for her sake, but I'm not sure what it means for us." Max realized he was probably saying too much, but he was still struggling to explain this situation to himself, let alone a seven-year-old. "I talked to Grammy and Gramps about it, and they said I should be honest with you, tell you she'd asked to see you and let you decide what you want to do."

"Um, well, I guess it would be cool to finally get to meet her. I mean, all the other kids have moms, so it would be nice to know mine."

Max's heart broke at his sweet innocence. "Then that's what we'll do."

"Only if it's okay with you, too. I don't want you to be upset or anything."

"I'm not upset, buddy. I just want to do what's right for you."

"You always do."

"You think so?"

"Yes! I have the coolest dad ever. All my friends think so."

If he'd ever received a better compliment, Max couldn't recall when. He held out his arms to his son, who came to him and surrounded him with so much love. "No matter what happens, it'll always be you and me against the world, right?"

"Yep." Caden pulled back to initiate the elaborate handshake they'd developed over the years.

"Love you."

"Love you, too."

"Now go take a shower."

"Do I gotta?"

"Same question every night followed by the same answer."

"Dad?"

"Yes?"

"When will I get to see my mom?"

"I'm not sure yet. I'll call her tomorrow and set up a time."

"Okay."

"If you take a shower and use soap, I'll let you stay up to play for a little while longer, and there might be ice cream, too."

"Yes!" Caden's fist pump was the last thing Max saw as he flew out of the kitchen to shower while Max did the dishes and wiped down the counters and table.

That had gone as well as could be expected, he supposed. Caden had processed the information and decided what he wanted to do. It was only natural that he'd be curious about the mother who'd been absent from his entire life, and Max knew it was in his son's best interest to have a relationship with her if that was possible. But he didn't have to like it.

And what the hell was he going to do about Caden disliking Lexi?

CHAPTER THIRTEEN

"The love we give away is the only love we keep." —Elbert Hubbard

*L*exi's first stop upon arriving back in Houston was at a cell phone store to replace the phone that had died the day before and wouldn't recharge. She'd used her computer to email her mom to tell her about the phone and that she'd be stopping to get a new one when she got back to Houston.

They'd wanted to pick her up, but she'd told them she'd get an Uber home, knowing how much they hated driving in Houston traffic. It'd been thirty degrees when she left Butler, but was seventy in Houston, which gave her temperature whiplash.

The minute her new phone came to life, she checked her messages and saw Max's from the night before, which she immediately replied to.

So sorry I didn't reply last night. My phone died at some point yesterday and wouldn't recharge. I just saw this message when I bought a new phone in Houston. I missed you, too, the minute I left last night. Hope all is well. Call me later!

While in the Uber home, she saw that he'd read the message, but he didn't write back. He was probably busy with Caden. During the long travel day, all she'd thought about was Max and his little boy, the weekend they'd spent together and how long it would be before she saw him again.

In the three days since she left Houston to go to her reunion in Vermont, she'd experienced every emotion on the spectrum. The one she was left with after reuniting with Max was pure joy, something she hadn't felt since the last time she was with him.

The Uber pulled into the driveway of the home she shared with her parents and grandparents.

"Thanks for the ride," Lexi said as she got out of the back seat and took her bags from the driver.

"You have a nice evening," he said.

"You, too."

All four of them were waiting at the door for her, making Lexi wonder if they'd been standing there waiting for her to come back since she'd left. She hugged and kissed them all and let them fuss over her, feed her and pepper her with questions about her trip.

"We were so glad you got to see Max and his family," her mom, Angie, said.

"That was definitely the highlight." Lexi used her new phone to show her parents and grandparents pictures of Max, Caden and Daisy.

"His little boy is so sweet."

"He really is. He turned seven this weekend, and the party was epic with all the Abbotts and their Coleman cousins and a million kids."

"I've never known anyone with a bigger family than the Abbotts had," her dad, Larry, said.

"They're all having kids of their own now. Elmer Stillman has forty-one great-grandchildren, with more coming."

"Wow," her grandmother, Carol, said. "How is Elmer? He and Sarah were our good friends back in the day."

"He's delightful as always and asked about you guys."

"He's got to be in his nineties by now. He was quite a bit older than us."

"If he is, you'd never know it. He looks exactly the same and is right in the middle of everything with his big family."

"That sounds like him," Carol said as she sipped from her after-dinner cup of coffee. "He was always a family man and took such delight in his grandchildren."

"Just like you do," Lexi said to her grandmother, smiling.

"Indeed. I love seeing you glowing with health and happiness again. It does my old heart good."

"Your heart is not old and thank you. It feels good to feel good again."

"Being with Max was wonderful?" Angie asked.

"Just like always, after I explained to him where I'd been and why. I realized I should've told him what was going on, because it was hard on him when I just disappeared. But after he said he wanted to see other people while we were in college..." She shrugged. "I found out this weekend that he still cared very much about me."

"He was always the nicest boy," Angie said. "We loved him and his family."

"He's still the nicest boy and a wonderful single father to Caden."

"What happened to the child's mother?"

"Shortly after the baby was born, she told Max she wasn't ready to be a mother. He's been a single parent ever since, but he gives tons of credit to his parents and siblings for supporting them both. His mom watches Caden after school and in the summers so he can work."

"What does he do for work?" Larry asked.

"He divides his time between the family sugaring facility and Christmas Tree Farm. The business has exploded since the catalog went live, and the town is full of people coming to visit and to find the handsome catalog models."

"I get that catalog," Carol said. "Those Abbott and Coleman boys are handsome."

"Yes, they are, even more so than they were when they were younger," Lexi said, standing. "I'm going to unpack and shower. Thank you for dinner."

"It's great to have you home, honey," Larry said. "We're so glad you had a wonderful time."

"Thanks. It was fun."

She cleared the table and loaded the dishwasher before she went into her room to unpack and check her phone to see if Max had responded.

Not yet.

Lexi showered, changed into pajamas and threw in a load of laundry. She was in bed scanning the day's headlines on her phone when he called an hour later. Her heart lurched with excitement when she saw his name on the caller ID, just like it used to back in high school when he'd call her every night after dinner.

"Hi," she said.

"How was the trip home?"

"Long. I left Butler at nine and just got home an hour ago, with a stop for a new phone."

"I wondered why I didn't hear from you last night."

"Sorry about that. I didn't realize my phone had died until after I got back to the rental. I didn't have your number to text you on my computer."

"No worries. As long as you're okay."

"I'm fine. Did you have a good day?"

"It was okay. Back to the grind after a fabulous weekend. And then I had to talk to Caden about Chloe."

"How'd that go?"

"He was curious, which I suppose is to be expected, and he said he'd like to meet her. He also loved the gift she sent, but Daisy didn't. She was growling and snapping at the truck. It was pretty funny."

Lexi laughed. "Poor Daisy."

"She'll eventually get used to life with a very busy boy. They're super cute together. She sleeps in bed with him. I know I shouldn't allow that, but Ringo used to sleep with me, so how can I deny him?"

"You can't."

"He asked if you're my girlfriend."

"Did he? What did you say?"

"That you were my girlfriend when I was in high school, and I hope maybe you will be again."

Her heart fluttered madly. "What did he say to that?"

"Nothing much. I think you're right about easing him in slowly to the idea. It's just been the two of us for all this time."

"I totally understand that."

"I do, too, but I'm ready for more—for myself and for him. I know it's a lot to ask someone to take on a seven-year-old, but he's a great kid."

"Yes, he is, and it's not a lot to ask. Not of me, anyway."

"When can you come back?"

"I'll figure that out soon and let you know."

"I hope it's soon. My bed is lonely after having you here."

"Max," she said on a nervous laugh. "When you say those things…"

"What?"

"You make me breathless. You always have."

His groan echoed through the phone. "Don't say stuff like that when we have no idea when we're going to see each other again."

Lexi laughed. "Stay strong. We'll figure this out."

"Do you promise?"

"Yeah, I do."

"I really missed you for all the time you were gone."

"I missed you, too."

"Let's make this happen, okay?" Max asked softly.

"Just give me a little time."

"I can do that, as long as we talk every day."

"Deal."

"I'll call you around the same time tomorrow?"

"That sounds perfect."

"Then I guess I'll talk to you then."

"Sleep tight and have a good day tomorrow."

"You, too."

The phone line clicked when he ended the call. This was crazy, to be as besotted by him as she'd been ten years ago after only a couple of days together. But it was the best kind of crazy.

It was why she'd fought so hard to survive her illness, hoping maybe she'd see him again and feel a fraction of what she had back then.

It was, she'd discovered, even sweeter the second time because of what they'd both been through. They had a deeper appreciation for how rare the connection between them was and how special it was to still feel the same way they always had.

Lexi slept better than she had in years that night, feeling rested and refreshed the next day as she did errands and made plans. She would move back to Butler in January and give her relationship with Max a real chance. After two days without him, she was already going stir-crazy wanting to see him again, which she told him when he called that night, right on time.

"I feel the same way. Like I made a huge mistake letting you leave, which is insane. You were only visiting."

"It feels insane to me that I left you, even for a short time."

"What's the plan, Lex?"

"I'm coming back for January. I'll talk to my parents tomorrow and tell them what I want to do."

"How do you think they'll take it?"

"My mom will be upset. Now that I'm well again, she wants to be with me all the time. We ran around together today, got our nails done, did some errands, and she was so, so happy. I haven't seen her like that in so long, I almost forgot she used to be that way."

"It's been hard on them. I've been thinking a lot about them and what it would be like for me if Caden got sick like you did."

"It was a nightmare for them, and I wouldn't still be here without all four of them stepping up for me the way they did. But now they have to let me go and live the life I fought so hard to have, and they will. It just won't be easy for them."

"Maybe they'll come back to Vermont, too."

"I don't know. My grandmother has terrible arthritis, which has been so much better since they moved to Houston. I can't see them going back to the cold, even if I do."

"Hmm, well, hopefully you guys can make a plan that works

for everyone. Maybe they could spend the summers up here or something."

"That would be nice. We'll see."

"Wherever we end up, there'd be room for them to visit any time they want. Make sure you tell them that."

"You're not getting ahead of yourself by any chance, are you?"

"Maybe a little, but it feels good to let my mind wander to you and me together forever with a sweet little family and house we've made a home."

"Max... You're doing it again."

"Doing what?"

"Making me breathless."

"Come back here. Don't wait until January. That's so far away."

"It's only like four weeks from now."

"That's forever!"

His urgency made her smile as her heart did the fluttering thing that had happened from the beginning with him. "I need to spend the holidays with my family, and then I'll be there."

"Fine, if you're going to be that way about it."

Lexi laughed. "Are you pouting?"

"Maybe a little."

"It'll go by fast. I promise."

"No, it won't."

"You're going to be busy at the tree farm and getting ready for Christmas yourself."

"Not too busy to hang with you."

"Soon, Max. I promise."

"You've got your appointment tomorrow, right?"

"Yes." One of the things she'd had to do earlier was blood work for that appointment, which always left her with a feeling of dread.

"Are you okay about that?"

"It's always nerve-racking, but I have no reason to be concerned. Jake, the oncologist, tells me that if I was sick again, I'd know it."

"Jake said that, did he? What's his story?"

Smiling, Lexi realized the crush she'd had on her doctor felt like a long time ago, especially since she'd seen Max. "He's happily married to Devon, who's also a doctor and a friend of mine. When you spend as much time with doctors as I have, they become friends. And that's something else I need to figure out if I'm going to leave Houston. I'll need new doctors."

"We can take you to Boston."

"I'll mention it to Jake when I see him tomorrow and see what he says."

"Will you text me right after your appointment, so I won't be worried?"

"Sure. Will you be able to see the text?"

"I'm working on the mountain tomorrow. Best cell service in the area, and I'll be waiting for that text."

"I'll let you know if there's reason to worry but try not to. This is part of my reality."

"It's going to take me a minute to get used to that reality."

"That's okay, we'll get you there."

"I'm so glad you're back in my life, Lex. It's like everything is right again, or something like that."

"For me, too. I'll text you tomorrow after the appointment."

"I'll be waiting and hoping everything is fine."

"Call me tomorrow night?"

"Wouldn't miss it."

THE NEXT DAY WAS PURE HELL FOR MAX, WAITING FOR THAT TEXT she'd promised him. As he trudged up the mountain behind Colton, all he could think about was what he would do if her illness came back right after they found each other again. The universe wouldn't be that cruel to them, would it?

The universe could be pretty fucking cruel sometimes, which reminded him that he needed to call Chloe. He'd do that when they took a lunch break.

"What's going on, Maxi-Pad? And don't say it's nothing."

"If you call me that stupid name, I'll never speak to you

137

again." Lucas and Landon had come up with that hideous nickname for him after middle school health class introduced them to maxi pads.

Colton grunted out a laugh. "Got your attention, didn't I? Now answer the question. What's up with you?"

"Lexi. She has a big doctor's appointment today, and she's going to text me after. She says it's perfectly routine, but after you have leukemia, is anything routine when it comes to doctors?"

"If she says it's routine, then you need to believe her. I'm sure she knows the difference by now."

"I feel like I'm coming out of my skin since she left, like I made a huge mistake letting her leave after we just found each other again."

"It wasn't your call whether to let her leave. Tell me you know that."

"I do. Of course I do, but it totally sucks after the way we reconnected over the weekend."

"So the little push your awesome big brother gave you yielded results?"

"Yeah."

"Aren't you glad you listened to me?"

"Shut up, Colton."

"Well, aren't you?"

"Yes! You were right. Is that what you wanted to hear?"

"Yep. Make sure you tell Lucy how right I was when you see her."

Max rolled his eyes.

"What happens now?" Colton asked as he peeled a banana that he pulled from his coat pocket.

"She says she's coming back in January, but that feels like a long time from now."

Colton stuffed the entire banana into his face. "What's stopping you from going there?"

Max gave him an incredulous look. "Other than my son and work?"

"Yeah, other than that. In case you haven't noticed, there's a rather large family surrounding you who could take care of Caden for a few days and cover you at work."

"It's the holidays. The tree farm—"

"Will be fine without you, as will Caden. If you want to be with Lexi, go be with Lexi. You're no good to me in this condition."

"What condition?"

"All sad-faced and pouty. It's not good for the trees to have your negativity around them when they're working so hard to produce sap by spring."

"Do you actually believe this nonsense you're spouting?"

"It's true. The trees are picking up on your vibe, and it's not good, so do me a favor and go to Houston to see your lady and come back when you're in a more positive frame of mind."

"You really think I should go there?"

"I really do. You're terrified that she's going to somehow slip through your fingers again, so don't let that happen. Go there and let her see you're dead serious about her. Lucy and I will take Caden."

"Um, thanks, but he comes back feral from every visit up here."

Colton grinned. "We'll make a man out of him."

"I'll ask Mom to keep him."

"So you're going to do it?"

The more Colton had talked about the idea, the more excited Max had gotten to make it happen. "Yeah, I think maybe I will, if you're sure you don't mind me missing a couple of days here."

"I don't mind, and Landon won't either."

"Thank you, for… you know, pushing me toward her the other day and now this."

"I'm a very wise man, Maxi. It's time you figured that out."

Before Max could formulate the proper reply to that, his phone chimed with a text from Lexi.

All good at the doctor. Talk to you tonight!

He was so relieved that his knees went weak. "She's okay."

"Go see her, Max. Give her no doubt about what she means to you."

"I'll talk to Mom after work."

Max responded to Lexi's text as soon as he could. *That's great news. Thanks for letting me know.*

Were you worried?

I was worried sick.

Don't do that! I told you not to.

I'll try harder next time.

She sent back heart emojis that made him even more determined to put Colton's plan into action. But first, he had to deal with Chloe.

CHAPTER FOURTEEN

"People protect what they love." —Jacques Cousteau

*M*ax found a stump to sit on and put through the call to the number that was still in his phone from seven years ago. Why hadn't he deleted it? He couldn't say.

"Max. Hi."

"Hey."

"Thank you so much for calling."

"No problem," he said, even though that was a huge lie.

She laughed. "I'm sure it was a big problem for you, and I'm sorry about that. I wasn't sure how best to reach out…"

"He loves the truck. Thank you."

"I'm so glad. I was hoping he didn't already have it."

Max didn't tell her that the reason he didn't already have it was because it was ridiculously expensive. "I talked to him about how you want to see him, and he said he'd be okay with that."

"Oh my goodness, Max. I'm so glad to hear that. I wasn't sure if you'd allow it, or if he'd want it. I just didn't know."

"I want to be clear. We're talking a visit, nothing more than that. I want to do what's right for him, and from what I'm told, letting him decide is the right thing."

"I understand."

"Do you, Chloe? Do you understand anything about what the last seven years have been like for me since you disappeared?"

It occurred to Max right in that moment that women tended to disappear from his life, and why was that exactly?

"No, I can't possibly know, and I'm sorry I did that to you. All I can say in my own defense is that I wasn't well mentally. I'm better now, but it's been a long journey. I'm not looking to upset your life or Caden's. I swear to you, that's not what this is about. I just want to see him and for him to know…"

"What?"

"That I love him. I always have, and I always will, and that I'm sorry for what I did."

He could hear the tears in her voice and felt like a monster for being so hard on her, but who could blame him for still being upset? "He's a wonderful kid, and he's happy. I won't let anyone or anything mess that up."

"I won't mess it up. I promise. When can we get together?"

"Next week?" He'd already decided to stay in Houston until Tuesday. "Wednesday or after is good for us."

"Wednesday it is. I can come there in the afternoon if that works."

"He gets out of school at three. I can pick him up and meet you at our place. We live at my grandfather's house now. Do you remember where that is?"

"I do. Your grandfather… Did he…"

"He's fine. He lives with my parents now."

"Oh good. I remember him as such a sweet man."

"Yes, he is."

"I'm glad to hear he's well. And the rest of your family?"

"Everyone is good. They're all married and have tons of kids who are like siblings to Caden."

"And you? Are you married?"

"No."

"Oh. Well… I um… I'm engaged."

"Congratulations. I need to get back to work. I'll see you at my house next Wednesday around three thirty?"

"I'll be there, and, Max… Thank you so much for this."

"You're welcome."

He pressed the red button to end the call.

"Who was that?" Colton asked when he emerged out of the trees, eating a protein bar. He never stopped eating.

"Chloe."

Colton stopped dead in his tracks. "How'd that go?"

"Fine, actually. She's going to come see him next week."

"Damn, my life is boring compared to yours."

"Be thankful for that."

"I am. Every day. My biggest issue this week was Coop putting slime on Molly's hair at school and how the dye in the slime turned her hair green."

"No way!"

"Yes way, and so now I'm paying for a very expensive hair salon to fix it, and Coop is doing extra chores to reimburse me—after he apologized to his cousin."

Max snorted with laughter. "Thank you for sharing that. I need a good laugh after talking to *her*. And you wonder why I don't want to leave Caden with you guys."

"I don't wonder."

Max laughed again. "You know I love your wild children."

"They're pretty wild and pretty awesome, but I worry about the teenage years."

"As you should."

"If I think it's a shit show now…"

Smiling, Max shook his head. "I can't even imagine that."

"I'm sure Lucy will leave me to deal with them alone."

"Would you blame her? That's why she keeps her place in the city."

"I know! We joke about that a lot."

"She's not going anywhere. For some reason none of us can fathom, she loves you and your feral brood."

"I'm very lucky she does, and I have a feeling you're about to get lucky like that, too."

"I'm ready, but I worry that Caden isn't."

"What do you mean?"

"He flat out told me he doesn't like Lexi."

"He *said* that?"

"Yep."

"Aw, he's worried he'll lose you to her."

"He'll never lose me to anyone."

"You have to keep telling him that. It's just been you two for his entire life. Ease her in slowly so he doesn't feel threatened."

"It's just so weird to hear him say he doesn't like someone."

"He can tell she's different, and that has him on edge. Keep telling him he's the most important person in your life and he always will be. That'll matter to him."

"When did you get so smart about these things?"

"Dude, I was always smart about everything. Just took you a while to realize the asset you have in me."

Again, Max snorted with laughter. He did that a lot during his workdays with the always-entertaining Colton.

"Did you or did you not get laid last weekend because of me?"

"I refuse to dignify that with a response."

"Which means you did. Do you need my address to send me the thank-you note you owe me?"

"You're so insufferable."

"Thank you. Lucy tells me that every day. You'll make sure Dad and Gramps know that the matchmaking torch has been passed to a new generation, right?"

"If you insist."

"I insist."

"Do you care if I bug out early so I can pick up Caden and spend some time with him?"

"Nah, go ahead. We're in good shape here."

"Thanks. I'll see you in the morning."

"I'll be here."

As Max trekked down the steep path that led to the sugar-house, he pondered what Colton had said about Caden feeling threatened. Caden had never seen Max with a girlfriend, and it was probably unavoidable for there to be bumps as he brought Lexi into their lives. He couldn't let his son turn against Lexi without giving her a chance.

When he got back to the sugarhouse, he called his mother.

"Do you mind if I pick up Caden today?" he asked her.

"Of course not. He'll be thrilled to see you."

"Great, thanks. I'm on my way."

"Come for dinner if you'd like. I'm making spaghetti and meatballs."

"Caden's favorite. We'll be there. Thanks, Mom."

"See you in a bit."

Max hung up the heavy coat he used to work on the mountain and changed into the lightweight down jacket he wore the rest of the time. When he was on his way down the mountain with classic rock blaring from the truck's speakers, he couldn't wait to see his son and spend a rare weekday afternoon together.

As Max eased the truck into the pickup line, he realized it'd been a while since he'd picked up Caden at school. His son would be looking for his grandmother's SUV, not his dad's truck. When he saw Caden standing with a bunch of other kids, he gave a soft toot and watched his son's face light up with delight.

All the hell and heartache he'd gone through with Chloe and the many challenges of single fatherhood were worth it to have his son look at him like he hung the moon.

Caden climbed into the truck and dropped his backpack on the floor with a thud. "What're you doing here?" he asked as he put on his seat belt.

Max kept the passenger-side air bag turned off so Caden could ride in the front seat.

"Took the afternoon off to hang with my best pal."

"Awesome! What're we doing?"

"I thought maybe we'd check out the rest of the stuff you got for your birthday."

"Yes!"

"And Grammy is making spaghetti and meatballs for dinner."

"Best day ever!"

Oh, to be seven years old again, Max thought. Caden was

always so happy with the simplest things, much as Max had been as a kid. He reminded Max of himself on many a day. It'd taken until Lexi disappeared without a trace for the blush to wear off the rose of life for Max. That'd been his first major disappointment, one so profound that he buried her and the memories of her deep inside so he could go forward without her. And then Chloe had happened and Caden was born, and he didn't have time to dwell in the past when the present had required his full attention.

Having Lexi back last weekend had opened all those old wounds and exposed them to the light. Being with her again had been amazing, especially now that he knew where she'd been and why. He wanted the same things with her he'd wanted back then, but he needed to make his son comfortable with the idea before it went any further.

"What else do you feel like doing before dinner?"

"Can we take Daisy to the dog park? My friend Luke was telling me that his dog loves that."

"Sure, that sounds fun." Max drove them home to pick up Daisy. "How much homework do you have?"

"One worksheet of spelling words and no math, thank God."

Max laughed. "I was the same way. Thankfully, Uncle Hunter was good with math and helped me with my homework."

"Now you tell me. I need to call him for help."

"That's a good idea."

"Yeah, cuz you still suck at math."

"Haha, and don't say suck."

"Why not?"

"It's vulgar."

"You say it."

"I'm an adult."

"I can't wait to be an adult so I can say whatever I want."

"You also have to work all the time to pay for everything, so enjoy being a kid while you can."

"Can I ask you something?"

"Sure. Anything. You know that."

"Am I going to see my mother?"

"I talked to her today, and she's coming next Wednesday. She said she's super excited to see you."

"Why can't she come sooner?"

"That was the first day we could both do it."

"Oh. Okay."

"Are you looking forward to meeting her?"

Max caught Caden's shrug out of the corner of his eye. "I guess."

"It's okay to look forward to it."

"You don't care if I like her?"

"No, Caden, I don't care if you like her. Why do you think I'd care about that?"

"Because. She hasn't been here, and I figured that might make you mad."

Max pulled the truck into the driveway and put it in Park. Then he turned to face his son. "I was mad when she first decided she couldn't be part of our lives. That made me really mad, but that was a long time ago, and we've done okay for ourselves, haven't we?"

Caden nodded.

"Being a single parent is hard work, but it's the most fun I've ever had, and I wouldn't trade the last seven years with you for anything. If you want your mom in your life, you can have your mom in your life."

"And you won't mind if I do?"

"Not at all, but I'll make you a deal. If you get to have your mom in your life, I get to have Lexi in my life."

Caden eyed him suspiciously. "Hmmm."

"It's only fair, right? We're both doing the other a favor. And besides, Lexi is really nice. I think you'll like her a lot when you get to know her better." Max waited for a second. "Do we have a deal?"

"I guess."

"You'll be nice to Lexi the next time you see her and give her a chance?"

Caden nodded. "Will you be nice to my mom?"

"Always."

147

"Even though you were mad with her?"

"She gave me the greatest gift of my life."

"Me?"

"Yeah, you," Max said, giving Caden's belly a poke that made him giggle. "Now, go get Daisy, and let's go to the dog park."

While Caden took off toward the house, Max stayed in the truck and thought about the conversation with Caden. His little boy was growing up, and things were changing for both of them. Max was determined that the most important things would never change, no matter what happened.

CHAPTER FIFTEEN

"Love knows not distance; it hath no continent;
its eyes are for the stars." —Gilbert Parker

*A*fter dinner, Max helped his mom with the dishes. "I have a favor to ask."

"What's that?"

"Colton has convinced me that I should go to Houston to surprise Lexi, and I was thinking about doing that this weekend, but only if you wouldn't mind having Caden."

"I wouldn't mind. Other than Sunday dinner, we have no plans except volunteering at the tree farm on Saturday. He can help us there."

"He'd love that. He's also got a couple of birthday parties." Max had talked to Landon earlier, who'd assured him he'd survive at the farm for a few days without Max.

"Nothing we can't handle. Go see Lexi. I agree with Colton that it's a good idea."

Max glanced at his mother. "Caden told me he doesn't like her."

"What? He barely knows her."

"That's what I said, too, and we made a deal. If he gets to have his mom in his life, I get to have Lexi in mine." They'd told his parents and grandfather over dinner that Caden would see his mom the following Wednesday.

"That's a fair deal."

"It's just been me and him—and all of you, of course—for his whole life. Things are changing for both of us, and I'm not sure how I feel about that."

"That was bound to happen eventually, no?"

"I suppose, but it's been a lot to process over the last few days."

"When it rains, it pours."

"That sounds like a Gramp-ism."

"I get most of my isms from him."

Max laughed.

"The one thing to remember about life is that change is inevitable, and it's not always a bad thing."

"I like things the way they are."

"But you liked having Lexi here with you, enough that you're already planning to go see her."

"I'm worried about Caden. He never says he doesn't like someone."

"He'll come around. He just needs to get used to seeing you with her."

"Part of me wonders…"

"What?"

"Maybe I'd be better off just leaving well enough alone. Caden isn't happy about her, so it might just be for the best—"

"No," Molly said forcefully. "He does *not* get to decide whether you date or care about a woman or even bring a woman into your lives. You're a loving, devoted father to that boy, and he's had you all to himself for his entire life. It's only natural that he might see her as a threat to the status quo, but he'll get over it."

"What if he doesn't?"

"He will. Don't you dare take a step back from Lexi because of what he said. He's *seven*, Max. If you start seeing her now, someday he won't remember much about the time before she was in your lives. And knowing her as we do, I have no doubt she'll make every effort to ensure his comfort around her."

"Are you sure about that?"

"I'm very sure. You've given that child *everything* and made us so proud in the process. It's time to take something for yourself."

Max hugged her. "Thank you for always having the advice I need."

"You got it, pal. Any time. It's okay for you to do something just for you. Caden will be fine this weekend and long term. Try not to worry."

He knew she was right but asking him not to worry about Caden was like asking him not to breathe.

IN THE END, IT WAS MUCH EASIER THAN MAX HAD EXPECTED TO drop everything for a long weekend in Houston. His grandfather had helped by giving him Lexi's grandmother's number so he could text to get her help in surprising Lexi. How funny would it not be if he got there, and she was somewhere else? Not funny at all.

Her grandmother had been delighted to be brought in on Max's plan and had even suggested they go to the beach in Galveston for the weekend. She'd sent him the names of places to stay, and he'd booked them a room right on the beach.

We're thrilled to see our girl back to good health and smiling like she used to when the two of you were together the first time, Carol had said in her last text to Max. *Looking forward to seeing you. She'll be so excited.*

The only thing keeping him from a clean getaway was Caden, who wasn't at all pleased to hear he was going away for the weekend.

"Why can't I go?"

"You've got two birthday parties and the sleepover at Chase's house that you've been looking forward to. That'll be much more fun than where I'm going."

"Where are you going?"

"To Houston, Texas."

"Why?"

"To visit Lexi."

Caden's displeasure with that news was obvious. "You just saw her last weekend."

"That wasn't enough. I want to spend more time with her."

"Why?"

"Because I like her. I've always liked her since we were kids. You're going to stay with Grammy and Gramps on Friday night and have a great time at the birthday parties, the Christmas Tree Farm, Chase's house and Sunday dinner. You'll be so busy, you won't even miss me. And when I get back, your mom will be coming to see you."

"I don't want you to go."

"Caden, come on… It's just a few days, and you'll have so much fun with Grammy and Gramps and Grandpa-Great." Max's heart broke when he realized Caden was crying. He hardly ever cried, except for when he was hurt. "Buddy…"

He sat up and threw himself at Max. "I don't want you to go."

While Max clung to him, he also clung to the words his mother had said earlier about deserving something for himself. "I want to make you a promise." Max pulled back so he could see Caden's face. "If I date Lexi, nothing will change between you and me. I swear to you. Nothing will change except maybe you'll have someone else in your life who loves you. But you and me? We're best friends, and that's never, ever going to change no matter what. Okay?"

His little chin quivered as he nodded.

Max hated that he'd upset him, but he supposed it was bound to happen whenever he started to date. He probably should've done it a long time ago so it wouldn't be such a big deal to Caden now.

"Are we good?" Max asked.

He nodded again.

Max held out his fist to initiate their special handshake. As they went through the elaborate sequence, Caden grinned, which was a relief. "No one else in the whole world knows our secret handshake, you know."

"Chase wants me to teach it to him, but I won't. Cuz it's ours."

"That's right, but you should make up another one for you and him, so he won't feel left out."

"That's a good idea. Maybe we can do that this weekend. Can he stay at Grammy's on Friday, too?"

Max was relieved that he'd come around to accepting the plan for the weekend. "I'll ask Uncle Will, but I'm sure that's fine." Max bent to kiss his forehead. "Get some sleep, buddy. Love you to the moon and all the way to Pluto."

"Pluto isn't really a planet anymore."

"It is in my world."

Giggling, Caden said, "Love you to the moon and your anus."

"We talked about that. Not funny."

"Yes, it is!"

"Nope." Max had to bite his lip to keep from joining in Caden's laughter. "Go to sleep." As he left the room, Caden was saying "your anus" in a singsong voice between giggles.

"I can't hear you."

"Yes, you can!"

"Sleep. Now."

Max waited until he was in the kitchen before he allowed himself a quiet laugh. The Uranus thing had started last fall when they covered the solar system in kindergarten. One of the other kids in Caden's class had explained to the class why the pronunciation of Uranus was so funny. Caden had trotted out the term "your anus" over dinner at the barn, which had resulted in his parents and grandfather laughing until they cried while Max had looked on in horror.

"This is what happens when you send kids to school," his dad had said.

The incident had made Max wish homeschooling was an option for them. As he finished loading the dishwasher, he thought about how Caden had cried over him going to see Lexi. That had gutted him and had him again questioning whether he was being fair to his son. He was so used to basing every decision on what was best for Caden that he'd forgotten how to think about what was in *his* best interest.

Lexi was in his best interest. Just as he had that thought, his phone chimed with a text. Thank God for Wi-Fi that kept him somewhat connected to the outside world. He pulled the phone from his pocket and smiled when he saw the text was from her. She'd included a picture of herself with a tabby cat.

Super cute—you and the cat. Who's your friend?

Our neighbor's cat Misty. She loves me. We spent so much time in the hospital that we couldn't have pets, so our neighbors let me borrow her whenever I need a fix.

We should get one when you move here.

She sent a GIF of a woman fanning her face.

Max sent laughter emojis. *Too much too soon?*

No... All I think about is moving to Vermont.

We're here, waiting for you to come back!

How is Caden and all the Chloe stuff?

Can you talk?

Yep.

Max called her.

"Hey."

"How's it going?"

"Better now that I'm talking to you."

"Is everything okay?" he asked.

"Yeah, it's just hard to be back here after being there with you."

Max wanted so badly to tell her about his plans for the weekend, but more than that, he wanted to surprise her. "Everything about my normal routine feels weird since you were here."

"Sorry about that."

"Don't be. It's not your fault that it was more fun when you were here than it is when you're not."

"All I think about is you and Caden and Butler and your family and Fred. It was so, so good to be home."

"It was good to have you home."

"You know that you're the main reason that Butler still feels like home to me, right?" she asked.

"I didn't know that until now, but I'm glad to hear it."

"This is kinda crazy, isn't it?"

"It's a good crazy. The best kind of crazy."

"Mary Jane texted to ask if we'd hooked up after the reunion."

"No way! What'd you tell her?"

"That it was nice to see her and Gig at the reunion."

"Haha, good deflection."

"She acts like we were besties in high school or something when we weren't."

"I'm sure they're all talking about us leaving together. People from Butler are very good at minding other people's business."

"Always have been, always will be. Has your family been asking questions?"

"Not particularly. They're playing it cool, for the most part."

"My family was thrilled to hear that I saw you and met your son and had a great time with you and your family."

"Give them my regards." Max wanted to tell her he'd give them his own regards on Friday, but he was sticking with the surprise. One more day to get through and then he'd be on his way to Houston. He couldn't wait. "I hate to say I need to go to bed, but I'm still exhausted from this weekend when you came to town and kept me up all night."

"*I* kept *you* up? I recall it being the other way around."

"We kept each other up," he said, "and I discovered I'm not as young as I used to be."

"Neither am I. I've been napping a lot this week."

"You're okay, though, right?"

"I'm fine, Max. I swear."

"Good. Let's keep you that way, okay?"

"That's the plan. Talk to you tomorrow?"

"I can't wait. Sleep well."

"You, too."

As he ended the call, he wanted to tell her he was still crazy about her, but that could wait until he saw her.

Two more days.

. . .

MAX FLEW FROM BURLINGTON TO ATLANTA FIRST THING FRIDAY morning. Because he'd had to leave the house so early, Caden and Daisy had spent the night at the barn. Hannah and her family had been there when he dropped Caden off, and Caden was so preoccupied playing with Callie and Colby that he'd barely noticed when Max said he had to go.

He'd kissed him goodbye and told him to be good for Grammy and Gramps.

"I will," Caden had said. "I always am."

"Love you."

"All the way to Pluto?"

"Yep—and don't say it."

Caden had given him a mischievous grin, and that's what Max had brought with him on the trip, holding that grin close to his heart as he ventured into the world without his sidekick. It felt almost unnatural to be going somewhere without him, but he was determined to enjoy the break from his responsibilities and to make the most of his time with Lexi.

He couldn't wait to see her. It'd been five days since he last saw her, and that felt like forever after reconnecting so completely the weekend before. It was the right thing to go there, to see her, to fully explore the connection with her that had never died.

But being without Caden for five days would be rough. It was the longest they'd ever been apart since his son was born. He hoped Caden would be okay for that long without him and wouldn't further resent Lexi for keeping his dad away. Jeez, he hadn't even considered that possibility when he made these plans.

With a two-hour layover at the massive Atlanta airport, Max found his departing gate and then went looking for lunch. Because he was on a mini vacation, he had a beer with his burger and fries and caught up on *SportsCenter* at the restaurant bar. When was the last time he'd looked at a TV that wasn't playing a kids' show or movie? He couldn't recall.

His whole life was Caden, and even though he knew that wasn't entirely healthy, it had worked for them. But now that he knew where Lexi was and that she'd never stopped thinking of him or caring about him, everything was different. The life he'd been leading before he saw her again didn't seem as full and satisfying as it had been only last week.

He'd gotten a taste of what it might be like to have someone of his own to love, and he'd liked it a lot, especially because that someone was her. It was funny how being with her again made it so clear to him that the reason he'd struck out with relationships was because he'd never stopped loving her. She'd lived in his heart all this time while he tried to move on from her, refusing to speak of her or think of her because of how painful it was to not know where she was or if she was okay.

Hearing what she'd been through had been gut-wrenching for him—and heartbreaking. He wished he'd known about it at the time, but in some ways, it was a relief to find out after the fact since he wouldn't have been able to do much to support her during that ordeal while managing single fatherhood, too. He would've worried himself sick over her from afar, so in a way, she'd done him a favor when she'd kept him in the dark.

He left a twenty and a ten on the bar to pay for lunch and returned to his gate, eager to get this last leg of the trip underway. In the gate area, he sat next to a young woman with a baby girl, who immediately wanted Max's attention.

"She's so cute. How old is she?"

"Nine months and full of beans," her mother said. She was blonde with brown eyes and reminded him a little of Cameron. "This is her first airplane trip."

"How exciting," Max said, giving the baby a finger to squeeze. "Do you live in Houston?"

"No, my parents do. I used to live here in Atlanta. Not sure where I live now."

Max didn't want to ask, but he couldn't help being curious. "Are you okay?"

"Not at all." She forced a smile as tears filled her eyes. "My husband confessed to having had an affair with a work colleague that's gone on for almost as long as we've been married, so I left him. And now I'm going home to my parents, and I don't know what we're going to do."

Holy crap. "I'm sorry that happened to you."

"Thanks. It's just a lot to process, you know? I never imagined I'd be a single parent to this little peanut."

"I know a little something about that. I've been raising my son on my own since he was a couple of weeks old." Max pulled out his phone and showed her a photo of Caden. "He just turned seven."

"Wow, he's gorgeous. Seven years on your own. How's that been?"

"My parents and extended family have been critical to my success. I couldn't have done it without them. My mom, in particular."

"I'll probably move back to Houston to be closer to my parents. It's just so overwhelming to consider it all right now. I only found out about the affair yesterday."

"That's a lot to deal with, and it's incredibly overwhelming at first. But it does get easier. I promise."

"I'm glad to hear that, because I can't seem to wrap my head around it all."

"The good news is you don't have to wrap your head around it all right now. You can take it one step at a time and figure things out as you go."

"Is that what you did?"

He nodded. "After the shock of his mother leaving wore off, I just powered through the days one at a time and tried not to get too far ahead of myself. After a while, you find a groove, and it stops being so daunting. And not that you asked me, but if your parents are willing to help, I think you'll be glad to have them nearby."

"They'd love to help. They're crazy about her."

"What's her name?"

"Adele. That was my grandmother's name."

"Beautiful name for a beautiful girl."

"I'm Jamie, by the way."

"Max. Nice to meet you."

"You, too. Are you from Houston?"

"No, I live in Vermont. My girlfriend is in Houston."

"She's a lucky girl."

"Thanks. I'm not sure if I should be calling her my girlfriend just yet. We dated in high school and reconnected at our reunion last weekend. I'm surprising her with a visit this weekend."

"So you broke up years ago and just saw each other again?"

"We never really broke up." He filled her in on why they hadn't seen each other. "Now that I know that she never stopped thinking of me or wanting to be with me, the time we spent apart seems to have disappeared, like it never happened. Not sure if I'm explaining this right."

"No, you are. I get it. She didn't stay away because she wanted to."

"Right."

"Are you worried that you'll go all in with her again and her illness will come back?"

"She tells me that after the transplant, she has as much chance of getting leukemia again as I do. So I'm trying not to worry about what *might* happen and live in the moment. I'm so glad to have her back in my life."

"That's really sweet, Max."

"My love life, such as it was, has been a bit of a mess since I was with her, and I think I've realized it was because I never really got over her."

"How could you have when you never really broke it off with her?"

"We agreed to see other people while we went to colleges on opposite coasts, but I never expected not to see her again for ten years."

"It's really sweet that you guys reconnected and that you're going to surprise her. That'll mean a lot to her."

"You think so?"

"I know so."

The gate agent made an announcement that would begin the boarding of their plane.

"Let me give you my number if you need to talk to someone who gets the single-parenthood challenge," Max said.

"Oh, that would be great."

They exchanged numbers, and he helped her with the stroller she was checking at the gate.

"Talking to you made me feel a lot better. Thank you. Your Lexi is a lucky girl indeed."

"Glad to help. I've been right where you are, well, except for the marriage-ending part, and I get it."

"Have a great weekend with Lexi."

"Thanks. I hope it all works out for you."

"It will. I'll make sure it does."

"That's the attitude."

"It really helped me to talk to you and to find out my life isn't over because this happened."

"Far from it. Keep in touch, okay?"

"I will."

CHAPTER SIXTEEN

"Love, having no geography, knows no boundaries."
—Truman Capote

*B*ecause she was boarding with the baby, Jamie was in the first group to get on the plane. Max waved to them as he went to his seat a few rows behind them. After he was settled in a window seat, it occurred to him that he'd become somewhat of an expert on single parenthood and that it might be fun to write about some of the things he'd learned. Maybe it would help people like Jamie who were just starting the journey and finding it overwhelming.

He certainly knew what that was like. Though he didn't often think about the bleak days after Chloe signed away her parental rights, it didn't take much to resurrect the feelings of shock and fear that had stayed with him for months afterward. At that time, he'd been quite certain there was no way he could raise a child on his own.

His big family had rallied around him, making it so he was never truly alone with the massive responsibility of raising a child. They had been an amazing source of support, but the reality was that for much of Caden's life, he'd been alone with him. He'd made all the big decisions for him, nursed him through every fever and cold and kissed him better whenever he skinned a knee or elbow. Not only had they survived, but they'd thrived.

Caden was a son anyone would be proud of, and Max was exceptionally proud of him—and himself, not just for surviving the last seven years, but for enjoying them, too. At first, the task had been so daunting, he hadn't fully wallowed in the joy of parenthood. That had come later, as Caden grew older and became his buddy as well as his son.

Max had looked forward to this break with Lexi, but after a short time away from Caden, he was already itching to get back to him. He reminded himself that he would talk to Caden on the phone while he enjoyed the time with Lexi. According to his mother, he'd earned the right to some personal happiness in addition to the parental happiness. He was still trying to convince himself that he could have both at the same time.

Caden's reaction to Lexi was worrisome, but Max hoped that in time, his son would get past the resistance when he realized nothing between them would change if she was part of their lives. At the same time, Max needed to accept that nothing between him and Caden would change if he allowed Chloe to be part of Caden's life.

The two-hour-and-ten-minute flight seemed to take forever, especially the part at the end when it took hours—or so it seemed—to get off the plane after it reached the gate. Being this close to her and still so far away was torturous as he made his way through the congested airport, following the signs for taxis and ride shares. Cameron had suggested he download the Uber app and use that when he got to Houston.

Twenty minutes later, he was in a car and on the way to the address Lexi's grandmother had given him. He'd texted her to tell her he'd landed on time and would be there shortly. She'd responded with thumbs-up emojis.

He was looking forward to seeing Lexi's parents and grand-parents again, but he couldn't wait to see *her*. After having spent last weekend with her, he wondered how he'd managed to get through a whole decade without her in his life. She'd refilled the space he'd kept open for her all that time without even realizing he was doing it. And now that he'd had a refresher course on all things Lexi, he wanted much more with her.

He wanted it all with her, and he'd never wanted that with anyone else.

A short time later, the Uber pulled up to a two-story home in a Houston suburb. "Here you are."

"Thank you."

"Have a great weekend."

"You, too." Max got out and hooked his bag over his shoulder as he went up the walk to the front door, which flew open.

Lexi's grandmother, Carol, hugged him in the doorway. "She'll be thrilled. She's talked all about you and your son and your family this week."

"That's good to know."

"It's so wonderful to see her smiling and happy again." The older woman blinked back tears. "It's been a long time."

"Thanks for helping me pull this off."

"My pleasure. Shall we go surprise our girl?"

He held out his arm to her. "Let's do it."

Lexi thought she was seeing things when her grandmother walked into the dining room with Max. It took a few seconds for her to blink him into focus and to catch up with the fact that he was there, in her house, with her grandmother, who didn't seem surprised at all.

He walked over and held out his hand to her.

Lexi took his hand and let him help her up and into his arms. Max was there. He'd left his home and his son and had come all the way to Houston to see her.

"You've left her speechless, Max," Lexi's dad, Larry, said with a laugh.

"So I see," Max said, smiling. "Are you okay, Lex?"

"I'm shocked."

"In a good way, I hope."

"In the best possible way."

They shared a warm smile, and she could tell he was dying to kiss her but never would in front of her parents and grand-parents.

"Oh, give her a kiss, Max," her grandfather, Jim, said. "We all know you want to."

Max shrugged and gave her a quick kiss that was nowhere near enough.

"How did you get here?" Lexi asked. "How long can you stay?"

"I flew from Burlington to Atlanta to Houston, and I can stay until Tuesday night."

"Oh my God!" She hugged him tightly, thrilled to have four days to spend together. "That's amazing."

"Good surprise?" he asked.

"Best surprise ever."

"You must be hungry, Max," Lexi's mom, Angie, said. "We were just about to eat. Have a seat."

"Thank you."

He joined them for a delicious chicken dinner, complete with mashed potatoes, stuffing and a variety of vegetables. "This is great," he said. "Thanks again, Mrs. Bradshaw."

"We're happy to have you, Max," she said. "And call us Angie, Larry, Carol and Jim."

"Thank you."

"They're trying to fatten me up," Lexi said, patting her belly. "And it's working."

"You look wonderful, honey," Larry said. "The picture of health again, which is such a relief."

Angie put a plate of brownies in front of Lexi.

"See what I mean?" Lexi asked Max, smiling. She still couldn't believe he was there. After last weekend, she'd missed him so much and had even questioned whether she'd done the right thing going to the reunion and reconnecting with him if leaving again had hurt so much.

Max got up to help clear the table.

"We've got it," Larry said. "You kids go for a walk or a drive or whatever you want."

"Thank you again for dinner," Max said.

"Such a pleasure to have you here," Angie said. "We've missed you."

"I missed you guys, too."

"You want to take a walk?" Lexi asked him.

"Love to."

They stepped outside into a warm late fall evening that would've required winter coats in Vermont.

"I can't get over how warm it still is here."

She took the hand he offered. "It stays warm most of the year. I miss the seasons in Vermont, but not the cold."

"I'd miss the seasons if I didn't live there anymore."

"I can't believe you sneaking to Houston without saying a word all the times we talked this week."

"It's called a *surprise*, Lexi."

"It was a good one, Max. You really got me. I wasn't sure if I was seeing things when you came in with Gram."

"She was my coconspirator. My grandfather still had her number, and he confirmed you'd be home this weekend."

"Thanks for going to so much trouble to surprise me."

"I couldn't wait to see you."

"You just saw me last weekend."

He dropped her hand and put an arm around her, bringing her in close to him. "That was a long time ago."

"I feel like I must be dreaming or something," she said. "To be with you again this way... It was all I wanted for so long."

"Everyone was all over me this week about what I was going to do now that I knew where you were and why you'd been gone. Colton was the one who told me I needed to come here. He made it sound so simple, which it was when I decided to do it."

"What about Caden?"

"He's with my parents and has lots of fun plans for the weekend. He'll be fine."

"Was he okay with you leaving?"

"Not entirely, but he'll forget all about that when he's with his cousins. He'll be fine."

"I don't want him to hate me."

"He won't. Don't worry."

"Did you see his mom yet?"

"We're doing that on Wednesday."

"How do you feel about that?"

"Strangely calm. I've decided that her being part of his life won't take anything away from what he and I have, and that it's in his best interest to know her."

"For what it's worth, I think you're doing the right thing."

"It's worth a lot. Did I mention that your grandmother told me we should go to Galveston for the weekend? So I got us a hotel room there starting tomorrow."

Her eyes lit up with happiness. "Remind me to thank her for putting that idea in your head."

"She thought we might enjoy some time alone."

"It's funny how things change, huh?"

Max laughed. "Your parents always wanted to hang out with us when we were at your house."

"I know! And now my grandmother is suggesting a weekend away together."

"We're not kids anymore, and after what you guys have been through, they're thrilled to see you moving on with your life."

"I told them I want to go back to Butler, and they said they do, too."

"Really? That's great news."

"We all want to be home again."

"What about your grandmother's arthritis?"

"She said she's on much better meds than she was when they lived in Vermont, and she misses it so much there."

"That's great. I'm glad for you that they're coming, too. We're still on for January?"

"That's the plan."

"I'll come drive the moving truck for you."

"Really? I was going to drive myself."

"Now you don't have to. Work shuts down the week after Christmas, so it's no problem."

"I can't believe this is happening, Max. That you're here, that we're picking right up like nothing ever changed."

"Nothing did change. It wasn't like we had a big meltdown and decided to never see each other again. Life happened. And now that we've found our way back to each other, all I want is more of everything with you."

"You promise I'm not dreaming?"

"I promise."

They turned the corner and walked into a park that they had all to themselves at that hour.

Max led her to a bench and turned to face her. "Kiss me."

She placed her hand on the face that had haunted her dreams during ten hellacious years and gazed into his eyes as she pressed her lips to his.

Max tipped his head and kissed her more intently, his tongue brushing against hers until she was clinging to him, lost to the kiss and him the way it had been between them since the first time they were together. Back then, they'd been so young that the desire had come almost as a shock to them. To go from having never experienced it to something so incendiary had been amazing and terrifying and wonderful all at the same time.

"Mmm." He withdrew slowly from the kiss. "I've needed that since the second you left the other day."

"I've needed it, too. Isn't it the weirdest thing to be completely addicted to each other again after just a few days together?"

"Weirdest, best thing ever."

Lexi leaned her head on Max's shoulder. "For sure. Being with you again has made the epic struggle to survive worth it."

Max tightened the arm he had around her. "Thank you for not dying."

Laughing, Lexi said, "You're welcome."

WHEN THEY RETURNED TO LEXI'S HOUSE, MAX CHECKED HIS watch and saw that he needed to call Caden to catch him before bed. "I'll just be a minute," he told Lexi.

"Take your time. Tell him I said hello."

"I will."

Max called the barn and wasn't surprised when his son answered the phone. "Hi, Dad. What's up?"

"That's what I'm calling to ask you."

"Grandpa-Great and I are watching *Cobra Kai*. Don't worry, he said it's okay for kids to watch."

Max smiled at how Caden knew exactly what he'd say. "How is it?"

"It's pretty cool. He said we'll watch *The Karate Kid* this weekend."

"I love that movie."

"He said that you guys have watched it a million times."

"At least a million. How was school today?"

"It was good. Joey got a bloody nose, and Maisy pinched Molly."

"Molly is having a rough week."

"I know," he said, giggling. "Cooper had to call and apologize to her, and he has to do extra chores to pay to get her hair fixed."

"It's not funny."

"It's a little funny. Admit it."

"I won't."

"How's Houston? And where is that anyway?"

"I told you. It's in Texas, and it's good. It's still warm here. Oh, and Lexi said to say hi to you."

"It's freezing here," Caden said, breezing over the message from Lexi. "Grandpa-Great says it's gonna snow like crazy tomorrow. Uncle Will said maybe we can ski this weekend."

"That'd be fun," Max said, feeling a pang about missing the first ski outing of the season. But there would be plenty of others.

"I gotta go. Grandpa-Great is gonna fall asleep if we don't finish this episode."

Max laughed. "You'd better get to it, then. Don't stay up too late."

"I won't."

"Love you, buddy, and I miss you."

"Love you, too."

"But you don't miss me?" Max asked in a teasing tone.

"I miss you. Don't be silly."

"Sleep tight, and I'll call you tomorrow night."

"Okay, bye, Daddy."

The line clicked before he could ask to speak to his mother, but she would call him if she needed to. What did it mean that Caden had totally ignored the message from Lexi?

"How's your boy?" Lexi asked when she joined him in the front living room, which looked like it rarely got used.

"He's good. Watching *Cobra Kai* with my grandfather."

"It's so wonderful that he has him in his life."

"They have a tight bond, just like he had with all of us. It's very sweet."

"Did you give him my message?"

"I did," Max said with a sinking feeling. "He was caught up in the TV show and didn't have much to say."

"I want him to like me."

"He will. It's just been the two of us for so long. It might be a bit of an adjustment to add someone to our duo."

"I don't want to cause any trouble for you with him."

"You won't. My mother reminded me that despite how it might seem, he's not in charge. I am, and if I want you in our lives, then you'll be in our lives."

"Not if it upsets him."

"He'll get used to it, and when he does, it'll be fine."

"What if he doesn't?"

"He will. It's been a crazy week for him. In addition to his mother resurfacing, he saw me with a woman for the first time. He's processing it. That's all it is." Max hoped he was right about that. He couldn't imagine Caden being intentionally rude to someone, especially a friend of his.

"I hope so."

"I've probably made a bit of a monster out of him by giving him my full attention for all these years. He's not used to sharing me with anyone."

"He's not a monster."

"I mean that in the best possible way. We've been a couple of bros, and now there may be a third member of our pack, and he's not sure how he feels about that."

"That's why I still say we need to ease him in slowly so he doesn't resent me."

"Probably, but I really hope he'll come around sooner rather than later. If it was up to me, you'd move in with us when you come in January."

"That's not a good idea, and you know it."

"I do know it," Max said with a sigh. "But I hope we can make that happen before too long."

"We have all the time in the world. We don't need to be in a big rush."

"I'm in a huge rush. Now that I have you back, I want everything right now. It's like I need to make up for all the time we missed, and I need to do it immediately."

"Do you think it feels urgent to you because I was sick?"

"No, I think it's because I have so many things I want us to do, like get married and have more kids and get a bigger house and do everything together." He stopped when he saw tears in her eyes. "What's wrong?"

"Everything is so right that I can't believe it."

"Believe it. We're going to make this happen." He caressed her face and gazed into her eyes. "Where're the parents?"

"Probably in the family room watching *Jeopardy!* and trying to outdo each other in yelling out the answers."

"That sounds like my parents and grandfather. My grandfather and my dad try to outdo each other with who's smarter."

"Who usually wins?"

"Gramps. My dad says he's the possessor of more worthless knowledge than anyone alive, to which Gramps replies, 'It ain't worthless if it helps me whup your ass, boy.'"

Lexi's laughter reminded him of how much he'd loved to make her laugh the first time they were together. "He's so cute. I love him."

"I do, too. I can't believe he's going to be ninety-one soon. He's unstoppable."

"Thank goodness for that."

"I need to keep him around forever. I honestly don't know what we'll ever do without him."

"You don't need to worry about that any time soon."

"I hope not."

Lexi tried to stifle a yawn, but Max caught her.

"You need to sleep."

She snuggled up to him. "Not yet."

Max put his arm around her. "Where am I sleeping?"

"With me."

"No way. I can't do that here."

"They don't care. We're twenty-eight, and they're thankful I'm alive."

"We're not manipulating them that way. I can sleep on the sofa."

"We have a guest room upstairs, across the hall from my room."

"Perfect." He kissed the pout off her lips. "We'll have three nights in Galveston, so quit your pouting."

"Will you at least tuck me in?"

"I'd love to."

"Let's say good night to the parents."

Max helped her up and held her hand as she led the way to the family room, where her family was, in fact, watching *Jeopardy!*

"Who's winning tonight?" Lexi asked.

"Your mother," Larry said. "She's putting the rest of us to shame."

"She usually does," Lexi said. "We're going to watch a movie upstairs, so we came to say good night."

"Let us know if you need anything, Max," Angie said.

"Thank you. I'll be sleeping in the guest room."

"That's not necessary," Angie said.

"Told you," Lexi said with a saucy grin. "Funny how a near-fatal illness changes things, huh?"

"Don't be sassy, young lady," Larry said with a grin. "And, Max, please make yourself at home here. We haven't seen Lexi happy like she's been tonight in a long, long time." His voice broke on the word *time*.

Angie reached for her husband's hand. "It's lovely to see," she said, smiling at them.

Lexi went to kiss them all good night. "Love you guys."

"Love you, too, sweetheart," Jim said gruffly. "Night, Max."

"Good night, and thanks again for having me."

"It's our pleasure," Carol said.

Lexi took him by the hand and led him upstairs. "We have the second floor to ourselves. Their rooms are on the main floor. They won't come up here to check on where you're sleeping, so you may as well sleep with me."

"You think you're so clever, don't you?" Max asked, amused by her.

"I'm very clever, and don't you forget it." She turned to him and ran her hands over his chest. "They know there's a very good chance we might've been married by now if things had gone differently."

"You think we would've been?"

"I'm almost sure of it. I wasn't going to last four years at Berkeley. I had already been approved to transfer to UVM when I got sick."

"You had? Really? Why didn't you tell me?"

"I wanted it to be certain before I said anything, but before I could tell you, I got sick."

Max sighed. "It's weird to consider that if you hadn't gotten sick, I might never have had Caden."

"Everything that's happened since we went our separate ways was meant to be, including him."

"I can't think of him any other way but meant to be, even though I wish more than anything that you hadn't been through such a horrible ordeal."

"I've realized that it was my destiny as much as Caden was yours."

"And now maybe we can be each other's destiny?"

She went up on tiptoes to kiss him. "I would love that."

CHAPTER SEVENTEEN

"Be of love a little more careful than of anything." — e.e. cummings

*M*ax had fully intended to sleep in the guest room until her parents told him not to be silly. That was how he ended up cuddling with Lexi in her bed while they pretended to watch a movie that neither of them was interested in. They were much more interested in kissing until they were breathless from wanting more.

"I can't do this in your parents' house," Max said as he kissed her neck.

Lexi ran her hand over his abdomen and down to cup his erection. "Yes, you can."

He groaned. "No, I really can't."

"They know what we're doing."

"Do you think that makes me feel better?" he asked on a laugh.

Lexi's giggle was the best thing he'd heard in a long time.

"What are you thinking?" she asked, her hand on his face.

Max gazed into her eyes as he kissed her. "You're amazing. You always were, but you're even more so now."

Her smile was a thing of beauty.

"I still love you," he said.

"I still love you, too. I never stopped."

"I didn't either. I can see that now. There was something keeping me from fully exploring other relationships, and I couldn't figure out what it was. The minute I saw you at the reunion, I figured out what it was."

"Are you going to tell me?"

Smiling, Max said, "I didn't think I had to come right out and say it was you. You're the reason I couldn't move on. I still loved you."

"I'm so glad you didn't move on."

"So am I. I would've hated to see you again and to find out where you'd been if I was with someone else."

"That was my greatest fear, that you'd be married or in love with someone."

"Never even came close."

"Not even with Caden's mom?"

"Nope. We were all about the physical."

Lexi winced.

"Sorry. You don't need to know that."

"It's fine. It's not like I didn't already know." She ran her hand over his bare chest, making him crazy with wanting her.

"I kept hoping it would be more with her because I wanted to feel that way again, you know? But we weren't meant to be."

"I'd say I was sorry about that, but…"

Max laughed and tickled her, making her scream with laughter. "Hush! They're going to hear us."

"So what?"

"Lexi…"

"Max, please make love to me. My parents would be thrilled."

"Stop it."

"Really. They would. They're so happy I survived that they want me to have everything I ever wanted, and what I want, more than anything, is you."

How could he resist her when she looked at him that way after confirming that she still loved him as much as he loved her? He couldn't. They pushed and pulled at clothes until all the important parts were exposed. As he slid into her, the feeling of homecoming was once again so profound, it took his breath away. She was his home. She had been since he was sixteen, and no one could take her place. He knew that now.

"Ah, shit," he whispered. "Forgot the condom."

She stopped him from pulling back. "I probably can't get pregnant, so that's not a concern."

"If you're sure it's okay…"

"I'm ninety-nine percent sure."

Being inside her with nothing between them was so amazing that he decided ninety-nine percent was good enough. "You feel so good."

"I missed this so much."

"There wasn't anyone else for you?"

She shook her head. "The only boy I ever wanted was in Vermont."

Max held her closer as he moved in her, more certain with every passing moment that he'd found his destiny the second he saw her again.

THEIR TIME IN GALVESTON WAS RIGHT OUT OF A DREAM FOR LEXI. They relied on room service, barely leaving their room except to spend a little time on the beach. On Sunday afternoon, they were dozing after making love when Max's phone rang. Lexi reached for it on the bedside table and handed it to him.

"Hey, Mom," he said, sounding as sleepy as she felt. He sat up. "What? When?" After another pause, "Oh my God. Are they okay?"

Alarmed by the tone of his voice, Lexi sat up, too.

"It might be tomorrow. We're in Galveston. Mom… He's going to be all right, isn't he? Please tell me the truth."

Seeing tears in Max's eyes, Lexi felt her heart race with fear.

"Yeah, okay. I'll be there as soon as I can. Keep me posted?" Another pause. "Thanks. Tell him I love him so much." His voice broke, and tears slid down his face. "Tell him… I love you, too."

As he ended the call, he got out of bed and started throwing clothes in his bag.

"What happened?"

"Caden was skiing with Will and Chase, and the boys collided with each other. They had to be airlifted off the mountain. They're taking them to Burlington, the only level-one trauma hospital in the state."

"Oh God… Max. I'm so sorry. Did she say how they are?"

"They were both unconscious on the mountain. I'm sorry. I have to go. I have to get to him."

"Of course you do."

They packed up their belongings and were on the road to Houston within fifteen minutes. While he drove, Lexi worked on her phone. "There's a flight tonight that would get you to New York City at eleven. We could rent a car there and drive the rest of the way."

"You don't have to come, Lex. I don't know what to expect."

"I'd like to be there to support you, if you'll let me."

"It's just that he's already uncertain about us, and this might not be the time." He glanced over at her, seeming tormented. "I'm sorry."

"I understand," she said, even though she didn't. Using the credit card he handed her, she booked a single seat on the flight out of Houston and then reserved a rental car for him in New York. "How long is the drive from New York to Vermont?"

"Six or seven hours to Burlington." His phone rang, and he pounced on the call, which was on speaker. "Hey, Will."

"Mom said she called you."

"Yeah, how are they?"

"I don't know." Will sounded awful. "Cam and I are on our way to Burlington. We're trying to hold it together."

"You haven't heard *anything*?"

"Not yet. I'm so sorry this happened, Max. They were having the best time, and then they both turned at the same second and slammed into each other. I was right behind them, but it happened so fast… So fast." His voice broke on the word *fast*.

"It was an accident, Will. It's not your fault."

"If anything happens to them… I don't know what I'll do."

"They're going to be fine. They have to be." Max would

simply cease to exist if that wasn't the case. "Will you call me when you get to Burlington or if you hear anything?"

"Yeah, I will."

"I'm on a flight to New York in two hours and will drive the rest of the way. I'll be there by the morning."

"We'll keep you in the loop," Will said. "I'm so sorry this happened when you were off on a well-deserved break."

"This is proof that parents don't deserve breaks. I should be there with him."

Lexi's heart sank. He would never forgive himself for not being there when Caden got hurt. If, God forbid, the worst happened… No, she couldn't go there. But he was. He was imagining what his life would be like without his little boy, and he'd never be able to separate where he was when it happened from that event.

She already knew how cruel life could be, but this was almost too much to bear. All she wanted was him and his son, and to be in their lives, but he would go home and maybe never look back. Her heart broke for him, for Caden and for herself. The only thing that truly mattered was that Caden and his cousin were all right. But she hadn't been happy like she'd been these last two weekends in so long, she'd nearly forgotten what it felt like. After having had this taste of perfection with him, how would she stand to be without it or him?

When Will ended the call with Max, Cameron called her father.

"Hi, honey," Patrick said. "How's it going?"

"Not great, Dad." She filled him in on the accident on the mountain. "We're on our way to Burlington now."

"Why there?" Patrick asked, sounding as panicked as Cameron felt.

"That's the state's only level-one trauma center."

"Dear God, Cam. Is it that bad?"

"We don't know."

"Mary and I will be there in a few hours. We're in Chicago for her cousin's wedding."

"I remember. Dad… Max is in Houston and on his way back to New York. He's planning to rent a car to drive to Burlington."

"I'll make the chopper available to him."

"I was hoping you'd say that," Cam said, choking on a sob. "He shouldn't drive all that way in a panic."

"Send me his number, and I'll make it happen."

"Thank you, Daddy."

"Anything for you, sweetheart. Tell me our Chase and Caden are going to be okay."

"I will as soon as I know more."

"We're praying for them, and we'll be there very soon."

"Love you."

"Love you more, and tell Chase that Pops is coming."

"I will. He'll be so excited."

Her son and father shared a special bond, and she'd hated to call Patrick with this news.

"We're coming, love."

"I'll send updates."

"Thank you."

As Cameron ended the call and sent her dad Max's number, her hands were shaking even harder than they'd been when she first got the frantic call from Will about the accident. They'd left Molly and Murphy with Will's aunt Hannah and rushed out of town, headed west toward Burlington.

"It was nice of you to think of the chopper for Max."

"I knew Dad would want to help."

Will reached for her hand and held on tight.

Cam had never seen him so undone, which only further shredded her nerves. "They're going to be okay, aren't they?"

"I hope so, but you need to prepare yourself…"

"For what?" she asked.

"For anything."

. . .

MAX'S HANDS WERE SHAKING SO HARD, HE PROBABLY SHOULD'VE let Lexi drive. But there was no way he could sit there and do nothing, so driving—even with shaking hands—was better. When his mother said Caden and Chase had been hurt in a skiing accident, Max had felt like all the bones had left his body, leaving him as panicked as he'd ever been.

And when he'd heard they were being taken to Burlington…

Only the most serious cases were treated there.

Max handed his phone to Lexi. "Will you call my brother Lucas? He's on my favorites."

She put through the call and put it on speaker for him.

"Hey, Max."

"What do you know?"

"I spoke with snow patrol on the mountain. He said one of them had an obviously broken jaw, and the other had internal bleeding."

"How can they tell that?" Max asked, feeling more frantic by the second.

"Blood was coming out of his mouth."

"Oh my God, Luc."

"I know it's easy for me to say don't panic, but they're young and strong, and it may not be that bad."

"It's bad when they're unconscious, isn't it?"

"It happens. Try not to spin up to worst-case until we know more. I'm on my way to Burlington, and I'll let you know the second I hear anything."

"Please, Luc…"

"We've got him, Max. We'll take good care of him until you can get here."

"I'm on a flight to New York tonight, and then I'll get a car."

"Are you sure you ought to drive all that way?"

"No, but it'll get me to him faster than waiting for a flight in the morning. I'll be fine. Just let me know if you hear anything more."

"I will. Be safe, Max."

"Take care of my boy."

"We will."

Max ended the call and handed the phone to Lexi. "I got a text while I was talking to him."

"It's from Patrick Murphy. He's making his chopper available to get you from New York to Burlington."

"Oh wow. That's amazing."

"Is he the billionaire?"

Max nodded. "Cameron's dad."

"Oh. I see. I had no idea."

"You'd never know it. She's as normal as can be."

"I'll cancel the rental car, then."

"Thanks." Max felt bad about discouraging her from coming with him, but he needed to be completely focused on Caden, and he knew his son wouldn't want her there. Not yet, anyway. Someday, maybe, but not now.

"We're going to George Bush Intercontinental," Lexi said, pointing to a sign.

Max pressed the accelerator, the need to get to his son more powerful than anything he'd ever experienced, even the love he felt for her. If he had to choose, Caden would win every time. In his right mind, he would've been sad to leave Lexi this way, but in his panic-stricken mind, he didn't care about anything other than Caden.

He never should've left him. If he hadn't, maybe this wouldn't have happened. Or he would've been there, too, and might've been closer to them, or a million other possibilities. Max would never leave him again after this.

At the curb outside Departures, Max left the car running and grabbed his bag out of the trunk. "I'm sorry about this," he said to Lexi when she met him at the back of the car.

"Don't be. Just let me know that you got there and how he is, okay?"

"I will." Max gave her a quick kiss and a quicker hug and then took off running toward the doors.

CHAPTER EIGHTEEN

*"Sometimes it's hard to be a woman giving all your love
to just one man."* —Tammy Wynette

*L*exi drove home from the airport feeling lost, set adrift and uncertain of what would happen next. They'd been so happy just a few short hours ago, and now she wondered if or when she'd ever see him again. Her heart was with him, Caden and Chase as well as their entire family, and she wouldn't relax until she knew the boys were on the road to recovery. That was the most important thing.

But... The way he'd cast her aside and taken off without looking back had hurt her.

She didn't want to be hurt by it, because she knew he was panicked over his son, but she was hurt, nonetheless.

After pulling into the driveway at home, Lexi sat for a minute, trying to find her game face so she wouldn't upset her family. The game face wasn't happening, she realized after ten minutes. She got out of the car, retrieved her bag from the trunk and went inside, surprising her mother when she appeared in the kitchen two days earlier than planned.

"What are you doing here?" her mom asked, coming to greet her with a hug and kiss.

"Max's son was hurt in a skiing accident in Vermont. He's on his way home."

"Oh no! Not serious, I hope?"

"We don't know anything other than he and his cousin were airlifted to Burlington after colliding on the slope."

"Dear Lord. The poor guy must be beside himself."

"He was."

"You didn't want to go with him?"

"I did, but he thought this wasn't the right time. Caden, his son, has been a bit uncertain about me. Max hasn't had a girl-friend since Caden was born."

"Ah, I see, so he's a little pushed out of joint at the idea of sharing his dad with someone."

"I guess."

"Your feelings are hurt because he didn't want you to go with him."

"Sort of, although all I care about is that his son and nephew are okay."

"Which is very noble of you, but you also care about him and want to be part of his life."

"Yes, I do."

"Then you must be patient. His son is his top priority always, but especially when he's hurt. And you may have to accept that you'll never come first with him. The child he's been raising on his own for seven years will probably always be first. Can you live with that?"

"Yes, of course I can. It was just kind of jarring to go from being blissfully happy with him to being cast aside."

"You weren't cast aside. He'd never want you to feel that way. It's hard to put into words what happens to a parent when their child is in any kind of danger. It's a feeling I wouldn't wish on my worst enemy."

"You don't have enemies," Lexi said, smiling for the first time since Max got the call from his mother.

"Still… You know what I mean. It's a terrible, awful feeling unlike any other I've ever had. When you got sick, I was quite certain I wouldn't survive it."

"You were a trouper."

"Eventually, but not at first. Have patience with him, Lex. He's a wonderful guy who clearly cares for you a great deal. We all saw that when he was here. Give him some time to deal with the accident and whatever his son needs. He'll be back for you. I'm sure of it."

Lexi wished she was as certain of that as her mother was, but for now, all she could do was wait and hope that she'd hear from him soon.

And while she waited, she would pray for his son and nephew—and for Max and his family.

THE NEXT FEW HOURS WOULD GO DOWN AS THE MOST STRESSFUL of Max's life. Nothing could compare to the hell of having to deal with people and mass transit when he was coming out of his skin with worry about Caden and Chase. He wondered for a second if he could give himself a heart attack or stroke or something equally unpleasant by stressing at this level. Before he boarded the flight, he'd tried to call the hospital directly, but a nurse had said there was no news yet as the doctors were still working on the boys.

It didn't help that the flight from Houston to New York was one of the roughest he'd ever been on, with the flight attendants ordered to stay seated for most of the trip.

The woman sitting next to him wept quietly as the plane bumped through the sky. She had long brown hair and hazel eyes.

"This sucks, huh?" Max asked her.

"So bad. I hate flying on a perfect day."

"The plane is designed for this, and we're perfectly safe."

"Intellectually, I know that. Tell it to my shaking hands."

"We're almost there."

"Not soon enough for me." She glanced over at him. "I couldn't help but notice that you seem really stressed. Is it the turbulence?"

"No, my son and nephew were hurt in a skiing accident, and I'm on my way home to Vermont."

"Wow, you must be frantic."

"I am, and the long, bumpy flight isn't helping anything."

"Have you heard anything about how they are?"

"The latest is they're both conscious and being evaluated in the Emergency Department. My nephew has a broken jaw, and my son has a couple of broken ribs and a collapsed lung along with some cuts in his mouth that caused some bleeding." He'd been relieved to hear that was where the blood had come from.

"Jeez. That's terrible. I'm so sorry."

"Thanks, but all we care about is that they're alive. My mom said it could've been much worse when she texted me. And thank God for onboard Wi-Fi."

"No kidding, right? How did it happen?"

"They turned at the same second and crashed into each other. My brother was right behind them and said it happened so fast, he couldn't do a thing."

"A freak accident."

Max nodded, grateful for the conversation that had calmed his nerves somewhat. "They're both great skiers. We've hammered safety into them since they were first on the bunny slope." He wondered how he'd ever stand to let Caden strap on skis again after this.

"Do you have a connecting flight to Vermont from New York?"

"Sort of. My brother's father-in-law is Patrick Murphy, the famous businessman. He's sending his chopper to pick me up at LaGuardia."

"That's great."

"It is. He's saving me six or seven hours on the road. My nephew Chase is his grandson."

"Ah, I see."

"He's a good dude. He would've done it for me even if Chase wasn't hurt, too."

"That's what family does."

"I haven't even asked what's bringing you to New York?" The conversation was helping to keep him calm as the flight stretched on interminably.

"I live there. I was in Houston for a college friend's wedding."

"Ah, I see. Two of my sisters-in-law are from New York. They moved to Vermont to marry my brothers, and then one of their sisters married my cousin."

"Wow, what a family affair."

"It gets better. Lucy, who married my brother Colton, and Emma, who married my cousin Grayson—their dad is also married to my aunt Hannah, Grayson's mom."

"Wait... I might need you to draw me a picture of that."

Max laughed, which he wouldn't have thought possible an hour ago. "Two sisters married my brother and cousin, and their dad married my aunt. Emma's mother-in-law is also her stepmother."

"My mind is blown."

"It's cool, though. They're all so happy together, and they deserve it."

"What brought you to Houston?"

"My high school girlfriend. We recently reconnected at our tenth reunion."

"That's amazing."

"It's been great so far. I've been a single dad to Caden since he was born, and he just turned seven."

"Has it been rough? Single parenthood, that is."

"Not as hard as it would've been without a lot of help from my parents, grandfather and siblings. I'm the youngest of ten and was the first to have a child, so my family rallied around us."

"*Ten?* Holy moly."

"Everyone says that."

"I've never met anyone who was one of ten."

"Well, now you have. My aunt Hannah has eight. Eighteen of us between her and my mom."

"That must've been fun growing up."

"It was. What about you? Big family?"

"I have two older brothers."

"Are you close to them?"

"We talk almost every day by text, so I suppose that counts as close these days. One lives in Phoenix and the other in Sacramento."

"Did you grow up in New York?"

"We did, on the Upper East Side."

"I haven't spent much time in the city, but my brothers get there once in a while."

The pilot came on the address system to announce their final approach into LaGuardia. "Sorry for the bouncy ride, folks. We do appreciate your business and hope to see you again soon."

"I hope they *don't* see me again soon," she said.

Max laughed. "I'm Max, by the way."

"I'm Toni. Nice to meet you."

"You, too. Thanks for talking to me. It helped."

She flashed him a warm smile. "Same."

As they were standing in the aisle waiting for others to deplane, Toni handed him a business card. "If you get back to New York, give me a call."

"Oh, thanks," he said.

"And all the best to your son and nephew."

"Thank you." Max sent his mom a text to let her know he'd landed in New York. *Be there soon.*

He's asking for you. We told him you're on the way.

Tell him I love him, and I'm coming.

Will do.

How's Chase?

Awake and alert. The broken jaw is the biggest concern. Will and Cam are with him.

Max was greatly relieved to know that both boys would recover—eventually. He realized he needed to give Lexi an update. *Landed in NY and on the way to Patrick's chopper. Both boys are conscious. Caden has broken ribs and a collapsed lung. Chase has a broken jaw. Both are awake and alert, which is a huge relief.*

The minute he was off the plane, Max ran through the terminal, following signs to the place Patrick had told him to meet the chopper. It was waiting for him in a section of the airport reserved for private aircraft. Max had to show ID to an agent at the doorway and was buzzed through to the tarmac.

He saw the distinctive black chopper with the PME initials on the side and jogged over to it.

"Max Abbott?" a man in uniform asked.

"That's me."

"Welcome aboard. We'll have you to Burlington in about ninety minutes."

That sure as hell beat six to seven hours. "Thank you so much."

"We're sorry about your son and nephew, but we're hearing they're going to be okay."

"Yes, they are, thank goodness."

They handed Max a headset to wear to mute the noise and so they could communicate with him if needed. As they lifted off, Max looked out the window at Manhattan in the distance. His phone vibrated with a text from Lexi.

SO relieved to hear they're going to be okay. I'm thinking of you and them nonstop. Please keep me posted. Love you. PS: I finally got through to cancel the rental car.

Max smiled as he read her text, comforted by her kind words and her love. *Thank you. I'm so sorry I had to leave the way I did. Was having the best time ever. Will make it up to you. I promise. Love you, too.*

She wrote right back. *No need to make it up to me. Caden is your top priority, and I totally understand that. I'm here if I can do anything for either of you. Xoxo*

Thanks for understanding. Means a lot to me. I'll try to call you later.

Call me any time.

Max felt better knowing she wasn't upset about the way he'd left her. He felt terrible about not bringing her with him, but he still felt this wasn't the time to try to force things between her and Caden. He would want Max's full attention, and that's what he would have until he was recovered from his injuries.

After that, Max would work on making the three of them into a family.

THE HELICOPTER LANDED ABOUT THREE MILES FROM THE HOSPITAL. Linc was waiting in his new Range Rover when Max stepped off the chopper in a remote field, seemingly in the middle of nowhere. But after having attended college in Burlington, Max recognized the location a short distance from downtown and the University of Vermont campus.

He jumped into the passenger seat of his dad's vehicle. "Thanks for meeting me."

"No problem. I'm glad to see you."

"Same. What a hellish day. I'm never leaving him again."

"Don't say that. Everyone deserves a break, especially single parents."

"Being far away from him when he was hurt is the worst feeling I've ever had."

"I understand that, but you can't be with him all the time."

"Yes, I can."

"No, Max, you can't," Linc said gently, "and you shouldn't be. As he gets older, he'll spend more time away from you, which is the natural order of things. You have a right to your own life."

Max shook his head. "I don't want my own life if it means I'm not there for him when he needs me."

"You're always there for him."

"I wasn't today."

"But we were. Will and Cam were. He was surrounded by people who love him almost as much as you do, and that will always be the case in our family."

"I know, but it should've been me."

"Max... I need you to hear me on this. You did nothing wrong taking a few days for yourself. It's good for Caden to have that time away from you. Remember when Mom and I went to London when you were in high school, and we left you with Gramps?"

"The time I broke my wrist skateboarding?"

"Right. How do you think we felt being across the pond when you were in the ER? I'll tell you—it was terrible. We felt awful that we couldn't be with you. But you were with the next best person with Gramps, and he took wonderful care of you until we could get there."

"Yes, he did," Max said, smiling at the memory of two days off from school with his Gramps tending to his every need.

"When you look back, do you think about how we weren't there when you broke your wrist?"

"I haven't thought of that in years."

"Exactly my point, and just think, if we hadn't been away when Charley fell off the mountain, she might never have gotten together with Tyler. That would've been tragic."

"For sure."

"Do you understand what I'm saying to you, son? You must forgive yourself for not being there today. You left him with people who love him. And not for nothing, I found I was a better father when I had a little time away to appreciate my ten hellions."

Max laughed. "I'm sure."

"How's Lexi?"

"She's great."

"I thought she might be with you when you got here."

Max winced at the reminder of how he'd rebuffed her offer to come. "I didn't think Caden would be receptive."

"Aw, Max. You gotta remember who's in charge."

"Him, right?"

Linc laughed. "Not hardly. In a day or two, when your boy is on the road to recovery, get your lady here to support you both. He'll come around."

"What if he doesn't?"

"He will. He doesn't know her yet, so he's threatened by her. Once he gets to know her, he'll see that nothing that really matters will change if she's part of your lives. That's what'll matter to him."

"You sure about that?"

"Maxwell, if there's one thing I know a thing or two about, it's kids. And yes, I'm sure."

They parked in a huge garage and made their way inside to the pediatric ICU. Having the boys in that unit spiked Max's anxiety. His dad led him right to Caden's room. Seeing his little boy in a hospital bed receiving oxygen through the thing in his nose had Max's knees buckling.

Linc's hand on his back propped him up.

Max stepped up to the bed, delighting in the way Caden's eyes lit up when he saw him.

"You're here," Caden said.

"I'm here. Sorry it took so long." He leaned over to kiss his forehead and breathed in the distinctive scent of his hair as relief flooded him. "How are you feeling?"

"My side hurts bad, and they said my lung collapsed. I'm not sure what that means."

"It's like a balloon when it pops." Max stroked his hair, filled with gratitude to be talking to him after imagining the worst-case scenario for hours. "But they fixed it so you can breathe."

"Chase got hurt, too."

"I heard."

"He's okay, though, right?"

"He's going to be. You both are, thank God."

"It was the weirdest thing, Dad. We were skiing, and then the next thing I knew, we were here. I heard we were on a helicopter. I'm bummed I missed that."

Max laughed. "We'll ask Patrick to take you for a ride on his helicopter. That's how I got here from New York."

"Was it sick?"

"So sick."

Molly came into the room and hugged Max.

"How's Chase?"

"He's doing well, but he's got to have surgery on his jaw. They're hoping to do that tomorrow."

"I hit his face with my helmet," Caden said, his chin trembling. "He knows it wasn't on purpose, right?"

"Of course he does, sweetheart," Molly said. "He feels bad that you got hurt, too."

"When can I see him?"

"Hopefully tomorrow," Molly said.

"You can stay, right, Daddy?"

"I'm not going anywhere," Max said.

CHAPTER NINETEEN

"Nobody has ever measured, not even poets,
*how much the heart can hold." —*Zelda Fitzgerald

*C*aden was released from the hospital two days later with orders to stay home from school and stay quiet for two weeks to give his ribs time to heal. They were holding Chase for one more day to work on his nutritional needs while his jaw was immobilized. The boys had seen each other on the second night in the hospital, which had raised their spirits tremendously.

Since Lucas and Landon had arranged to get Max's truck from the airport and back home the day before, Max and Caden drove to Butler with Linc and Molly. Elmer had stayed in Butler to take care of all the pets while the others were away and was looking forward to welcoming them home.

Max had left the hospital only long enough to go to his parents' lake home in Burlington to shower and change into clothes his mom had brought from home since he'd packed for much warmer weather in Houston.

The getaway with Lexi in Galveston felt like months ago rather than only days. They'd had a few quick conversations and had been texting a lot. Max appreciated her kind thoughts for Caden and Chase and how she asked frequently how *he* was doing while taking care of his son.

He missed her terribly, and as soon as he got Caden settled at home, he planned to ask her to come up. His dad's words from the other day had stayed with Max. Linc was right that Max deserved a life of his own in addition to being Caden's dad, and now that the crisis had passed, he was able to see that more clearly than he had during it.

Max glanced over at his son, who was asleep. He looked tired and pale, but otherwise, he was doing well despite a lot of pain from his broken ribs. It would take a long time before Max's nerves fully settled from the events of the last few days, but he was taking his lead from Caden, who'd rolled with serious injuries with his usual wit and resilience.

"Mom. What day is it?"

"Wednesday."

"Shit. Chloe is coming today." Max sent her a text. *Hey, sorry for the short notice, but we can't do it today. Can we move to next week? Sorry.*

She wrote back a few minutes later. *Disappointed, but sure. Same time next week?*

Yes, and thank you.

"I moved it to next week."

"You didn't tell her he got hurt?" Molly asked.

"Why would I? I've never told her the many times he had fevers or when he had pneumonia."

"I guess that's true."

He glanced at Caden to make sure he was truly asleep before he continued the conversation. "I don't see anything changing just because she's reappeared and wants to know him. She'll never be his mother the way you've been mine."

"No, she won't be, but she did give birth to him, and that means she'll always be his mother."

"I respect that, and I appreciate it every day. But that's as far as my obligation to her goes."

"Hmmm," Molly said.

"What does that mean, Mom?"

"I read her letter, son. She's grown up a lot in the last seven years, and you may need to make space for her in your son's life, starting by telling her he got hurt."

"What if she decides she wants joint custody and uses that information against me?"

"You have full custody, Max," Linc said. "She's not going to be able to change that. Check with Grayson to see what he thinks to be sure, but I think that ship has sailed for her."

"Your points are well taken, and I'll talk to Gray."

Molly turned in her seat so she could see him better. "I never considered the custody question, and you're right to be cautious about that."

"Did you just tell me I was right about something?" Max asked, grinning.

"There's a first time for everything."

Max laughed at the way she said that. "I'll try not to get too cocky."

"The thing is, I've never had to consider how my actions might affect the custody of my children, so I didn't properly appreciate that concern."

"Not everyone gets lucky being married to the father or mother of their children for fortysomething years."

"No, they don't, and in case I forget to tell you this every day, that child is very lucky to have you as his daddy."

"And he's lucky to have you guys as his grandparents."

Molly smiled and then turned back to face the front.

Max composed a text to his cousin Grayson. *Hi there, on the way back to Butler with Caden and my parents. Thanks to you and Emma for all the texts and well-wishes over the last few days. We're very thankful that he and Chase are doing so much better. I wanted to let you know that I recently received a gift for Caden along with a letter from his mother, Chloe. She told me how she has worked hard to get to a point where she feels like she'd like to see him, and I've agreed to let her because Caden wants to meet her. That was supposed to happen today, but I put it off until next week. My mother thought I might want to inform Chloe that Caden is injured, but I'm concerned about her end game and maybe using that against me if she's gunning for some form of custody. Anyway, can we catch up tomorrow to discuss? Thanks, Gray!*

His cousin responded a few minutes later. *So happy to hear Caden is on his way home. Hope Chase is right behind him. Thank God they're both ok. Will call you tomorrow.*

Thanks again, Gray.

"I'm going to talk to Grayson about Chloe tomorrow," Max told his parents.

"Good," Molly said. "He'll know how to handle it."

When they got home, all the lights were on in Max's house, and the driveway was full of SUVs and pickup trucks. "Looks like there's a welcome-home party for Caden," Max said.

As he carried Caden inside, Max wasn't at all surprised to find most of his siblings and their partners jammed into the small home he shared with Caden. Every available space was covered with food.

Caden perked up at the sight of his aunts and uncles, who swarmed around him, making a fuss and surrounding him with love, as they had all his life.

Max got him settled on the sofa, covered with a blanket and propped up with pillows supporting his injured left side.

"Where are all the kids?" Caden asked.

"Either at school or with my mom," Dani said. "We thought the adults would be enough for today."

Elmer poked his head in the door. "Is the patient ready to see his best pal?"

"He is," Max said.

Elmer led Daisy into the crowded house, and she looked around until she found Caden, her eyes widening and her tail wagging madly when she saw him. "Remember what we talked about, Miss Daisy. Nice and gentle with your boy."

Caden held out a hand to her, and she came over to sniff and lick him, making him giggle.

Somehow, the puppy seemed to understand that he was hurt and nuzzled him gently. She ended up on the sofa, parked between Caden's legs, the two of them happy to be reunited.

"I missed you, girl," he said as he scratched behind her ears.

195

"We made everything," Max's sister Hannah said. "Dig in."

"Thanks, guys." Max fixed a small plate for Caden and then went back for some of Ella's chicken and Charley's mac 'n' cheese for himself.

"We knew there wouldn't be room for everyone, so we made this an OG mission while the kids were in school," Landon said, meaning "original gangsters."

"Good call," Max said.

"So, how'd you leave things with Lexi when you had to come running home?" Charley asked.

Max paused mid-bite. "Um, well, she knew I needed to get home as fast as possible. We've been talking."

"Did you have fun in Houston?" Ella asked.

"Uh-huh."

"Girls, leave your brother alone," Molly said.

"We're just making sure he doesn't mess this up, Mom," Charley said.

Max scowled at her. "I'm not going to mess it up. Now go away."

"We're keeping an eye on things," Lucas said for himself and his twin, who nodded.

"We won't let him mess it up," Landon said.

"Oh my God," Max said with a groan. "The last kind of help I need is from you two."

"Which of us are happily married and which of us is *not*?" Landon asked. "Hmm?"

"Boys, please, stand down," Colton said. "I've got this taken care of."

Max rolled his eyes.

"How quickly you forget, young grasshopper," Colton said to Max. "Who was the one who pushed you in her direction when she was here?" Colton held his hand to his ear. "What's that? I can't hear you saying, 'Colton did that.'"

"I blame you two for this," Molly said to her husband and father.

"What'd we do?" Linc asked, full of innocence.

"What didn't you do? Now they all think they have some sort of right to butt into other people's relationships."

"We do have that right," Charley said. "It's in the Abbott family rulebook."

"Which none of you has ever read," Molly said with a pointed look for her daughter.

"We wrote that book," Lucas said, with a high five for his twin.

"You all can go now," Max said. "Caden needs his rest."

"Why would we leave when things are just getting interesting?" Hunter asked.

"I expect better from you," Max said to his eldest sibling.

"Really? Why?"

The others cracked up laughing. Thankfully, they moved on to other topics and left Max alone about Lexi. Now that the crisis with Caden had passed, he was feeling badly about the way he'd left her so abruptly and declined her offer to come with him. They'd been wrapped up in each other in bed a few minutes before that, so he could only imagine how much it had hurt her to have him take off without her.

He winced thinking about that, even though he still felt it had been the right thing for Caden. But it hadn't been the right thing for him—or her. Now that they'd found each other again, all he wanted was to be with her as much as he possibly could. He would tell her that as soon as his family left and he got Caden tucked into bed for the night.

Max couldn't wait to talk to her.

WHILE MAX TENDED TO HIS SON, LEXI HAD BEEN MAKING PLANS to move home to Vermont as of early January. She was on a tight budget and would shop for used furniture at secondhand shops when she arrived. All she needed was a bed and a few kitchen items to get by for a while.

She'd also been doing some research about online classes so she could pick up her education where she'd left off when illness struck. Finally, she'd been job hunting, applying for several jobs within the Abbotts' company, which was the town's largest employer.

Her mom came to the door of her bedroom, where Lexi was seated at her desk. "I thought you might want a cup of that Sleepytime tea you like."

"Thank you."

"What're you up to?"

"Making plans."

"To move home?"

Lexi nodded and took a sip of the tea.

"Us, too. I hired movers today, and we're putting this house on the market next week."

"Are you prepared to go back to those winters after living here?"

"That'll be an adjustment, but I miss the New England seasons. I never thought I'd miss snow, but I do."

"Me, too, even though I'm always cold."

"You'll have Max to keep you warm."

"I hope so."

"You sound uncertain."

Lexi shrugged. "It may not happen. His son isn't digging me."

"He must barely know you," her mom said. "You were only there a few days. How much time did you spend with him?"

"Not much."

"It's the *idea* of you he doesn't like. He isn't opposed to you. He's opposed to any woman who takes a portion of his father's time and attention from him. I suppose that's to be expected when it's just been the two of them for all this time."

"I worry that he'll never accept me as part of their lives."

"He will. It just might take some time and finesse on your part."

"How so?"

"Small doses at first until he gets used to having you around. Take the time to really get to know him and his interests. Participate in things he likes to do and make him see you're no threat to him or his relationship with his dad."

"I can do that."

"Sure, you can. It'll be fine, but it won't happen overnight."

"It's strange how I hoped I'd see Max at the reunion, but I never thought for a second that he'd be a single father."

"Did that change how you felt about him?"

"No, it only makes me admire him more. He's done such a great job with Caden and has their lives running so smoothly. Part of me wonders if I should just leave them alone and focus on getting my own life back on track."

"Why can't you do both?"

"I can, it's just that I want to be sure that Max is committed to bringing me into Caden's life before we go any further. It can't happen without him."

"If you ask me, from what I saw of him, Max is very committed to you and to making this work."

"I guess we'll see. Sometimes I worry that it was too much to hope that we could just pick up where we left off and go forward like the last ten years didn't happen."

"You were both dealing with big things during those years. Now you can focus on what's next together."

"Is it that simple? Can we see each other twice in a decade and make this work long term?"

"If it's what you both want, absolutely. I remember telling your dad when you and Max were first together that you were going to marry him someday. I kept waiting for you to tell us you'd taken a pass on Berkeley so you could stay with him."

"I should've. Everything might've been different if I had."

"You still would've gotten sick, and he might not have had Caden, which he would say was meant to be. Life gets in the way of plans all the time, and that's what happened to you two, but I've always thought you and Max belonged together. Why do you think I encouraged you to go to the reunion? I was so hoping for exactly what's happened."

"Apparently, his family pushed him just as hard to go. I'm not sure if they were hoping he'd see me, but they wanted him there."

"They were probably hoping you'd show up. No doubt they

saw what we did with you two, a forever kind of love that happened long before either of you was ready for it."

"I want this to work out so badly, Mom. Other than surviving my illness, I've never wanted anything the way I want him."

"I know, sweetheart, and I have a good feeling you two will make a go of it. That's a big reason why we want to be back in Butler, so we can be there to watch you live your happily ever after with him."

"Your faith that it will happen is very reassuring."

"Good."

"What if…"

"What, honey?"

"What if we make a go of this and the cancer comes back?"

"It won't."

"And you know that for certain?"

"No, but I feel confident that you've beaten it, and I've chosen to believe the worst is behind us."

"I probably can't have kids, and he'll want more."

"You have the eggs frozen, and there're other ways to have them besides the natural way. If I know Max at all, I'd bet he'd rather have you than six kids with someone else."

Lexi's phone rang, and she pounced on it, checking the caller ID. "It's Max."

Her mom got up and kissed Lexi's forehead. "I'll let you talk to him."

"Thanks again for the tea—and everything else."

"Love you, sweet girl."

Lexi took the call. "Hi there. Did you get home okay?"

"A couple of hours ago. My siblings were all here with food to welcome us home."

"Caden must've enjoyed that."

"We both did. Gramps brought Daisy home, too, and they're asleep together in Caden's bed."

"Everything is as it should be."

"Almost everything."

"What do you mean?"

"You should be here, too. I'm sorry that I discouraged you from coming the other day. That must've felt like a slap in the face considering what we'd been doing right before my mom called."

"You were thinking of Caden and getting to him. I understand."

"I should've brought you with me."

"Don't beat yourself up, Max. You were in a panic."

"You're being too forgiving. I'm sure you were hurt when I left without you."

"Please don't stress about that. You've got enough going on."

"I want you here with us. I miss you."

"I miss you, too, and I'm making plans to move home."

"I can't wait."

"You sound exhausted."

"I am. Three nights sleeping on a recliner in the hospital and worrying about the boys has me worn out."

"How's Chase doing?"

"Much better. The jaw injury is a big deal, so they had to get some additional support for that before he could leave the hospital."

"I hope they can get home soon."

"Hoping for tomorrow."

"Weren't you supposed to see Caden's mom this week?"

"I put that off until next week."

"Ah, I see."

"I don't want to wait weeks to see you again, Lex."

"It'll go by so fast."

"Every minute will drag until then."

She laughed. "Quit being dramatic. You have a lot to do getting Caden back on his feet and preparing for the holidays."

"I don't want to do any of it without you here. It only took a few nights of sleeping with you to get me addicted to it."

"Max," she said with a sigh.

"What?"

"You're making me breathless again."

"I miss you like crazy."

"I miss you, too, and the next few weeks will go by fast, I promise."

"No, they won't."

"Yes, they will."

"Are we having our first fight?"

Lexi laughed. "Nah, you just need to accept that I'm always right, and then we'll never fight."

"Um, well…"

She laughed again.

"You always were too quick for me, Lex."

"I'm just right for you."

"Yes, you are, and now that I've found you again, all I want is everything."

"Easy does it," she said.

"We're going to have it all. I know it."

"That would be lovely, but one step at a time, okay?"

"We're going to have our second fight if you keep up this slow-and-steady-wins-the-race theme."

"I'm going to keep it up, because you know as well as I do that it's what we have to do."

"I can't talk right now. I'm mad at you."

"Whatever," she said, giggling. "Go to bed and get some rest."

"Hey, Lex?"

"Yes, Max?"

"When we have kids, they're going to have to have the letter X in their names, okay?"

Her heart skipped a beat when he said that. "What part of 'one step at a time' are you not hearing?"

"The part where you're gonna make me wait to have it all with you."

"I won't make you wait that long."

"You promise?"

"I promise."

CHAPTER TWENTY

"Children begin by loving their parents; as they grow older they judge them; sometimes they forgive them." —Oscar Wilde

The following Wednesday, Max cleaned the house while Caden rested on the sofa watching *Paw Patrol* and working on some of the schoolwork his teacher had sent home so he wouldn't fall behind. Max wanted his home to be standing tall when Chloe visited for the first time so she would see a single father who had his shit together.

And thank God he worked for the family business and could be out of work while Caden needed him.

After speaking with Grayson the other day, he felt much better about sharing the news of the accident with Chloe.

"The document she signed giving up her parental rights was airtight," Grayson had said. "She gave full custody to you in front of multiple witnesses. Even if she's had a come-to-Jesus since then, she'd have zero chance of taking you to court to upend the custody agreement. It's entirely up to you as to how much she gets to see Caden, and I have no doubt she's gotten that same information if she's consulted with a lawyer."

Max had been so reassured by Grayson's input that he'd shared the news of Caden's accident with Chloe by text.

Oh my God, she'd responded. *I'm so glad he and his cousin are all right. You must've been terrified.*

I was, he'd replied. *I'd like to never go through that ever again.*

I'm sure! Thank you for letting me know. Please tell him I hope he feels much better, and I can't wait to see him on Wednesday.

I will, thanks.

So now it was Wednesday, and he was going to see Chloe for the first time in seven years and introduce her to their son. The whole thing was surreal, to say the least.

A knock on the door had Max putting down the mop to admit his grandfather, who'd come by every day to see Caden since he'd been home.

"How are my boys today?" Elmer asked.

"The boys are good and so is the girl," Caden said of Daisy, who sat up with excitement when she saw Elmer come in. She'd been amazingly well behaved and gentle with Caden.

Elmer had a treat for Daisy and a bag of penny candy from the store for Caden. "Got your favorite, chocolate raisins," Elmer said.

"Thanks, Gramps."

"You're welcome, buddy. How're you feeling?"

"A lot better. Dad said I can go back to school next week."

"Only if Dr. McKinley says it's okay," Max said.

"I gotta go see him tomorrow," Caden said.

"How's the homework coming?" Elmer asked, taking a seat next to the sofa.

"Not great, but Dad said if I get it done before dinner, I can have two scoops of ice cream for dessert."

"That sounds like a pretty good deal to me." Elmer ruffled his hair. "I'll let you get to it. Time's a-wastin', my friend."

"If you were really my friend, you'd do it for me," Caden said with an impish grin.

Elmer howled with laughter. "I'm the best friend you'll ever have, but I ain't doing your homework."

"Fine. Be that way."

"Glad to see him getting his sass back," Elmer said when he joined Max in the kitchen.

"Me, too. I never thought I'd be so happy to see him be sassy."

"Accidents have a way of reminding you of what's important."

"Indeed. Have you been to see Chase today?"

"Just came from there. He's very unhappy about the food situation, which is all liquid for the time being."

"Poor kid."

"Your mom is making some of the tomato soup he loves, and Cameron has the smoothie machine going full steam."

"That's got to be a heck of a challenge."

"It is, but he'll be back to fighting form in a few weeks, and then you got to get them right back on that mountain, so they won't be afraid of it."

"Ugh, I don't know about that."

"They love it the way you and Will do. You can't let them lose that. Get them back on the horse, my friend."

"We'll see." Max glanced around his grandfather to make sure Caden was occupied by the TV and the homework. "His mom is coming today."

"I might've heard something about that. How you feeling about it?"

"Oddly fine."

Elmer nodded. "Because she doesn't mean anything to you anymore, except as the person who gave you the greatest gift of your life."

"That she did, and I'll always be thankful to her for him."

"If you can stay in that mindset around her, it'll all be fine."

"That's the goal. Thanks for coming by, Gramps." Max hugged the older man. "We look forward to seeing you every day."

"Glad to see our boy bouncing back quickly. I'm too old for a scare like the one he and his cousin gave us."

"Me, too," Max said, smiling.

"Damned kids."

"Right?"

"Caden, I'll see you tomorrow. Be good for your dad."

"I always am."

"Love you, buddy."

"Love you, too."

Max waved Elmer off from the front door and then went to see how Caden was making out with the homework.

"I think he might be my favorite person in the whole wide world," Caden said. "After you, of course."

"It's okay if he's first. He's first on a lot of people's lists of favorites."

Max was thankful his grandfather had lived long enough that Caden would remember him, not that he wanted to think about a time when Elmer wasn't right in the middle of everything in their lives.

He spent more than an hour helping Caden finish his homework and then made turkey sandwiches for lunch.

"What time is my mom coming?" Caden asked.

"Three."

"What time is it now?"

"One. How many hours until three?"

Caden gave him a withering look. "Duh. Two. That's baby math."

"Just making sure you're staying sharp while you're out of school."

"It was cool that the whole class sent me a card and those sick cookies."

"It was very nice of them. They miss you."

"I know."

Several of his friends had called to check on him, which had made Caden so happy. "You'll be back there soon."

"Hey, Dad?"

"What's up?"

"What if my mom doesn't like me?"

Max was flabbergasted by the question. "Caden, buddy... Of course she'll like you. Everyone likes you."

"But what if she doesn't?"

"You don't need to worry about that. She's going to be so happy to see you that she'll probably cry."

"You think so?"

"I'll be surprised if she doesn't. I would if I hadn't seen you since you were a baby."

"Tell me again where she's been all this time."

"Do you remember us talking about where babies come from?" Max had given him the highest-level view he possibly could after Caden had seen two sheep humping in a neighbor's yard.

"Ew, yes, disgusting."

"Sometimes when people make babies, the babies aren't planned."

"Like I wasn't, right?" That had come up when a friend's mother had a surprise pregnancy and he'd asked how that was possible.

"Right. The second we knew we were having you, I was so excited to meet you. Your mom was scared. Her family wasn't around like mine is, so she didn't have a lot of support. She was still really young and didn't feel ready to take care of a baby."

"Weren't you really young, too?"

"I was, but I had my wonderful parents and great big family supporting me the whole way. Your mom didn't have that."

"Why not?"

"I'm not sure, buddy, but they weren't close like the Abbotts are."

"That's sad."

"It is. We're very lucky to have such a wonderful family."

"What's she like? My mom?"

"Well, I haven't seen her in a long time, but when we were in college, she was sweet and funny and pretty." That was until she became pregnant unexpectedly, and then she'd changed dramatically, not that Caden needed to know that.

"What should I call her?"

"Why don't we ask what she prefers?"

"Okay."

Max leaned in to hug his son. "Don't worry about anything. She'll be thrilled to see you, and she'll love you like everyone else does."

"She's not going to try to take me away from you, is she?"

Shocked, Max pulled back. "What? No. Why would you think that?"

"I heard you talking to Grammy about it in the car the other day."

"You were asleep."

"I could hear you."

"I'm sorry you heard that, but I talked to Grayson, and he said there's no chance of anything happening to change our current situation." Max was furious with himself for talking about that when Caden was nearby. "I hope you haven't been worried about that."

"Not really. I knew you wouldn't let that happen."

"I'd never let that happen, so don't worry. She may want to see you occasionally, which is fine, but she can't take you away from me. And I don't think she'd ever try to because she knows that's not what's best for you."

"Okay."

"Can we talk about something else?"

"Sure."

"My friend Lexi..."

"Your *girl*friend, you mean?"

Max smiled. "Yeah, my girlfriend."

"What about her?"

"I want you to do something for me. Something really important."

"What?"

"I want you to give her a chance before you decide you don't like her just because you think she's going to change things between us or something like that." Max felt it was important to continue this conversation since she'd be living near them before much longer. "You should know by now that nothing and no one could ever change things between us. We're always going to be best friends and buddies, no matter what."

Caden appeared to give that some thought. "Is she coming here?"

"She's moving back to Butler after Christmas. Having her in my life again makes me happy, but I can't truly be happy if you're not. So it would mean a lot to me if you would give her a chance."

"I will."

"Really? You promise?"

He nodded. "You do a lot to make me happy, so I guess it's only fair that I do the same for you."

"Thank you. I promise you that nothing between us will change if we see your mom once in a while or if Lexi is in our lives. You'll just have more people who love you, which is always a good thing." Max caressed his son's soft hair. "No one will ever love you as much as I do."

Caden smiled. "I love you, too."

"Why don't you go get cleaned up? Your mom will be here in a little bit."

"I can't believe I'm going to meet my mom."

"I know. It's exciting." Max helped Caden up from the chair, noting that he was moving more easily than he had since the accident. "Call me if you need help."

"I'm fine."

After Caden left the room, Max sat back in his chair feeling amused, amazed and relieved after the conversation with his son. From the start, he'd been the most incredible kid, full of spunk and sass and curiosity for people, places and adventure. Max felt sorry for everything Chloe had missed with their son, but he hoped that maybe she could be part of his life going forward.

Before he'd gotten her letter, the thought of allowing her into their lives would've been preposterous to him. But people grew and changed and evolved, and he hoped the new version of Chloe would be someone he'd want in his son's life.

Chloe arrived right on time at three o'clock, driving a white SUV and wearing jeans, boots and a sweater with a navy blue down vest. Her hair was darker than he recalled, her blue eyes clear and her smile bright. It was almost shocking to Max to see how great she looked, because his most recent memories of her had been colored by her utter misery over the pregnancy and childbirth.

Max went out to greet her.

"Hi, Max," she said, smiling. "It's good to see you."

"You, too. You look great."

"So do you, but then again, you always did."

"Thanks. Caden is excited to meet you."

"That's nice to hear. I wondered if he'd be angry with me."

"He doesn't have that in him."

"I guess that makes me lucky. How's he feeling?"

"Much better."

"And you? Having him hurt must've been awful."

"Worst thing I've ever been through, but as long as he and Chase are okay, that's what matters."

"He's close with Chase?"

"Very. They're like brothers."

"He must have a lot of other cousins by now."

"There's twenty-six grandchildren at last count, and that doesn't count the Colemans."

"Wow. And he's the oldest, right?"

"He's inherited a few older cousins since Landon married a woman with a daughter and Charley and Tyler took in his nieces after their parents died. The younger ones look up to Caden, though." Max glanced back at the house. "Before we go in, I just wanted to know what you're hoping to have happen."

"I'd like to see him occasionally, maybe go to one of his games or to his school for whatever goes on there. I'm not asking for anything more than to be in his life, however you and he see fit. I know it's more than I deserve—"

"I don't hold it against you, Chloe. You did what was best for you and Caden, and it was a long time ago. He's been the greatest blessing of my life. I wouldn't change anything."

"Thank you for stepping up for him the way you did. I've always been so thankful to you and your family for doing what I couldn't."

"You're welcome. Come meet your son." Max led the way inside, where Caden and Daisy were seated on the sofa. When

Chloe followed him in, Daisy moved closer to Caden. "Caden, this is your mom, Chloe. Chloe, this is Caden."

"Oh," she said on a long exhale. "Look at you. You're so handsome, just like your daddy."

Max went to give Caden a hand up.

Caden offered his hand to Chloe. "It's nice to meet you."

She shook his hand as tears filled her eyes. "It's nice to meet you, too. I'm sorry it took so long."

Caden shrugged. "You're here now."

"Yes, I am, and I'm so happy to see you. I want you to know that I've thought of you every day." Her voice caught. "And I've always loved you."

"Thanks. This is Daisy. My dad gave her to me for my birthday."

Chloe bent to pet Daisy, who had followed her boy. "It's nice to meet you, Daisy."

"Thank you for the truck you sent me. I love it."

"I'm glad you do. My nephew told me that it was the coolest truck ever, and that's what I wanted for you."

"How old is your nephew?"

"He's nine. I also have nieces who are six and four."

"They're my cousins, then?"

"They are."

"Do you have other kids?"

"No, just you, but I'm getting married next year, so I might have more."

"Do you want to see my room?"

"I'd love to."

"Come on. I'll show you."

As she went past Max, Chloe placed her hand on her heart and gave him a look that left no doubt in his mind how much it meant to her to be with her son.

While Max stood in the doorway, Caden showed his mother his favorite toys and treasures, including the trophy from his first Little League season and his Student of the Month certificate from school.

"These are all my cousins with my grandparents and my

grandpa-great." He handed her the photo Max's cousin Izzy had taken a year ago of all the Abbott grandchildren. "My cousin Murphy hadn't been born yet."

"That's a big crowd," Chloe said as she scanned the photo. "Who are the older girls?"

"My aunt Charley's nieces. Their parents died in an accident, and they came to live with Aunt Charley and Uncle Tyler."

"Oh, I see. That's so sad for them."

"It was," Caden said, "but they're doing better. They're fun to hang out with."

"Tell me who all the others are and who they belong to."

Like the Abbott family expert he was, Caden pointed to each child and told Chloe their name and who their parents were.

"How fun for you to have so many cousins," Chloe said.

"I love them so much. And we have the Coleman cousins, too. Every summer, we have a big cookout at Grammy's house with all the Abbotts and Colemans. Grammy calls it the madhouse."

"How many Coleman cousins are there?"

Caden glanced at Max.

"Fifteen so far," Max said. "We expect there'll be many more before all is said and done."

"Wow, that's a lot of kids."

"It is a madhouse," Caden said, "but it's fun. That's my favorite day of the whole summer."

Max hadn't heard him say that before.

Chloe asked him about school and sports and who his friends were and what kind of pizza he liked.

"Meat lovers," Caden said. "The more meat, the better."

Max and Chloe shared a laugh, the first one ever as parents to the most exceptional boy who'd ever lived.

"Just like your dad," she said with a smile for Max.

She stayed for two hours, until they could both see that Caden was getting tired. "I should go, but I want to thank you for such a lovely afternoon, Caden."

"Thanks for coming."

"I'd like to see you again sometime, if that's all right with you and your dad."

"It's all right with me," Caden said. "Is it okay with you, Dad?"

"Sure. We'll make that happen."

They walked her to the door.

"What should I call you?" Caden asked her.

"What do you want to call me? Anything is fine with me."

"Um, well, you're my mom, so I guess I should just call you that."

Chloe's eyes filled with tears. "I'd love that. Could I hug you?"

"Sure."

A huge lump landed in Max's throat as he watched them hug. Chloe kissed Caden's forehead. "I'll be in touch."

"Okay."

"Bye, Daisy," Chloe said, bending to give the dog a pat on the head.

Max walked her out. "So that's our son."

"I'll never have the words to tell you what this has meant to me, Max. Thank you."

"You're welcome. And I mean that… You're welcome in our lives, Chloe. All I ask is that you don't disappoint him."

"I won't. I promise."

"Okay, then. I guess we'll talk soon."

"Thanks again, Max. Not just for today, but for raising such a wonderful boy. He's…" She shook her head when words failed her.

"Believe me, I know. Raising him has been the honor of my lifetime."

Chloe hugged him, and he let her.

"I'll be in touch," she said when he held the car door for her.

After he waved her off, he went back inside. Caden and Daisy were on the sofa with the TV tuned to a *Drake & Josh* episode. That had been Max's favorite show as a kid. He'd shared it with Caden, who also loved it.

"How're you feeling, pal?" Max asked.

"Fine."

"Good visit with your mom, huh?"

"Yep. She's nice. And pretty."

"She really loved you, but I knew she would."

"That's good. I liked her, too. What's for dinner?"

Max was relieved to have gotten through the momentous visit with Chloe without any apparent fallout for Caden. "What do you feel like?"

"Duh. Spaghetti."

"Then spaghetti it is."

CHAPTER TWENTY-ONE

"Whatever souls are made of, his and mine are the same."
—Emily Brontë

Max and Caden returned to work and school the following Monday, and the next few weeks flew by in a whirl of holiday preparations and festivities. They attended parties at school, at Cub Scouts and at Hunter and Megan's house while working long shifts at the Christmas Tree Farm, which was one of Caden's favorite holiday traditions.

Max was on him constantly not to overdo the activity, but Caden was almost back to normal by Christmas Eve, as was Chase, who was now allowed to eat soft foods. The excitement level was through the roof as the family gathered at the barn for Christmas Eve for their annual sleepover. That tradition had started five years ago, after Linc reconnected with his siblings on an emotional trip to Philadelphia right before his father died. The entire family had spent Christmas Eve at the barn, and it'd been so much fun, they'd done it every year since.

The barn got more crowded as the family grew, but they found room for everyone, with air mattresses all over the place and every bedroom occupied.

Max, Caden and Daisy were in his dad's study, sleeping on the sofa and an air mattress.

Long after Caden was asleep, Max was still texting with Lexi, counting down to the twenty-eighth when he would fly to Houston to drive with her to Vermont. He couldn't wait to see her. The last few weeks had felt endless as they made plans and talked for hours every night. They were stuck texting tonight so he wouldn't wake Caden or anyone else.

She was spending Christmas with her family as they, too, prepared to move back to Vermont.

I'm looking forward to next Christmas when you can join the holiday madness at the barn. Head count: forty-six people. Hunter said tonight that we need to bring in some RVs next year before we burst at the seams.

It's such a sweet tradition. I'm looking forward to being number forty-five.

The volume, though... Are you sure you're ready for this???

Haha, quit trying to scare me away. It's not going to happen. Did you work out a time for Chloe to see Caden?

They're going to lunch the day after Christmas. Their first outing without me.

How do you feel about that?

I'm fine with it. She's been in regular contact with us, visited a few more times and hasn't asked for anything unreasonable. I keep telling myself that having her in his life is what's best for him.

It is. You're doing the right thing for him.

It's amazing how much she's changed.

We all grow up eventually.

I guess so.

You'd better get some sleep. Your boy will have you up early.

Last year, the kids were up at four thirty.

Stop it! No way.

Yep. The entire house was awake by five.

OMG. LOL.

Still looking forward to it?

I can't wait for all of it. Love you so much, Max Abbott.

Love you, too, Lex. So much. Looking forward to everything. Call me when you can tomorrow.

Will do. Merry Christmas.

She responded with all the Christmas emojis, and Max fell asleep smiling, full of excitement for the week ahead.

IN A BEDROOM UPSTAIRS, COLTON ABBOTT WAS TRYING TO MAKE love to his gorgeous wife, but she wasn't having it.

"If you wake them up," Lucy said in a harsh whisper, "I'll kill you, and I'll make it hurt."

His low chuckle came out louder than he'd intended. But how was that his fault? She was funny.

She elbowed him in the gut. "You think I'm joking?"

"I know you're dead serious," he whispered. "Ha. I made a joke."

"Go to sleep."

"Not yet. You've got me all worked up."

"You did that to yourself."

"No, you did it by crawling in bed with me wearing flannel. You know what that does to me."

"The passing breeze does the same thing to you."

"Only when you're the one causing the breeze to pass." His hands slid under her pajama top and up to play with breasts that were lush and full after having given birth to their three sons. He kept thinking the fiery attraction between them would eventually fade, but instead, it only grew more intense the longer they were together. "I love you so, so, so much, my Lucy in the sky with diamonds. You have no idea how much."

"I can feel just how much."

"That's just a fraction of the total."

"Are you calling your precious manhood a fraction of anything?"

"Allow me to rephrase that."

Her silent laughter made the bed shake.

Colton played with her nipple. "I want to love you, Luce. I want you so bad."

"Tomorrow, when we're home and the hellions aren't sleeping two feet from us."

"I can't wait that long."

"Honestly, Colton…"

"Honestly, Luce."

"Fine. Make it quick."

"I'm so good at quick."

"You're good at all of it."

He stopped short. "You think so?"

"Yes, Colton, I think so. That's why I married you."

"Is that the only reason you married me?"

Though the room was dark, he could imagine her rolling her eyes at him, as she did many times in an average day. He loved driving her crazy. "Time's a-wasting, my friend. Your spawn will be up in a couple of hours, and if their mother doesn't sleep, it's not going to be a merry Christmas for anyone."

"Hey, Luce?"

"Yes, Colton?"

"Just so you know… You're the best thing in my whole life. You and the devils. I love you so, so much."

"I love you, too."

"Even when I'm driving you bonkers?"

She ran her fingers though his hair. "Even then."

Colton kissed her and loved her to a quiet orgasm that had them gasping from the power of what they created together. As it had been from the start, sex with Lucy was almost a religious experience. As he came down from the incredible high, he kissed her and rubbed his nose against hers. "Love you forever and ever."

"I'll love you longer."

"No way."

"Yes way."

"Sleep, Colton. I need sleep."

He withdrew and made his chest available to her, wrapping his arms around her to keep her close, thankful for every second he got to spend with the incomparable Lucy Mulvaney Abbott.

✳

HUNTER WAS ABOUT TO GO LOOKING FOR MEGAN WHEN SHE snuck into the bedroom, where their kids, Carson, Cory and

Claire, were asleep on an air mattress. It'd taken Hunter more than an hour to get them to sleep, as they were not used to sleeping together and had been full of beans at bedtime.

"Where've you been?" he asked her in a whisper.

"I had to run home for a minute."

"I would've done that for you."

"It was something I had to do myself so I wouldn't spoil the surprise."

"I'm intrigued."

"Can you come to the kitchen for a minute?" That was the one room in the house where no one was sleeping.

"Yep." He got out of bed and followed her to the kitchen, stepping over Charley and Tyler's girls, who were asleep on air mattresses in the dining room.

"How were the kids at bedtime?"

"Terrible, but funny. We knew the sleepover would be dicey. Claire wanted to sleep between the boys, but they didn't want her touching them, which hurt her feelings."

Megan stifled a laugh. "Business as usual, huh?"

"Poor Claire can't catch a break with those boys. I'm working on getting them to be nicer to her, but it's a long-term project."

"They'll get there."

"It's just so strange for me because I was always so close with my sisters."

"They will be, too. They'll be so protective of her. I'm sure of it."

Hunter put his arms around her and rested his forehead against hers. "Since you're the wisest person I know, I'm going to believe you're right and hope for the best." He lifted his head to kiss her. "Now, about this surprise…"

She retrieved a gift bag off one of the chairs in the kitchen and handed it to him.

Hunter was surprised by how heavy it was. He pulled the tissue paper out and found three inches of paper held together by a big binder clip. Glancing at her, he said, "Is this what I think it is?"

As she nodded, her smile was so big it could probably be seen from space.

"You *finished* it?"

"Earlier today. I had to go home to print out the last three chapters."

"Oh my God, Meggie. You did it! You wrote your book while running a business and raising three kids and being the best wife and mom ever." His heart was so full of love for her, he could barely contain it all. He set the bag on the table and reached for her. "I'm so, so proud of you, and I can't wait to read it."

"I couldn't have done it without you and the info you gave me about search and rescue and the story ideas. I've already got three more books planned."

Hunter hugged her tightly. "Best Christmas present ever."

"I also want to thank you for all the times you took care of the kids so I could write. When I say I couldn't have done this without you, I mean it."

"We're a team, babe. Whatever you want is what I want."

"Not every author has a husband like you. Some of the women in my writing group talk about how their husbands don't take their writing seriously. I never have anything to add to those conversations, because my husband is amazing."

"Watching this dream come true for you has been one of the most exciting things I've ever experienced."

"Look," she said, flipping to the second page where the dedication said, "For my husband, Hunter, the love of my life who makes everything possible."

Hunter's eyes filled with tears as he kissed her. "Thank you for that. I'm so honored. What happens next?"

"I find an editor and a cover designer and make a plan to publish it in the next few months."

"You decided to pursue the indie path?"

She nodded. "I'm too busy to be beholden to someone else's deadlines. I don't want it to turn into another chore that has to get done every day, which it will if I chase the traditional route."

"We'll have the biggest party ever when your book is published."

She kissed him and hugged him. "I can't wait for that."

"Me either. Merry Christmas, my sweet love, the soon-to-be published author."

"Merry Christmas, best husband ever."

NOLAN ENTERED THE BARN THROUGH THE MUDROOM, BRINGING Dexter and his massive dog/moose bed with him. He tossed the bed on the floor and pointed to it. "Go to bed. Right now, or I'll make a stew out of you."

"No, you will not! Don't say that to him!" Hannah joined them, wearing her favorite flannel Christmas pajamas, with her long, dark hair down around her shoulders. She went to Dexter, who nuzzled her while giving Nolan a "fuck you" look over Hannah's shoulder.

Nolan had never imagined he'd be competing with a moose for his wife's affection, but by now, he shouldn't be surprised.

"Was someone making a ruckus because his family left him alone on Christmas?" Hannah asked as she hugged and kissed Dexter.

The neighbors had called to tell them something was wrong with Dex, which had sent Nolan out into the frigid darkness to retrieve their "family member," as Hannah referred to him. As if it wasn't enough to have more than forty humans and twenty dogs sleeping in the barn, now they had a moose, too.

"You felt left out, didn't you, sweetie?" Hannah asked, cooing at him.

Dex was blissed out with love for her.

Nolan certainly understood that, not that he'd ever cop to having anything in common with that GD moose.

"Did Daddy bring your food and water bowls?"

"All his crap is in that bag," Nolan said.

"His things are not *crap*," she said, with a glare for Nolan.

"I went and got him, Hannah. Now, can we please go to bed before our human animals wake up at the butt crack of dawn?"

"Let me get him settled first." She sweet-talked Dexter until he was stretched out on his bed, receiving the sweet loving

Nolan had hoped to get some of before Dex ruined his evening. This wasn't the first time Dexter had cock-blocked him, and it most definitely wouldn't be the last.

When Hannah was satisfied that Dex was settled in for the night, she followed Nolan out of the mudroom, closing the door to the kitchen. "I need to leave a note on the door that he's in there, so he doesn't scare anyone."

After she'd done that, Nolan put his hands on her hips from behind and steered her upstairs to her childhood bedroom, where their kids, Callie and Colby, were asleep.

When he'd closed the door behind them, Hannah turned to him and put her arms around his neck. "My hero. Thank you for going after him."

"You're welcome." He had much more he'd like to say about how that freaking moose would be the death of him, but he'd learned to keep his comments about Dexter to himself.

She tugged on a handful of his hair. "I'd better never hear you tell him you're going to make stew out of him again, you got me?"

"I thought I was your hero?"

"You were until the stew threat."

"I'm very sorry about that," he said, even though he wasn't one bit sorry.

"You need to tell him that."

"I'll take care of that first thing in the morning. Now, can we talk about something else besides that moose?"

She raised the brow that got his motor running every time she used it to get her way with him, which was daily. "You mean my baby Dexter?"

"Yes, him, the bull moose you've turned into the biggest lapdog in the history of lapdogs."

"He's one of the best things to ever happen to me in my entire life."

"I know that, Hannah, which is why I left a warm bed on Christmas Eve to go get him for you. I deeply regret the stew comment. Now, can we please go to bed?"

"A, you do not regret the stew comment. And B, yes, we can."

"It's a good thing I love you so much," Nolan muttered under his breath.

"What was that you said?"

"Love you so much, Hannah, and Merry Christmas."

"Merry Christmas, Nolan, and I love you so much, too, except for when you're threatening to turn my baby into a stew."

He climbed into bed after her and put his arm around her. "You caught me in a weak moment."

"No, I didn't. We all know how you feel about Dex, especially since he bit you on the bum. Callie asked the other day why Daddy doesn't like Dexter."

"I do like him. I even love him a tiny little bit, although less since he bit me. He's just a gigantic pain in my ass, even when he's not biting me there."

"Then you must think I'm a gigantic pain in your ass, too, then."

"No, I don't. You're just a tiny, little pain in my ass."

Hannah poked his chest. "That's not funny."

Laughing softly, he grabbed her finger and brought it to his mouth to nibble on. "Yes, it is."

"No, it isn't. If you love me, you love Dexter. That's all there is to it."

"Yes, dear."

"Did my father tell you to say that any time you need to pacify me?"

"I can neither confirm nor deny that," he said on a yawn. "Go to sleep, my sweet moose-whispering baby mama. Tomorrow is your favorite day of the year, and you've got your whole family here."

Homer Junior let out a snore on the other side of Hannah, making his presence known.

Nolan had failed miserably in getting him to sleep in his own bed. Thank goodness Dexter had gotten the message that he wasn't sleeping with them.

"Nolan?"

"Hmmm?"

"There was a time," she whispered, "not that long ago, when I honestly thought I'd never be truly happy again. I was okay with that because I figured I'd had my great love with Caleb, and I needed to be satisfied with the peace of mind that had been a long time coming after he died."

Nolan held his breath, waiting to hear what else she would say.

"But with you and our kids and Dex and Fred and Homer Junior… I've never been as happy as I am with our little family, so thank you for putting up with me and Dex and everything else I do that drives you crazy."

He hugged her tighter. "Hannah, sweet, sweet Hannah… I had no life at all until I had you and look at me now. A husband to the most gorgeous woman in Butler, father of two beautiful kids, a dog and a moose. You drive me crazy in all the best ways, and in case you didn't know this already, there's nothing I wouldn't do for you, even fetch your GD moose on Christmas Eve."

He felt her lips curve into a smile against his neck. "Thank you, Nolan."

"You're welcome, Hannah."

CHAPTER TWENTY-TWO

"Come live in my heart, and pay no rent." —Samuel Lover

"Chase is finally asleep," Cam whispered to Will, yawning as she joined him in bed after checking on their kids. "He's so excited, I thought he'd never sleep."

"I'm just so thankful to have him back to full health," Will said, yawning right along with her, "that I don't care if he's up all night."

"Shhh, don't say that, or he will be."

Murphy and Molly had been asleep for hours, but Chase had been a holdout.

"He's so excited to see your dad tomorrow," Will said.

"My dad is equally excited to see them all."

The man who had once been an absent, remote father was a devoted, hands-on grandfather to their children.

"He wants to know how long he has to wait until he can pick them up in the chopper and take them to New York for a weekend."

"A few more years," Will said. "I'm not ready for that yet."

Cameron cuddled up to him, arranging herself the way she did every night, with an arm and leg sprawled over him. "Neither am I. I'd miss them too much."

"Funny, isn't it, that there are days when we'd do anything for a break from the madness, but when someone who loves them as much as we do offers to take them off our hands, we're like, no, not yet."

"I know," Cam said with a little laugh. "We're silly to say no to that."

"How about if we let him and Mary stay with them at our house for a few days and we run away together after Christmas?"

"That I could get on board with, as long as we don't go far."

"I might've already arranged this with your dad, Mary and a lovely bed-and-breakfast in Stowe. We're leaving on the twenty-eighth, so we don't miss game night, and we'll be back on the first."

Will anticipated Cameron's squeal of excitement and kissed her to drown out the noise. "Good surprise?"

"The very best surprise ever. I can't wait for some time alone with you."

"And maybe after four nights with the hooligans, your dad will stop asking when he can take them to New York for a while."

"No doubt," she said with a grunt of laughter. "Mary will save his ass."

"As she always does."

"Remember when you saved my ass?" she asked, pressing against him suggestively.

He cupped his favorite ass and gave it a squeeze. "Best night of my whole life, except for every night since then."

"Me, too. Best night ever. I still have those suede boots you rescued."

"I know. Remember when I suggested you get a new pair?"

"That didn't go over well. I'll never part with them—or you."

"And I'll never part with you, love of my life, mother of my children, maker of magic."

"This is my favorite night of the whole year, being here with our whole family. Thank you for giving me that, Will."

"Thank *you* for giving me everything."

She moved so she was fully on top of him and kissed him. "Definitely my pleasure."

LUCAS AND LANDON SNUCK INTO THE BARN SHORTLY AFTER ONE a.m. A fire department colleague had dropped them off after the holiday party at the fire barn. They'd had such a busy December that they'd had no choice but to have the party late on Christmas Eve, after everyone had spent the earlier part of the evening with their families.

"What the actual fuck?" Landon asked when he tripped over something in the mudroom.

Lucas turned on the light and gasped when he saw Dexter sleeping on a gigantic bed.

"Moo," Dexter said, visibly annoyed by the disruption.

"Only in this house would you find a full-grown bull moose sleeping on a dog bed in the mudroom," Lucas said.

Landon snorted out a laugh. "Right?"

When he burped and then hiccupped, they cracked up.

"*Moo*," Dexter said more insistently this time. In other words, *get the hell out of my bedroom.*

They tiptoed through the house to bedrooms on the second floor, whispered good night and then entered their assigned rooms.

It was crazy, Landon thought, how he missed Amanda and their kids after being apart for only a few hours, during which they were asleep anyway. On a normal night at home, he'd sit up watching TV after they went to bed, feeling thankful that they were upstairs. That was all he needed to feel content, to know they were close by.

He dropped his clothes into a pile on the floor and stepped around the air mattresses of sleeping children to get to his love. The first thing he noticed when he slid into bed with her was that she must've used different shampoo, because it didn't smell right. And she was curvier than usual, too, and what the hell, why were her boobs so big?

And then a scream came from across the hall that had

Landon launching out of bed and running for the door, tripping on the air mattress and nearly falling in his haste. He opened the door to find his naked twin standing outside the door, looking completely undone.

"Wrong room, bro," Lucas said. "Your wife is over there."

"Oh my God. I just felt up Dani."

Lucas's brows narrowed into a thunderous expression. "Get out of there. Right now."

Amanda came to the door across the hall. "You freaking idiots," she said on a hiss. "Landon, get over here."

Landon put his hand over his bare junk and gave her a sheepish grin. "Yes, dear."

Dani came to the door. "What's going on?"

"Your husband was in my bed, and my husband was in yours," Amanda told her.

"I suppose it was only a matter of time." Dani grabbed Lucas's arm. "Get in here before you wake up the whole house."

"Hey, baby," Lucas said, "I missed you."

"Shut your mouth and get in bed."

"I love when you're stern with me."

She gave him a push into the room and shut the door.

Amanda dragged Landon into their room. "Just when I think you two can't top yourselves…"

"We like to keep things interesting."

"If you wake up one of these children, I'll neuter you."

"Gulp." He got into bed and waited for her to join him before turning toward her.

"You stink like beer and whiskey."

"Love you, too, and I'm sorry I touched the wrong boobies. I was just wondering why she smelled different when I heard you scream and came running."

"And I bet you noticed her boobs are bigger than mine."

"I noticed no such thing."

"Don't make it worse by lying to me. I'm going to find a bigger penis to feel."

He guffawed. "Good luck finding one bigger than mine."

"Shut up, Landon."

"I'm just saying… Good luck with that."

She pinched his lips closed, making him laugh.

He drew her in close to him and kissed her bare shoulder as he breathed in the familiar scent that he'd know anywhere as his love. "Sorry for the mix-up. There's only one Amanda Abbott, the only one I want to grow old with."

"If you ever touch someone else's boobs again, you won't live long enough to grow old."

"Yes, dear." He kissed her neck. "Merry Christmas, love."

"Merry Christmas, Landon."

"WHAT WAS ALL THAT?" LINC ASKED WHEN MOLLY RETURNED TO bed after investigating the screaming.

"Your jackass sons got in bed with the wrong wives."

"Need I ask which jackasses?"

"No, you don't."

Linc lost it laughing. "Those two…"

"They're grown men with wives and children, and they're still nitwits."

"And we wouldn't have them any other way."

"Thank God for Amanda and Dani. They're a couple of saints."

Linc put his arm around her. "Indeed, they are."

"Landon was bare-ass naked in the hallway, hand over his privates and a wild look in his eyes as Amanda pulled him into their room."

"Too bad you didn't get video of that."

"I want to scrub the sight from my brain," she said with a giggle.

"Just when we think we've seen everything with this family," Linc said.

"They go and top themselves."

"This is my favorite night of the year, having them all sleeping under our roof."

"Mine, too, even with the chaos."

"What would the Abbotts be without a little chaos?"

"They get that from your people," Molly said, as she always did when the kids behaved outrageously.

"You'd like to think so, wouldn't you?" he asked with a chuckle. "My people were far less unruly than your people. After all, there're no moose whisperers in my family. She gets that from your people."

"The moose whispering is uniquely hers," Molly said of their eldest daughter.

"Speaking of moose, there's probably one in your mudroom by now. Nolan was going after Dexter when I went to bed. Something about him raising a ruckus at home."

"Of course there's a moose in my mudroom. Wouldn't be Christmas without Dexter."

"This family is batshit crazy," Lincoln said, chuckling.

"To quote the great Lincoln Abbott… We wouldn't have them any other way."

WADE ABBOTT WOKE FROM A SOUND SLEEP AND COULDN'T FIGURE out where he was for a second, until he recognized his childhood bedroom, which was really a closet that he'd repurposed. A few years ago, in anticipation of the Christmas sleepover, he'd added a second bunk above the first one, which was where he and Mia were sleeping while their kids, Carlee and Corbin, slept below them in the bed that had once been Wade's.

"Why are you awake?" Mia whispered.

"Not sure. Something woke me up."

She was pressed to his right side without much room to spare in the twin bed.

They slept in a king-sized bed at home but used about this much of it on a regular night, so it was no hardship to sleep in the small bed for one night. Everyone looked forward to the big Christmas Eve sleepover, even, surprisingly, Wade, who was known as the family loner. Growing up, he'd commandeered the former closet out of desperation to have a space away from his raucous family.

As a father of small children, peace and quiet were in short supply, so his original family didn't get on his nerves the way they used to.

Wade turned toward Mia and put his arm around her. "Our sixth Christmas already," he whispered. "How is that possible?"

"Best six years of my life."

"Mine, too."

"Did you talk to your mom earlier?" he asked her.

"Just for a minute. We got to say Merry Christmas."

"I'm sure she appreciated the call." Mia and her mother had never recovered from the deception her mother had perpetrated for most of Mia's life, keeping her from her devoted father, Cabot.

"She did. In other news, I have a present for you that I'm hoping you'll like."

"I'll like any present you get for me. You know that."

"This one is a little different. It's a big commitment."

"I'll admit I'm curious."

"I'm pregnant."

"You… you're… Wow," he said on an exhale. "I didn't see that coming."

"Me either," she said with a laugh. "I thought we were done, and then I missed a period and took a test and… well… Merry Christmas, Daddy."

Wade smiled as he kissed her. "Best Christmas present ever."

"Is it? I wasn't sure how you'd feel about it. We already have our hands full with two kids and busy jobs."

"I'm thrilled." He put his hand on her face and caressed her soft skin with his thumb. "You make the cutest babies. How could I not be excited about another one?"

"We didn't plan this one."

"We also didn't do much to stop it."

"That's true."

"I used to lie awake in this room and dream about how my life might unfold, but nothing I could've imagined for myself

231

could match the life I have with you. It's right out of the best fairy tale I've ever read, and now we have another little person to look forward to welcoming next year."

"I'm glad you're happy about it." Mia rested her head on his chest. "I used to picture the man I might marry, and he looked nothing like you."

Surprised, he asked, "What did he look like?"

"He was big and burly with a beard and tattoos."

"So basically you dreamed about Brody?" He referred to the man she'd helped put in prison after he was abusive to her, among other offenses.

Mia's soft laughter rocked them both. "What can I say? I had a type until I met this amazing guy at a yoga retreat, and my type instantly transformed."

"Nice save," he said dryly.

"You know I love you more than I've ever loved anyone in my whole life except for our kids."

"I do know that, and it's the best thing to ever happen to me. You're the best thing."

"Same goes."

"Merry Christmas, sweet Mia."

"Merry Christmas, Wade."

"How much sex is being had in this barn tonight?" Charley asked Tyler as he moved in her, driving her wild the way he always did.

"Probably a lot," he said without missing a beat. He was good that way. The ultimate multitasker. "But I'm worried I'm not doing a very good job if you're having random thoughts in the middle of sex with me."

"You're doing a very good job. As always. I'll be sure to leave you another five-star review afterward."

"Gee, thanks," he said, smiling as he kissed her. "I live and die by those reviews."

"Don't you dare die. There isn't another man alive who could put up with me. Just ask my brothers. They'll tell you."

"There isn't another man alive who'd ever love you like I do."

"That makes me a very lucky girl."

"I'm the lucky one." He propped himself up on his muscular arms as he made love to her. "Once again, you stepped up for me and the girls during the holidays, doing recital hair and makeup, preparing for *The Nutcracker*, baking cookies, shopping, wrapping, decorating the house and never missing a beat at work."

"I love doing all of it."

"Have I properly thanked you for taking in my nieces and loving them like they're your own?"

Charley held out her arms to him and held him close as they chased the big finish. "Every day."

Tyler kissed her to keep her quiet and then collapsed on top of her. "It'll never be enough."

"I love every minute with you and the girls. You know that."

"I do, but still… You never wanted kids, and then you brought two heartbroken kids into our home without a single hesitation."

"I have a thought about that."

"Are you going to share it with me?"

Charley ran her hands over his back, soothing him as they came down from the incredible high they always found together. "I think, it's possible, that I never wanted kids of my own because, somehow, I knew I was going to be called upon to finish raising someone else's children. Maybe I suspected the universe had other plans for me."

"You really think so?"

She shrugged. "It's the only explanation I can think of for why I always knew I wouldn't have kids of my own."

"Whatever the reason, you've become such a wonderful second mom to them, and they love you so much. Almost as much as I do."

"Who'd have ever thought that falling off a mountain would turn out to be the best thing to ever happen to me?"

"I knew. Not the falling-off-the-mountain part, but I knew if you'd only give me a chance, we could have something amazing."

"You were right. You're always right."

"Could I please have you say that again so I can record it?"

"Absolutely not. Hey, Ty?"

"Yeah, baby?"

"If you, you know, wanted to get married at some point, I'd be down with that."

His entire body went still in the second before he raised his head to make eye contact. "Really?"

Charley was immediately shy and uncertain, two emotions she rarely experienced, especially with him. She nodded since the lump in her throat made it hard to speak.

"When and where? You say the word, and I'm there."

"Maybe in the spring?"

"Are you proposing to me?"

"Do you want me to?"

"Hell yes. And make it good. I've waited a very long time for this."

Charley giggled. "Tyler Westcott, love of my life, will you finally make an honest woman out of me and marry me in the spring?"

"Hmm, let me think about it."

"Tyler!"

He lost it laughing. "Yes, Charlotte Abbott, love of this life and all the ones to come, I'll marry you in the spring. With bells on."

She hugged him tightly.

"Did you get me a ring?" he asked.

She poked his side.

"I'm a traditional kind of guy, which means I'll be getting you a ring to seal this deal."

"You don't have to."

"Oh yes, I do, because I'm only getting married once, and we're going to do it right. What changed, sweetheart?"

"I'm not really sure, but at some point in the last few months, I started thinking more about how maybe we should get married."

"I'd marry you tomorrow if we could."

Charley caressed his handsome face. "Thank you for being

patient with me and never pushing me to be anyone other than who and what I am."

He kissed her softly. "I love who and what you are, and I always will."

GAVIN RETURNED TO THE BEDROOM HE WAS SHARING WITH ELLA and their kids, carrying a mug of the peppermint tea that was the only thing that helped with nausea when Ella was pregnant. She had put the light on in the closet so he could find his way to the bed without spilling the hot tea on their sleeping little ones.

He handed it over to her.

"Thank you."

"I hope it helps."

"Me, too."

They'd been planning to take a test after the holidays to confirm what they already knew after three previous pregnancies. The nausea had kicked in two days ago, which was the final piece to the puzzle.

"Four kids," Gavin said for the hundredth time in the last few days. "We're going to have *four kids*."

"I told you I wanted a big family before we got married."

"I know, and don't get me wrong. I'm thrilled. But wow. *Four.*"

"Good thing you have a few more months to prepare yourself."

"How are you so calm and cool about this?"

"Because I'm so happy. All I've ever wanted is what I have right now—you, our kids, another on the way, my family, the store, this town. It's my dream come true, and it just keeps getting better all the time."

"I love how you can say that when you feel awful."

"Eh, it'll pass. It always does, and the result is worth a few months of feeling lousy."

"You're my hero," he said, kissing her hand. "I hope you know that."

"And you're mine. I couldn't do any of this without you."

Gavin tucked a strand of her dark hair behind her ear. "You're the superhero. When I think of where I was before you decided we were meant to be... You saved my life, Ella."

She kissed him. "And you saved mine, because I never would've been happy with anyone but you."

CHAPTER TWENTY-THREE

"Love is a great beautifier." —Louisa May Alcott

*M*ax was awake before Caden and took a second to text Lexi before madness ensued in the barn. *Merry Christmas, love. I can't wait to spend it with you next year.*

He was surprised to see her writing back. *Same to you. I was just thinking about next year and wondering what it will be like.*

Chaos. You haven't lived until you've experienced the full Abbott family on Christmas morning.

I think it's a wonderful tradition, and I can't wait to be there.

I can't wait to see you. How many more days?

THREE!

That feels endless.

It'll be here before we know it, and then we can see each other every day. Can't wait.

You're not overdoing it getting ready to move, are you? he asked.

Nope. My parents have been a great help, and some of my dad's golf buddies came over tonight to move the furniture I'm taking to the truck. I've just got the mattress in my room now for the last few nights.

It's getting real.

I know. I'm so ready!

My parents are taking me to Burlington on the 28th so I won't have to get my truck at the airport when we get back. They'll spend a few days at their house there to decompress from the holidays.

That's great! I wondered if we'd have to go to Burlington when we got back to VT. What's Caden doing while you're gone?

He's hanging with Lucas and Dani and their family. The kids are excited.

Has he been skiing again?

Not yet. We told him and Chase we'd take them soon. Not sure I'm ready for that, but they are, and we don't want them to be afraid of it. It's their favorite thing.

Now that they know what can happen, they'll be extra careful.

I hope so. What are you guys doing today?

Nothing much. Exchanging gifts and having dinner. Some of my parents' friends are coming over after dinner to play cards.

That sounds fun and relaxing. Unlike Christmas at the barn.

Cherish these memories. The kids won't be little for much longer.

I know. It's already going by so fast.

Caden popped up from his spot on the air mattress. "It's Christmas! Let's get going, Dad!"

Caden is awake, so I have to go. I'll call you later?

Can't wait. Love you. Tell everyone I said Merry Christmas!

You do the same. Love you, too.

"Who are you texting with?" Caden asked.

"Lexi."

"Oh."

"She said to tell you Merry Christmas, and she's looking forward to seeing you soon."

"When is she coming again?"

"I'm going there in three days to help her drive the moving truck to Vermont."

"How come I never met her before she came here?"

"Remember how I told you she was sick for a long time?"

"Oh right. Is she okay now?"

"She's doing great and is excited to get home to Vermont. She was living in Houston to be close to the hospital that treated her."

"I'm glad she's okay. Can we open presents now?"

Max appreciated that Caden was asking about her and took that as progress. "Yeah, buddy. Let's do that."

CHRISTMAS AT THE BARN WAS THE USUAL THREE-RING CIRCUS WITH kids and dogs—and a moose—underfoot, presents, laughter, music and food. Everyone was abuzz with the news that Charley had proposed to Tyler and Lucas and Landon had gotten into bed with the wrong wives during the night. They would never live that down.

The Colemans came over after dinner, which brought the crowd to nearly one hundred people.

Elmer Stillman sat amid the madness surrounded by grandchildren and great-grandchildren, smiling from ear to ear the way he always did when his family was around.

Landon brought the horses and sleigh from the farm and took all the kids for rides. Later, Colton had organized a massive snowball fight that helped to wear out the young ones before their parents took them home.

As Max drove a sleepy Caden home at nine o'clock, his ears were ringing from the noise, but it had been another amazing Christmas with everyone pitching in to help so Molly could enjoy the day, too.

Thankfully, Caden went to bed without much fuss, exhausted after the wild twenty-four hours with his cousins. Tomorrow, he was having lunch—alone—with Chloe, and Max had spent all day trying not to think about that. He had no concerns about them spending time together, but he would feel better when Caden was back home with him where he belonged.

He cracked open a beer and went to the sofa to call Lexi.

"Hi there," she said, sounding sleepy. "How was your day?"

"Extremely chaotic. In other words, typical Abbott Christmas. How about you?"

"Much quieter, thank goodness. I'm exhausted."

"I told you not to wear yourself out. I'm coming to help in two more days." Now he wished he hadn't planned to stay in Butler for the annual family game night on the twenty-seventh.

He could've left for Houston tomorrow instead of waiting until the twenty-eighth.

"I'm fine. Just tired."

Hearing her admit to being tired put a knot of fear in his stomach. Would it always be this way? Any time she mentioned feeling off, would he go right to worst-case scenario? "I should let you get some sleep. We can talk in the morning."

"I think I'll take you up on that. I can't keep my eyes open, which is weird because I took a three-hour nap this afternoon."

That information had alarm bells ringing for Max. What the hell? Why was she so tired? "Call me when you wake up."

"Will do. Love you, Max. Merry Christmas."

"Love you, too. Looking forward to saying Merry Christmas in person next year."

"Me, too. I can't wait."

"Sleep tight." He ended the call with a sinking feeling inside. Was she sick again? And what in the world would he do if she was?

While Caden went to lunch with Chloe at Kingdom Pizza, Max cleaned the house and changed the sheets on both beds. The work helped to keep his mind off Caden being out with his mother and his worries about Lexi, who hadn't called him yet or responded to any of his texts that day.

At twelve thirty, he finally texted her grandmother to check on her.

She's still asleep, which is odd. Let me go check on her.

Max's anxiety spiked through the roof hearing she was still asleep at twelve thirty. By the time she called fifteen minutes later, he was worried about his own health as well as hers. "Hey," he said, grabbing the phone. "Are you okay?"

"Yeah, wow. I slept like a dead woman."

"That's not funny."

"Oh, sorry," she said with a giggle. She sounded much more like herself this morning. "Didn't mean to make you worry."

"I was worried. Should you check in with the doctor about the sleeping?"

"Nah, it's fine. I've just been pushing it lately, between the move and the holidays. I feel much better today than I did yesterday."

"That's good," he said, releasing a deep sigh. "What are you up to today?"

"Just a few errands. Picking up medical records to bring with me, closing my bank account here. That kind of stuff."

She had sold her car and would buy a new one in Vermont. It was all coming together, and she was moving home. Finally.

"I can't wait for you to be here all the time."

"I can't either. These last few days have been endless waiting for you to get here."

"I'm coming soon, honey, and then we'll have it all."

"I'm so excited to have it all with you, Max Abbott. I feel like I've waited my whole life for that."

"Same, sweetheart."

"What are you boys up to today?"

"Caden is at lunch with his mother."

"Oh. Wow. How're you holding up?"

"It's fine. He's comfortable enough with her by now to do that, and he wanted to go. I suppose I need to get used to sharing him with her occasionally. Everyone tells me that's what's best for him."

"It is, for sure."

"I'm trying to roll with it."

"You're doing all the right things for your boy."

"I hope so."

"How's he feeling?"

"Back to normal and wants to ski again. We're doing that tomorrow to break the seal, as Will put it."

"Good idea. Don't give them time to become afraid of it."

"That's the thinking."

"I'd better get myself out of bed and get moving with this day. I've got a long to-do list."

"Don't wear yourself out. You hear me?"

"Yes, dear," she said with a laugh. "I hear you."

"Hey, Lex?"

"Yes, Max?"

"I just really can't wait to see you."

"Same."

EVEN THOUGH HE WAS CRAZY BUSY WITH CADEN, SKIING, vacation week playdates with cousins and Abbott game night, Max felt like the time was marching in reverse as he counted down to the morning when he would leave for Burlington with his parents.

Game night was the usual shit show, with accusations of cheating, game pieces being thrown at siblings and kids playing Twister until they were a sweaty mess. It was awesome, but Max wanted it to be done so he could get going.

"You're tightly wound tonight, baby brother," Hannah said when she sat next to him after they'd had cake to celebrate Callie's birthday.

"Just ready to get to Houston and be with Lexi full time."

"I'm happy for you." She rested her head on his shoulder. "I always wondered if that loose end was the reason why nothing else seemed to work out for you."

"She was the reason. I see that now. I didn't allow myself to think about her or talk about her or even miss her, because it hurt too much. I pressed on, but I never got over her. She was a gigantic question mark in the back of my mind, always there even when she was nowhere to be found."

Hannah looked up at him with tears in her eyes. "That's lovely, Max."

He shrugged. "It's how I feel."

"You should tell her that."

"Maybe I will."

"I always liked her for you. You two reminded me of how Caleb and I were back in the day."

"Really?"

"Oh yeah. For sure."

"Wow, you guys were the gold standard of high school romance."

"You and Lexi were right there with us. I was always sorry it didn't work out with you guys."

"I was, too."

"When you asked us to stop asking about her, my heart broke for you."

"I had to do that for self-preservation. She'd taken off somewhere and was staying away intentionally, so what could I do about that?"

"You did the only thing you could."

"Can I be honest about something?"

"Of course."

"I'm scared shitless of her leukemia coming back."

"Which is totally understandable."

"She's been really tired lately. Sleeping for hours and hours. I know the move is stressful and she's still recovering, but my brain is spinning with terrible scenarios."

"When was the last time she had a checkup?"

"Recently. It was all good."

"Then there's probably nothing to worry about. Moving is exhausting under the best of circumstances. Add the holidays and recovering from everything she's been through. It's no wonder she's exhausted."

"You're right."

"Duh. I'm always right. Ask Nolan."

Max nudged her with his elbow and then rested his head on hers. "We're so close to having it all—finally. Is it normal to be scared that something will go wrong?"

"It's normal to be anxious when you're so close to having everything you've ever wanted. It's not normal to wallow in awful scenarios."

"I'll try not to do that."

"She's fine. You're fine. Caden is fine. It's been a lot lately. It's no wonder your nerves are shot."

"Yeah, it has been a lot. From Lexi coming back into my life, finding out what she's been dealing with all this time, Chloe reappearing, Caden and Chase getting hurt… It's a wonder I'm not drooling."

"Take the time with Lexi on the road to relax a bit and enjoy yourselves. Everything will be all right. Your big sister says so."

"Then that must mean it's true."

"Of course it does."

"Love you, Han."

"Love you more, Maxi."

THE FLIGHT TO HOUSTON WAS DELAYED BY TWO INTERMINABLE hours in Burlington, but at least this flight was smoother than the last one had been. Caden had been so excited to spend a few days with Lucas's family that he'd barely noticed when Max left. That'd been a relief. He'd been worried that his son would be upset about him going to see Lexi again, but that had never materialized.

Maybe he was getting used to the idea of his father having a girlfriend.

Max could only hope so as he stood in the aisle, waiting forever for people to get their crap and get off the plane. It was like they knew he was dying to see his love after weeks apart and were trying to make the final minutes as torturous for him as they could be.

Once off the plane, he broke free of the crowd and jogged toward baggage claim, where they'd planned to meet. As he took the escalator down, he looked for her and spotted her at the same time she saw him.

The smile that lit up her sweet face and the feeling of homecoming that came with it were all Max needed to be absolutely certain he was doing the right thing going all in with her. He held her for the longest time, breathing in the scent of her hair that brought back so many memories.

"Thought you'd never get here," she said as she held him as tightly as he was holding her.

"Seemed to take forever."

When someone bumped into them, Max put his arm around

Lexi to leave the madness of the airport. They held hands as she led the way to her mother's car in the garage. Before they got in, he leaned her against the car and kissed her.

"Hi," he said.

She smiled, but she looked pale and tired, which worried him. "Hi there. Thanks for coming."

"Guess what?"

"What?"

"From today on, together forever. How does that sound?"

"It sounds like a dream come true."

CHAPTER TWENTY-FOUR

"With our love, we could save the world." —George Harrison

*L*exi barely made it through dinner with her family before she said she needed to go to bed. "I'm so sorry," she said to Max, looking tearful. "I don't know why I'm so tired lately."

"It's fine," he said, forcing a smile for her. "I'll be up after a bit."

"Don't fight over *Jeopardy!* in front of Max," she told her parents and grandparents.

"We'll try to behave," Jim said.

After she went upstairs, Max looked to the others for answers. "What's going on with her?"

"We aren't sure," Angie said, brow furrowed in worry. "Her recent checkup was perfect, but she's been asleep more than she's been awake lately."

"So you're worried, too?"

"We are," Larry said. "She'd been doing so well. We're chalking it up to the move and hoping she'll feel better once that's behind her."

"You'll make sure she doesn't overdo it on the road, right?" Angie asked Max.

"She won't have to do anything but enjoy the ride."

"We'll give you all our numbers just in case," Angie said.

Max wanted to ask in case of what, but he was afraid of what they might say. His stomach was in knots as he killed time before bed, watching TV with Lexi's family. "I'm going to check in with my son and then head to bed," Max said. "We're hoping for an early start tomorrow."

"We'll see you in the morning," Angie said.

He went into the front living room to call Lucas's house.

"Hey, how's it going in Texas?" Lucas asked when he answered the phone.

"Okay. I guess. Lexi is really run down. I'm hoping she's okay."

"Moving is a drag, even when you're not recovering from a serious illness. I'm sure she'll bounce back in a few days."

"I really hope so. It's concerning. She went to bed at seven."

"Hmm, that is odd, especially when you guys hadn't seen each other in weeks."

"Yeah. Are the kids still up?"

"They are. Here's Caden."

"Hey, Dad."

"Hi, bud. How's it going there?"

"Good. We had spaghetti for dinner with really good meatballs that Aunt Dani made from scratch and brownies for dessert."

"Sounds good."

"It was! Tomorrow, we're going to ski, but Uncle Lucas said not to worry because we're not leaving the bunny slope."

"I'll try not to worry."

"How long do I have to stay there? I feel fine, and I've learned my lesson about looking before I turn."

"For a little while."

"It's *so* boring."

"It's better than not skiing at all, isn't it?"

"I guess. When will you be home?"

"Aiming for New Year's Eve."

"Cool. Call me tomorrow?"

"I will. Love you, pal."

"Love you, too."

Lucas took the phone from him and told the kids to go brush their teeth and to use toothpaste. "Did Mom have to tell us to use toothpaste?"

"She probably had to tell you."

"Ha. Very funny. Are you okay with us going skiing?"

"Of course."

"Okay. Just making sure."

"Go and have a good time, and if you want to let him off the bunny slope, I'm fine with that."

"I'll see how it goes."

"Thanks again for having Caden this week."

"We love having him. He and Savvy have the best time together, and he's sweet with Sierra and Sawyer, too."

"He loves hanging with you guys."

"Safe travels tomorrow."

"Thanks. I'll check in tomorrow night."

"Sounds good."

"See you."

MAX WAS AWAKE AT SEVEN THE NEXT MORNING, BUT LEXI WAS still sound asleep. He tried kissing her, but she never moved. "Hey, Lex," he whispered, giving her shoulder a gentle shake.

She moaned.

"We need to get moving. We wanted to get an early start today."

The only thing left in her room was the mattress she was leaving behind. She'd bought a new one that would be delivered when she arrived in Vermont.

"Lex."

Her eyes opened and then closed again. "Tired."

"How can you be tired when you slept for twelve hours?"

Her shoulder lifted in a shrug.

"You can sleep in the truck."

"'Kay."

"Lexi." Their nineteen-hundred-mile drive would take twenty-nine hours, and Max was eager to get going.

"I'm awake." She forced herself to rally, to get up and shower and get dressed while he took several of her bags downstairs. Then he took a quick shower, packed his bag and grabbed her last bag on the way out.

He found Lexi in the kitchen, sipping coffee with her parents and grandparents, and noted the deep, dark circles under her eyes and the unusual pallor. As soon as they got to Vermont, he would insist she see a doctor, because something wasn't right.

Her family waved them off a short time later, promising to see them in Vermont in a month or two. Their house was on the market, and they'd begun packing up to move.

Lexi had nodded off shortly after they drove away from her house, which put Max's nerves further on edge.

Driving the rental truck was easy enough, but the ride was hardly luxurious. He felt every bump in the road, but Lexi never stirred.

She was still asleep when he stopped in Louisiana for gas and later when he stopped in Mississippi to use the bathroom and get something to eat.

When he returned to the truck with chicken tenders and fries, he tried to nudge her awake.

"Lexi, wake up. You're scaring me."

"Mmm," she said without opening her eyes. "Sorry."

"I got some food."

"Smells good."

"Have a few bites."

She seemed to force herself to wake up and to eat a few bites. "I have no idea why I'm so wiped out. It's weird."

"Was it like this when you were sick?"

"Sometimes, but mostly after I had chemo. Haven't had that in more than eighteen months now. Doesn't make sense."

"Do you want to use the restroom while we're stopped?"

"Sure." She released the clasp on her seat belt and started to get out of the truck, stopping suddenly. "Whoa. Head rush."

"Wait for me. I'll help you down." Max went around the truck and opened the passenger door to give her a hand.

The second her feet hit the pavement, she fainted.

What the hell?

In a panic, Max dropped to the ground to cradle her head. "Lexi!"

"Is she okay?" someone asked from behind him.

"I don't know," Max said. "She fainted."

"Do you want me to call the rescue?"

Max was so afraid of what was happening to her that he could barely croak out a "yes" to tell the other man to go ahead and call.

Something was wrong, and the thought of what it might be had him gripped with fear.

Lexi came to and couldn't figure out where she was. Her eyes darted around and landed on Max, sitting across from her.

The scream of a siren jolted her out of the fog.

"What happened?"

"You passed out."

"I did?"

He nodded, looking as tense as she'd ever seen him.

"My stomach…"

"What about it?"

"I feel like I'm going to be sick."

An EMT held a bag for her to vomit into.

For the first time since exhaustion had overtaken her, she was truly afraid of what was happening. She hadn't felt this bad in a long time. Not since…

No, don't go there. It's not that. You just had a perfect checkup a few weeks ago.

Though she could tell herself not to panic, her heart beat fast and hard, and her stomach ached. What the hell was going on?

They arrived at the hospital and were taken to a treatment room in the ER.

A nurse named Beverly came in, rolling a computer on a

stand. "What's going on, darlin'?" she asked in a thick Southern accent.

"I'm not sure. Apparently, I fainted at the rest stop."

"She's also been sleeping a lot. Like twelve hours at a time, and that's not enough."

"I should mention that I had a stem cell transplant for leukemia nineteen months ago. I was in remission as recently as three weeks ago."

At the mention of the word *leukemia*, the nurse's expression became much more serious. "Let's figure out what's up and get you on your way."

They took tons of blood and sent it off to be checked.

"I put a rush on it," the kind nurse said. "It could be a virus or so many other things, such as anemia."

"That would be better than the dreaded L word."

She patted Lexi's shoulder. "Try not to worry."

"That's easier said than done," Lexi said to Max after the nurse left the room.

"Sure is."

Lexi held out a hand to him.

He took hold of her hand and sat on the edge of the hospital bed.

"Sorry to do this to you," she said.

"Don't be sorry. I just want to hear that you're okay."

"Can you grab that pink thing over there?" Lexi said, pointing. "Hurry."

He handed her the plastic bowl a second before she threw up.

She'd never eat a chicken nugget again.

Max held her hair back and then rinsed out the bowl.

"Chicken nuggets on an empty stomach wasn't the best idea I ever had."

"Probably not."

She took the clean bowl from him. "Thank you, and I really am sorry. You didn't sign on for this."

He took a wipe out of a package on the counter and gently cleaned around her mouth and then handed her a cup of ice water with a straw. "I signed on for all of it, so quit that right now. You got me?"

"I got you," she said with a weak smile.

He returned to perch on the edge of her bed and held her hand. "And you're not getting rid of me, so don't go there." He kissed the back of her hand for emphasis. "Whatever comes next, I'm here for it. Good, bad, ugly. Whatever. I've spent my entire adult life with a hole in my heart where you used to be, and I don't want to be without you ever again. So no more talk of what I signed on for, okay?"

Lexi blinked back tears. "I'm so lucky to have found you twice in a lifetime."

"We're both lucky, and it's only going to get better from here. I promise."

By the time Beverly returned, Lexi's nerves were all but shot. Despite the recent positive news from her medical team and Max's reassurances, she was scared senseless of a relapse that would ruin everything right when her life was finally moving in a direction she'd longed for during her illness.

"It's not leukemia," the nurse said, smiling. "But you are pregnant."

Lexi's mouth fell open in total shock. *Pregnant.* She hadn't considered that for a second after being told the odds of conceiving were low after chemo. "What?"

"Oh my *God*," Max said as a huge smile lit up his handsome face. "Lex! We're *pregnant!*" He let out such a loud whoop that the nurse shushed him. "Sorry," he said sheepishly, "but this is the best news *ever.*" He leaned in to hug her as tightly as he could. "We're having a baby!"

Tears slid down her cheeks as pure joy filled her heart. She and Max were having a baby!

He brushed away her tears and kissed her. "Best news ever."

"Y'all are too cute," Beverly said.

"They told me I probably couldn't get pregnant after treatment," Lexi said, astounded by the news. "I... I froze eggs before..."

"Well," Beverly said, smiling, "*they* were wrong."

. . .

THEY TOOK AN UBER BACK TO THE REST STOP.

"I'm still in shock," Lexi said when they were on the road again. "That's normal, right?"

"Sure is. This is my second time being shocked by a baby, so I can attest it's entirely normal."

Lexi turned in her seat to look at him as he drove them toward Alabama. She'd been given fluids to make her feel better and told to acquire prenatal vitamins, which they planned to do when they stopped for the night. "You said all the right things back there, but I wouldn't blame you for being upset about this. After all, I told you we didn't need birth control."

He reached for her hand and brought it to his lips. "I'm not at all upset. I'm thrilled."

"What will Caden think?"

"He'll be excited to be a big brother," Max said.

Lexi hoped that was true. "He's had you all to himself, and now he'll have to share you with me and the baby."

"It'll be okay. He'll have months to get used to the idea. What about you? This isn't what you had planned either."

"My brain is spinning. I'm signed up for classes that start in January, and I've applied for some jobs."

"You don't have to work if you don't want to."

"Yes, I do."

"No, you really don't." He shifted in his seat, seeming uncomfortable. "So here's the thing… Since the catalog debuted, the family business has exploded. Like, we've gone from a two-million-dollar-a-year operation to like fifty million last year. It's insane and growing every year."

"*Whoa.* I had no idea."

"Since my parents bought out the rest of my mom's siblings years ago, my grandfather, parents and all of us kids are the owners, so we get dividends every year. Big dividends. My grandfather directs his to the rest of the family so everyone benefits, so when I say you don't have to work, I mean it."

"That's amazing. You've all worked so hard to build up that business. I'm so happy for you."

"Be happy for *us*. We can do whatever we want. If you want to just focus on school, you can do that."

"It's very generous of you to want to take care of me."

"I do want that. I'll get you added to our health insurance ASAP."

"I have good insurance that my parents have paid for to keep me covered while I was sick."

"I can take that over now."

"Max... You don't have to do all that. I've sort of been looking forward to having a job for the first time since I was a teenager working for your family store on the weekends. I loved that job."

"We can find you something in the company," he said, glancing at her. "Whatever you want, but you don't have to."

"I want to. I've never had a chance to be independent, and I'm not saying I want to be independent of you. That's the last thing I want. I just want to know that if I had to take care of myself, I could."

"You'll never have to."

"Still... I've missed out on so many things. Just having a job again will be a luxury to me. Does that make any sense?"

"It does, and I understand that you have things you want to do. I'll never stand in the way of that, but you may find it's too much to work and go to school while you're pregnant. If that's the case, I just want you to know you don't have to work if you don't feel up to it."

"That's very good to know, and I appreciate your generosity."

"I'm not being generous, Lexi. We're going to be a family. You and me and Caden and our baby and other babies we're going to have. What's mine is yours."

Lexi fanned her face. "I'm going to need a minute to get my head around all this."

"Take all the time you need. I'm not going anywhere except to Vermont with you."

"In case I forget to tell you later... the day I fainted at the

Mississippi rest stop will always be one of the best days of my entire life."

"Mine, too, but I could've done without the ambulance and the emergency room."

Lexi giggled. "Sorry about that."

"I'll let it go this one time because I got a baby out of it, but in the future, let's keep the drama to a minimum for the sake of Max's nerves, okay?"

She laughed again. "I'll see what I can do about that."

"Thank you."

"I was so sure the leukemia was back," she said softly.

"So was I. It was all I could think about."

"We'll always be a little extra thankful for this baby because he or she wasn't that."

"Yes, we will." He took his eyes off the road to glance over at her. "What do you want it to be? Boy or girl?"

"I'm still so shocked to be pregnant that I'll take either as long as he or she is healthy. What about you?"

"Either is fine with me, but I wouldn't say no to a little girl who can wrap me around all ten of her tiny fingers."

"I'd really like to see that," Lexi said with a sigh.

For the rest of her life, Lexi would never forget this miraculous day.

CHAPTER TWENTY-FIVE

"Love is a smoke made with the fume of sighs."
—William Shakespeare

When they stopped for the night in Alabama, at a hotel off Interstate 59, they went straight to bed after the long, emotional day.

"I should tell my parents about the baby," Lexi said, yawning. "They were worried about me being so tired."

"You can call them tomorrow."

"Let's not tell anyone except our families for now, though, okay? A lot can still go wrong."

Max placed his hand on her abdomen. "Nothing will go wrong. Look at the odds our baby has already beaten. This little one is determined to join us."

"I hope you're right."

"Try not to worry," he said, kissing her softly. "Today, we dreaded the worst news and got the best news. I think your luck is changing, my love."

She looped her arms around his neck and drew him into a much more serious kiss. "My luck changed the day I came back to Butler and found you still there and still single."

Max leaned his forehead on hers. "I was waiting for you, and I didn't even realize it."

"I'm so glad you waited for me. I would've been crushed if you'd married someone else."

"Never even came close to marrying anyone else. But I do plan to marry you. As soon as I possibly can."

Her eyes filled with tears that made her laugh. "Does pregnancy make people an emotional disaster area?"

"It does. My mom said she cried nonstop the whole time she was pregnant with us, which was years when you add it all up."

"She's a superstar."

"Indeed, she is."

"Do you think I'll be a good mom?"

"You'll be a great mom. You have a great mom—and grandmother."

"Yes, I do. They'll be so excited. It's nice to give them something happy to think about after all the years of hell we went through together."

"The baby will make all the hell worth it."

She nodded and then raised her head to kiss him.

"You need to get some rest, baby mama."

"I need you more than I need sleep."

"What'd they put in that IV?" he asked with a smile, noticing she had a bit of color in her cheeks and had eaten a good dinner when they'd stopped for food earlier.

"Whatever it is, I feel so much better."

"I'm glad you do, but you still need your rest."

She hugged him tightly. "I missed you so much these last few weeks. I kept waiting for something to happen to mess up our plans."

"Nothing will mess up our plans." He fell into a kiss that managed to be sweet and sexy at the same time. "All this time… I was waiting for you. Now that I have you back, I'll never let you go."

Lexi worked the T-shirt she'd changed into up and over her head, leaving her bare except for panties.

Max sat back and took a greedy look at her. "You're already curvier than you were," he said, cupping her breasts and teasing her nipples. He bent to touch his tongue to the left one, and she

257

nearly levitated off the bed. "Is someone extra sensitive, perhaps?"

"Yes," she said, sounding breathless. "It's never felt like that before."

"Let's see if it works on this side, too."

It did. In fact, she was sensitive all over, which Max discovered one kiss at a time until she was writhing under him and pushing on the boxer briefs he'd left on for bedtime.

"Is my baby mama feeling needy?"

"Very. Hurry up, will you?"

Max choked on a laugh. "Is this the kind of wife you're going be? Demanding that I service you on a moment's notice?"

"Yes, can you deal with that?"

Grinning, he said, "I think I'll manage somehow."

"Could you start now, please?"

"Yes, dear."

They moved quickly to remove the underwear that stood in the way of what they both wanted, and as he sank into her heat, Max had no doubt that he was exactly where he belonged, with the woman he was always meant to love. It'd never been like that with anyone else but her, and to know he had a lifetime to spend with her made him happier than he'd ever been.

"Max? Are you okay?"

"I'm great," he said, kissing her. "Just making sure this isn't over before it begins."

"It's okay if it is. I'm not going anywhere either."

"That's good to know."

They moved together with the easy rhythm of a couple together a long time, which in some ways they had been. Yes, he'd been with other women and even had a child with one of them. But none of them had ever touched his heart the way Lexi had from the beginning.

He could see and feel how much she loved him in every look and caress and hoped she felt the same coming from him.

"Max," she said on a gasp as her fingertips dug into the muscles of his back. "Don't stop."

"I won't. I'll never stop."

She came with a loud cry that shattered his control.

Someone banged on the wall, startling them. "Shut the hell up over there! People are trying to sleep!"

Lexi laughed so hard, she shook with it. "Oh my God," she whispered.

"I guess we got a little carried away," Max said, laughing with her.

"Just a little."

"If they knew what we've been through to be together, they might be more forgiving," he said as he withdrew from her and snuggled her into his arms.

"And it's our first time doing it in a hotel."

"That, too. Lots of firsts to look forward to." He loved the way her hair brushed against his skin, setting off goose bumps. "You know what's cool about finding out about the baby in Mississippi?"

"What?"

"My parents met there."

"They did? Really?"

"Uh-huh. They were volunteers on an affordable housing project for a summer, and that's how they met."

"I never knew that."

"They'll think it's cool that it happened there. Not the part about you fainting, but the baby."

"Do you think they'll be excited about another grandchild when they already have so many?"

"Definitely. They say all the time that grandchildren are the best thing to ever happen to them."

"My parents will be so excited. I think they'd sort of resigned themselves to never being grandparents because it was such a long shot."

"I can't wait to tell them."

"I can't wait for everything."

LEXI CALLED HER PARENTS THE NEXT MORNING AS THEY CRUISED toward Georgia. She put the phone on speaker so Max could hear, too.

"Hi, honey," her mom said. "I thought we might hear from you last night."

"Sorry I didn't call. We had kind of an eventful day yesterday."

"How so?"

Lexi could hear the worry in those two little words. She'd given her mom plenty of reason to worry and was looking forward to providing some joy now. "We stopped at a rest stop in Mississippi, and when I got out of the truck, I fainted."

"What? Oh my God! Lexi…"

"It's not what you think."

"How do you know?"

"Max called an ambulance, and I was treated in the ER."

"They checked your blood counts?"

"Everything was normal except for the fact that I'm pregnant."

"*What?*" her mother asked on a long exhale. "Lexi… That's why you've been so tired!"

"Sure is."

"Hold on, I have to tell Dad, Gram and Grandpa the news. Lexi is *pregnant*. That's why she's been so tired!"

Lexi smiled at Max as they listened to the excitement coming from Houston. "I'm only about four weeks along, so it's very early. We're not telling anyone besides you and Max's parents. I wanted to tell you so you wouldn't worry about how tired I've been anymore."

"This is the most exciting news, sweetheart."

"It really is. We're so thrilled and shocked and excited and all the things. I thought I couldn't get pregnant, so we weren't exactly careful."

"What a blessing this is after all you've been through."

"Hello? Is this my mom who used to tell me I'd ruin my life if I got pregnant?"

"That was a very long time ago. A lifetime ago. And now I'm simply delighted for you, for Max, for us, for his parents. For everyone."

"Thanks, Mom."

"I hope you enjoy every second of your new life, Lex. If anyone deserves all the good things, you surely do."

"We all do. So much to look forward to. Hurry up and get to Vermont, will you?"

"We're coming, sweetheart. Are you going to call Max's parents?"

"Right after this."

"They'll be so excited. Drive safely. We love you."

"Love you, too."

"Let me know where you land tonight."

"Will do." Lexi ended the call with her mom. "That was fun."

"Yes, it was." He handed her his phone. "Let's continue the party with my parents."

"Let's do it. Is 'Barn' them?"

"Uh-huh."

"I love that you have your parents in your favorites as Barn."

"It's fitting, right?"

"Sure is." She made the call and put the phone on speaker.

"Hey, Max," Molly said. "How's the trip going?"

"Very well. We're almost to Georgia."

"Making good progress."

"Are Dad and Gramps around?"

"They're right here."

"Put the phone on speaker so I can tell you what happened yesterday."

"Hang on," Molly said. "Okay, we're all here. What happened yesterday?"

"Don't sound worried. It's a good thing. A great thing. Lexi passed out at a rest stop in Mississippi."

"Oh my goodness! Is she all right?"

"She's great—and she's pregnant."

"She… Oh, Max. How wonderful!"

"What a difference seven years makes when I come to you with a surprise baby," Max said drolly.

"Stop that," Molly said with a sputter of laughter. "You're all grown up, and this is amazing news. How's Lexi feeling now?"

"Much better since she got IV fluids, but she's still tired."

"She will be for a while yet. The first trimester tends to be that way."

"That's good to know, Molly," Lexi said.

"We couldn't be happier for you both."

"We're pretty excited," Max said.

"I could hear it in your voice from the minute you said hello."

"Lexi thought she couldn't have kids after her treatment."

"What a miracle," Molly said.

"It's a total miracle," Lexi said. "And the biggest and best shock ever."

"How cool is it that we found out in Mississippi?" Max asked.

"Very cool indeed," Molly said, sounding tearful. "Caden will be a wonderful big brother."

"I know. I can't wait to tell him. Keep this between us for now, okay? It's still early days, and Lex is superstitious."

"No one will hear it from us. I'll muzzle your father."

"Hey," Lincoln said indignantly. "I heard that."

Max laughed. "You're the weak link when it comes to family gossip, Dad."

"I'm hurt."

"Truth hurts."

"Congratulations to both of you," Lincoln said. "We're so happy for you."

"Thanks, Dad."

"And Gramps," Elmer said. "I'm excited, too. I've been waiting for this for you for a long time, pal."

"Don't go thinking you can check out because little Max is finally settled, you hear me?"

"I ain't going nowhere, son. I've still got a lot of work to do around here."

"Yes, you do. It's starting to rain, so I need to focus on driving. We'll see you in a couple of days."

"Can't wait," Molly said. "Drive safely, and congratulations again."

"Thanks. Love you guys."

"Love you, too."

. . .

MOLLY PUT THE PHONE ON THE TABLE AND THEN DID A LITTLE happy dance that included clapping and cheering.

"What's going on with your wife?" Elmer asked Lincoln.

"Not sure. I was going to ask you what's happening with your daughter."

"Gentlemen, what you see here is a full-on celebration of a plan well designed and executed."

Elmer glanced at Linc. "What's happening?"

"I have beaten you both at your own game, so you'd better just suck it up!"

Linc eyed her suspiciously. "Start talking. Leave nothing out."

"When I heard about the reunion, I tracked down Lexi's mom and made sure they knew about it. We agreed to do everything we could to make sure those kids were both at the reunion. It took a little bit of convincing, as you know, but in the end, all it took was for them to see each other again to pick right up where they left off." She punctuated her words with another fist pump, a twirl and a squeal.

"Never seen her quite like this," Elmer said, sounding concerned.

"Neither have I," Linc said.

"I *knew* he'd never stopped caring about Lexi," Molly said. "I knew it, and I was *right!*" More twirling and cheering ensued. "And now they're *pregnant!* Whoop!"

"Did she say she's beating us at our own game?" Linc asked Elmer.

"I believe she just seriously smoked us on our most vexing challenge," Elmer said.

"I smoked your *asses*, boys!"

"We're never going to hear the end of this," Lincoln said on a moan.

"I'm moving in with Hannah," Elmer said.

"Ha, ha, ha, ha, *ha!* You two think you're all that and a bag of chips, getting all the kids paired up and married off, but meet the master."

"She has *one win*, and suddenly, *she's* the master?" Elmer asked, scoffing.

"I am the master."

"I never knew you were so full of yourself, love," Linc said.

"Sure, you did. When I am right, I'm right, and I knew if he could see her again, that'd be all it would take. Angie felt the same way, that Lexi had never gotten over Max. They gave her an early Christmas gift of the weekend in Butler and presented it to her as a done deal." Worn out from her celebrating, Molly dropped into a chair. "I thought I was going to have to drive Max to that reunion myself and make him go, but the wager worked. An Abbott can never resist a wager."

"Well played," Lincoln said. "Very well played. But you're not the master."

"Not even close," Elmer said. "But you've clearly *learned* a few things from the masters."

"Whatever," Molly said with an eye roll that encompassed them both. "All I care about is that Max is back with the only woman he's ever loved, and now there's a baby, too!" She lifted her hands in the air in a raise-the-roof motion. "Best day ever."

"Are you planning to tell Max and Lexi how you and Angie shamelessly manipulated them?" Linc asked.

"Oh, um, I don't think they need to know that."

"Is that so? How much is our silence worth to you?"

"You aren't serious," Molly said.

"Are we serious, Elmer?"

"Dead serious."

The phone rang, and Molly jumped on it. "It's Angie!" She took the call and had a good scream with the baby's other grandmother.

Max had stood silently by as each of his older siblings had found their true loves. Molly had been hoping for this kind of happiness for her youngest child for a long time. This really was the best day ever.

CHAPTER TWENTY-SIX

"Love is a better teacher than duty." —Albert Einstein

On the morning of New Year's Eve, Molly called Lucas's house.

"Morning," Lucas said when he took the call.

The sound of screaming kids in the background brought a smile to his mother's face. She'd spent most of her adult life surrounded by screaming kids and wouldn't have had it any other way. "Morning. How's it going over there?"

"Business as usual, as I'm sure you can hear."

"Could I have a word with Mr. Caden, please?"

"Yep. Hey, Cade, phone for you."

"Is it my dad?"

"Nope. It's Grammy."

"I wanna talk to Grammy," Sierra said.

"After Caden," Lucas said. "Here you go, Mom."

"Hi, Grammy," Caden said. "What's up?"

"I was wondering if you might like to have a lunch date with your old Grammy. I'm missing you since you've been on vacation."

"You've seen me almost every day," he said with amusement.

"I know, but it's not the same when there's millions of other people around. Besides, it's raining, so you won't be skiing."

"Can we go to the diner?"

"Wherever you want."

"You're not old, Grammy, but you sure are silly."

"I'll pick you up at noon, you charmer. And let's keep this our little secret, okay?"

"Okay. Here's Sierra."

She chatted with Sierra, Sawyer and Savannah before she got Lucas back and told him she would pick up Caden at noon.

"Got it. See you then, Mom."

Molly went out of her way to spend one-on-one time with all her grandchildren, but she had a special place in her heart for Caden. He'd made her a grandmother and then lived with them for the first four years of his life. She didn't play favorites, ever, but he was her special pal—and he knew it.

The thing she loved best about Caden, though, was that he knew he was special to her, Linc and Elmer, but he never acted that way in front of the other kids. He was always kind and generous toward them, and she was counting on his kindness for the mission she had planned for today.

A little before noon, she packed her oversized purse with colored paper, crayons, pencils and other art supplies and headed to Lucas's to pick up Caden. She didn't go in so the other kids wouldn't get upset when she left with Caden. Instead, she waited outside for Luc to walk Caden out.

Caden carried his duffel bag while Luc brought his skis and another big bag of toys Caden had brought with him.

"You don't travel light, kid," Molly said.

"Haha, Uncle Lucas said the same thing."

"What do you say to Uncle Lucas for having you this week?"

Caden threw himself at his uncle, wrapping his arms around him. "Thank you so much for such a fun time. I love staying here."

"We love having you. Any time, buddy."

"And thanks for getting me off that bunny slope," Caden said in a loud whisper.

Lucas gave him a playful bop on the head. "Shh, that's our secret."

"Not anymore," Molly said.

"Have a nice time with Grammy," Lucas said as he held the back door for Caden.

"Tell your kiddos I'll see them at dinner tomorrow."

"Will do."

Molly backed her SUV out of the driveway and headed toward town. "What's going on in the back seat?" she asked Caden, as she did every day when she picked him up at school.

"Nothing much. When will Dad be home?"

"Later today."

"I can't wait."

"I bet he can't wait either. He misses you when he's away from you."

"I miss him, too. Why does it take so long to drive from Houston?"

"It's almost two thousand miles."

"Is that a lot?"

"Sure is. Here, let's count off a mile, starting now. I'll let you know when we've gone a mile." She drove the car along the winding mountain road that led to town. "Right... now. That was a mile, and your dad and Lexi had to drive two thousand of them. You see why it's taking so long?"

"I guess so."

Molly glanced at him in the mirror and saw that he was looking out the window, a contemplative expression on his cute little face. He reminded her so much of his father at the same age, and since Max had been her last baby, he, too, held a special place in her heart. She so admired the way he'd stepped up as a full-time father. He'd done such a beautiful job raising his son, and she was thrilled to see him getting some much-deserved personal happiness with Lexi.

They parked behind the store and crossed Elm Street holding hands on the way to the diner.

Molly knew the days were numbered in which Caden would want to hold hands with his grandmother in public, so she was enjoying every minute while she could.

Megan greeted them with a smile and a wave from the other end of the restaurant as they slid into a booth.

"What do you feel like?" Molly asked.

"My usual."

"A boy cannot live on chicken nuggets alone."

Caden flashed a grin that was all Max. "He can sure try."

"Haha," Molly said.

Megan came over to take their order. "Nice to see you guys."

"You, too," Molly said. "Are you still floating over finishing your book?"

"I can't believe it's done. It took years."

"We're all so proud of you."

"Thanks, Molly. What can I get you guys?"

Molly ordered a grilled cheese, while Caden asked for his usual.

"Coming right up," she said.

While they waited for the food, Molly withdrew the art supplies and paper she'd tucked into her purse and put them on the table. She pushed the paper toward Caden. "I was thinking you should make a welcome-home card for your dad and Lexi."

"Does it have to include her? Couldn't it just be for Dad?"

Molly had suspected he might say that, thus the reason she'd invited him to lunch. "Your dad really cares about her a lot. He has since he was just a little bit older than you are now. If she hadn't gotten sick, they probably would've gotten married, and you wouldn't be here."

"How come?" he asked, his blond brows furrowing in confusion.

"Your dad never would've dated your mom if he was with Lexi."

"Oh."

"I want you to do something for me."

"What?"

"I want you to think about what your dad has done for you since you were a baby. Other than the time he's at work, he's been with you. He hasn't had much time for a life of his own that doesn't include you, which was fine with him because he loves you so much. But now, he has a chance to have you *and* Lexi, which will make him even happier than he already is. Don't you want that for him?"

"I do, but…"

"But what, honey?"

"I don't want everything to change," he said, his chin quivering.

"Sweetheart, the things that matter most will never change. Your dad will love you as much as he always has. That could never change. Do you see how happy Uncle Will and Aunt Cameron are together, or Uncle Lucas and Aunt Dani?"

He nodded.

"Don't you want that for your dad, too?"

"I guess."

"You're the most generous boy I've ever met. Do you know that?"

"Really?"

"Uh-huh. You take such good care of your baby cousins. You don't care if they break your toys or pinch your toes or pull your hair."

"I love them."

"I know you do, and you love your dad. That's why I want you to be just as generous to him as you are to your cousins. Can you do that for me?"

He nodded, even though he didn't seem completely sold.

She nudged the paper and crayons closer to Caden. "In eleven short years, you'll leave for college, and your dad will be all by himself. We don't want him to be lonely, and you know he would be if he was all alone after you move out."

Caden took the paper and opened the box of crayons.

Megan brought an ice water with lemon for Molly and a chocolate milk for Caden.

"Thank you," they said.

"Another thing I want you to think about," Molly said after Megan had moved on, "is how cool your dad has been about your mom coming back into your life."

Caden looked up at her. "What do you mean?"

"It isn't easy for him to share you with her, but he did it because it's what you wanted. If you share your dad with Lexi, you'd be doing what's best for him. You see how that works?"

"I think so."

"Sometimes doing what's best for the people we love isn't always the easiest thing, but it's the generous thing. It would make your dad very sad if you weren't nice to Lexi simply because you don't want things to change. One thing about life is that things are always changing, but change doesn't have to be scary. Sometimes it can be awesome, like when you have more people in your life who love you."

Caden worked on the card while thinking about what Molly had said. "What if Lexi doesn't like me?"

"She already likes you."

"How do you know?"

"Because you, Caden Abbott, are a great kid, and anyone would be lucky to have you in their lives."

He rolled his eyes. "You're my grammy. Of course you think I'm a great kid. You have to think that."

"No, I don't, and I wouldn't say it if it wasn't true. I have a lot of experience with kids."

Caden snorted with laughter.

"*A lot.* I know good kids, and you, my friend, are the best of the best. Lexi will love you as much as the rest of us do. I have no doubt. She's a really nice person, and I think, if you give her a chance, you might love her, too."

While they talked, he'd drawn a rainbow. Under it was a boy, a yellow dog and a picture of their house. He wrote, *Welcome Home Dad and...* "How do you spell Lexi?"

"L-E-X-I."

He wrote it down. Inside, he signed the card: *Love, Caden and Daisy.*

"You did a great job. That will mean a lot to them."

"I want my dad to be happy. He's a great dad."

"Yes, he certainly is. He's one of the best dads I've ever known."

"And you've known a lot of dads."

"That's right."

Megan brought their food to the table and set it down while Molly collected crayons and stashed the card to the side to keep it safe. Megan placed the ketchup next to Caden. "Can I get you guys anything else?"

"I think we're set. Thanks, Megan."

"Thank you," Caden added.

"You're welcome. Enjoy."

As they were finishing their lunches, a truck drove down Elm Street, beeping the horn.

"I believe that's your dad and Lexi," Molly said as she put cash on the table to pay the bill Megan had left. "Should we go find them?"

"Yes!" Caden said.

Before she could grab the card he'd made, he had it in hand and was heading for the door, dragging his coat.

"Thanks, Megan," Molly said with a wave for her daughter-in-law.

"Have a great day!" Megan said.

Molly followed Caden out of the diner, feeling pleased with the way their conversation had gone. She hoped it helped to smooth the way to happily ever after for Max and Lexi.

MAX PULLED THE TRUCK INTO THE DRIVEWAY AT LEXI'S childhood home, located about three miles from his place. "Home sweet home."

She'd been practically bouncing in her seat for the last twenty miles. "I'm so excited!"

"I never would've known."

"Haha. Let's get this done!"

"You, my love, aren't lifting a finger. My brothers and I will be moving you in."

"They don't have to do that!"

"Yes, they do. I've helped them move numerous times. They owe me." He made a call to Lucas. "We're here. Will you call the boys?"

271

"Yep. Be right there."

"Thanks, bro." To Lexi, he said, "All set."

"Did you plan this in advance?"

"Hell yes, I did. I texted him earlier to say we were coming and to get the boys together to move you in."

Lexi leaned across the center console and crooked her finger at him.

He leaned in to meet her halfway. "Yes?"

"A little closer."

Max smiled as he kissed her.

"Thank you."

"Welcome to the Abbott family, where there're six brothers available as needed."

"It's the seventh one who holds a special place in my heart."

A knock on the driver's-side window had them pulling apart.

Max was thrilled to see Caden grinning at him.

He opened the door—carefully—and reached for his son, so happy to see him after the long days apart. "How'd you find me?"

Caden hugged him fiercely. "Grammy knew where to look."

"She's a smart grammy."

Caden thrust a piece of paper at Max. "I made this for you."

Max took the paper and was surprised to see it was a welcome-home card for him—and Lexi. "That's great work, buddy. I love it." He handed it to Lexi. "It's for you, too."

She took it from him and teared up when she saw he'd included her. "Thank you, Caden. That's a beautiful card. It's so good to be home in Butler."

"Are you guys gonna stay in the truck all day?"

Max ruffled Caden's hair. "Nope. We've got moving to do, and you can help."

LEXI COULDN'T BELIEVE HOW MANY ABBOTTS SHOWED UP TO HELP her move into the garage apartment at her childhood home. Not only did all of Max's brothers come, but his cousin Grayson was there, as well as Max's three sisters, his parents and grandfather, who supervised. Even Nolan and Skeeter came from the garage to pitch in.

With so much help, they had most of her things in the apartment in less than half an hour.

"This is amazing," Lexi said, battling more tears. She was already sick of the pregnancy hormones that had her teary-eyed constantly, or so it seemed. "Thank you all so much."

"This is what family does for family," Molly said, hugging her. "And you're family."

"You're going to make her bawl her head off, Mom," Max said, laughing at Lexi's reaction to such a sweet gesture from his mom. "Colton, follow me to St. J to drop off the truck."

"Yes, sir," Colton said, saluting Max.

"You want to come for the ride?" Max asked Caden.

Caden gave him an uncertain look. "Would it be okay if I stayed here?"

Max eyed him curiously. "Sure. I bet Lexi would like more help inside."

"I'd love that," Lexi said, pleased that he'd asked to stay with her.

"I'll be back soon," Max said.

She put her hand on Caden's shoulder. "We'll be here."

Most of the others left to go back to whatever they'd been doing before Max summoned them.

Lexi thanked them all with hugs and promises to return the favor any time.

"We'll see you tomorrow at New Year's Day dinner," Molly said, hugging her again.

"Looking forward to that and everything else."

"Welcome home, Lexi," Lincoln said when he hugged her. "We're so glad to have you back in town."

"It's great to be here. It's all I wanted the whole time I was sick, to get back home to Butler and Max."

"We couldn't be happier to have you, sweetheart," Elmer said when he hugged her. "Congratulations on all the great news," he added in a whisper.

"Thank you, Mr. Stillman."

"Elmer."

"Elmer. That'll take some practice."

"We've got all the time in the world to practice."

After they waved off Molly, Linc and Elmer, Lexi and Caden went upstairs to her apartment.

"You've got a lot of work to do in here," Caden said as he surveyed the stacks of boxes.

"I sure do."

The family had placed all the furniture, and her new bed was set to be delivered the next day, but there were boxes stacked everywhere. She'd brought an air mattress for her first night.

"Where should we start?" Lexi asked him.

"Probably kitchen and bathroom."

"You're a wise young man."

"Grammy says those are the two most important rooms in the house."

"She's right. Let's start in the kitchen."

Lexi pulled the tape off a box labeled KITCHEN and opened it to find the silverware and cooking tools she'd bought at a discount store in Houston. The only money she had was the small inheritance she'd received from her father's parents when they passed, so she had to be frugal until she started working.

She'd heard what Max had said about not having to worry about money, but she meant it when she told him she wanted to be independent. This would be the first time she'd ever lived on her own, and while she looked forward to sharing her life with him, she wanted some time in her own place before they made a home together.

A previous tenant had left a silverware organizer in one of the kitchen drawers, so she put Caden in charge of unloading the stainless-steel pieces from the box and into the drawer.

"How's your vacation been?" she asked him.

"Great! We finally got to ski the big hill again, and I hung out with my cousins a lot."

"That sounds like fun."

"It was. I wish we didn't have to go back to school so soon. Why does vacation go by so fast, but school is so slow?"

Lexi laughed as she unloaded a motley collection of coffee mugs into one of the kitchen cabinets. "That's a very good question." She loved having him all to herself so they could get to know each other better.

"It's so weird how that happens. Vacation flies by and school drags."

"Because one is something you want to do, and the other is something you *have* to do. Big difference."

"I guess so. Did you like school?"

"I loved school. I'm looking forward to getting back to it in January. I'm going to take a few classes online."

"And you're doing that because you want to?" he asked, seeming incredulous.

"Believe it or not, I do want to. Your dad told you I was sick for a long time, right?"

"Yeah, I'm sorry about that."

"Thank you. It was a drag. The whole time I was sick, all I could think about was getting back to my old life, which included school."

"And my dad."

"And your dad."

Caden was quiet after that, so Lexi waited to see if he might say anything else.

A full minute later, he said, "He's a really good dad. A great dad."

"Yes, he is. All he talks about is you and how proud of you he is."

"That's nice," Caden said with a smile.

"Can I say something?" Lexi asked.

"Sure."

"I love your dad. I really, really do. I have since I was about fifteen, if I'm being honest. I never stopped loving him the whole time we were apart. But you—you're his whole life, and I'd never do anything to get in the way of what you two have together. I promise you that."

"I'm not his whole life."

"Yes, you are, Caden. He'd choose you over anything and

anyone."

"I want him to be happy."

"I do, too, which means we both want the same thing. What do you say we work together to make that happen?" She extended a hand to him and held her breath, waiting to see what he would do.

When he reached out to shake her hand, Lexi exhaled.

"I hope you and I can be good friends," she said.

"That'd be cool."

"I think so, too."

CHAPTER TWENTY-SEVEN

*"Love is the joy of the good, the wonder of the wise,
the amazement of the Gods."* —Plato

*A*s he drove the moving truck to St. Johnsbury, Max wondered what was up with Caden wanting to stay with Lexi while he was gone. Once he was in Colton's truck on the way back to Butler, Max said as much to his brother.

"I thought that was odd, too, especially since you just got home," Colton said. "I heard he and Mom had a lunch date at the diner. Maybe she had something to do with it."

"He made a nice card welcoming both of us home. I didn't expect that either."

"He's trying to make room in his life for her, in his own seven-year-old way."

"It's very sweet of him."

"I'm sure it's a relief, too," Colton said. "Since he didn't take her initial presence all that well."

"Not at all, and I was worried that was going to be a problem now that Lexi lives in town."

"Is he the reason why she didn't move in with you guys?"

"Partially. She also wants the chance to live on her own for a while. She's never gotten to do that. She's got a lot of lost time to make up for after being sick for so long."

"Ah, I see. Are you okay with that?"

"Sure. I'm just happy to have her back in my life."

"And who do you have to thank for that?" Colton asked, holding his hand to his ear as if trying to hear better.

"Mom? She pushed me to go to the reunion."

"Oh please, who pulled your head out of your ass when you were *cleaning Caden's room* instead of hanging out with the only girl you've ever loved?"

"I think that was Lucas."

"Shit," Colton said with a laugh. "You're full of it."

"Thank you for giving me a push toward her, oh wise one."

"Now we're talking."

"Can I tell you something that you'll swear you won't tell anyone else?"

"That's a tall order for me."

"I mean it, Colton. No one else."

"Not even Lucy?"

"*No one.*"

"Fine. If you're gonna be that way about it."

"I am. Do you promise?"

"Yes. Now what is this state secret I'm being forced to keep?"

"Lexi is pregnant."

Colton looked over at Max, making the truck swerve. "Whoa. Is it yours?"

"Shut the fuck up. Yes, it's mine. She thought she couldn't have kids after the treatment, so we weren't careful."

"Well, that'll speed things up for you guys."

"For sure. Hopefully before the baby arrives, we can find a place together or add on to Gramps's house. In the meantime, she wants to live alone for a bit, and I want Caden to have time to get used to us together, so it works out."

"Sounds like it. Congrats, Max. I'm truly happy for you and Lexi."

"Thanks. We're excited, and hearing she was pregnant was a lot better than hearing the cancer was back."

"I'm sure it was." Colton glanced over at him. "Are you going to be able to live with the worry of that happening?"

"If it means I get to live with her. The odds are pretty good that she's going to be fine."

"That's great news all around."

"It feels so good to have the big question answered, you know?"

"I do know. I remember what that was like when I realized that Lucy was the only chance I had to be happy in this life and somehow was lucky enough that she felt the same way."

"We're all still trying to figure out why she picked you," Max said with a laugh.

Colton chuckled. "Me, too, brother. Me, too. But thank God she did."

"We're thankful for that, too."

"It takes a special woman to handle me, and Lucy is very, very special."

"Enough already."

"What? I'm just saying that asking a sophisticated woman like her to move to a mountaintop and live without indoor plumbing for years was not your average ask."

"No, it wasn't, and you're a lucky man."

"And I know it. It's worked out well for all of us, hasn't it?"

"Yeah, it really has."

"Thanks to Dad and Gramps."

"Oh jeez, don't let them hear you say that. They're insufferable enough as it is. At least they had nothing to do with me getting back together with Lexi."

"I wouldn't be so sure about that. They've gotten very crafty over the years. Anything is possible."

"I don't care how it happened as long as it did."

THE NEXT FEW MONTHS WOULD GO DOWN AS THE HAPPIEST OF Max's life. Lexi started her classes in mid-January and began working part time at the store on the days she didn't have class. They'd waited until the three-month mark to tell everyone else about the baby, but before they did that, they had to tell Caden.

He'd gotten used to having Lexi around, and the three of

them had fallen into a nice routine that included dinner together just about every day. They went on hikes and spent time with Max's extended family and had helped her parents and grandparents move back into their Butler home in late February.

Max couldn't wait to finally share the news about the baby with Caden, which they planned to do after dinner. He and Lexi had made stew over the weekend, and they were having the last of it with bread and salad he'd grabbed at the store on his way home.

Lexi was picking up Caden on her way home from work, and they were due to arrive any minute.

Max was excited and nervous. He thought Caden would be pumped to be a big brother, but he wasn't entirely sure. He'd ordered a Big Brother shirt online and they were going to give it to him as a gift to tell him the news. He and Lexi had talked about it endlessly and had decided on that as their plan. She'd assured him that she felt confident Caden would be happy, but Max wasn't as certain.

He'd been an only child for almost seven and a half years. That was a long time to occupy center stage. Caden was a special kid, and Max didn't say that because he was his. Everyone said it —grandparents, teachers, coaches, Scout leaders and the parents of his friends. People had nothing but nice things to say about him, a fact that Max took tremendous pride in. He was counting on his son to come through for him at this critical moment.

Lexi was starting to show, so they couldn't wait any longer to tell Caden the news.

Tonight was the night.

When he saw the headlights sweep over the yard, Max decided to stop being nervous and focus on the joy. He was so happy to see them both after a long day apart.

Caden burst into the house, and Daisy ran to him, jumping into his arms to lick his face the way she did every night when they got home. Soon, she'd be too big for him to hold. He loved the way she made Caden laugh with everything she did. "Easy, girl. Give a man a chance to get in the door, will ya?"

Lexi came in after him, carrying Caden's backpack and the

bag she took to work at the store. Her face was flushed from the cold and fuller now due to the pregnancy. She had never been more beautiful to him than she was carrying their child.

Max hugged her and gave her a quick kiss as he relieved her of the bags. They were careful not to overdo the PDA in front of Caden. "Hi."

"Hi there."

He loved the way she smiled at him, the way she looked at him, the way she loved him. Being back with her again had made his already satisfying life complete in so many ways, it would take hours to list them all.

"Are you guys hungry?" Max asked.

"Starving," Caden said, as he did every night.

"Feed Daisy, and then you can eat."

Max was trying to get Caden in the habit of feeding Daisy twice a day, and so far, he was doing well, but sometimes he had to be reminded.

While Daisy chowed down on puppy food, Max served up the stew he and Lexi had made. They'd discovered cooking was another thing they enjoyed doing together. In fact, he enjoyed doing everything with her and couldn't wait until they lived together full time.

She was at their house most nights for dinner and often helped Caden with his math homework, which was a relief to Max. She'd helped him with his math homework back in the day, too. He still sucked at it as badly as he had then.

They had slowly started to feel like a real family, and he gave her credit for not forcing herself on Caden, but rather allowing their relationship to grow organically.

As they enjoyed the stew and salad, Max glanced at Lexi.

She gave him a hesitant smile that lit up her eyes, letting him know she, too, was feeling all the things about what they needed to tell Caden.

Max cleared his throat and took a sip of the beer he'd opened. "So, um, Caden… Lexi and I wanted to talk to you about something."

"Are you getting married?"

"Uh, well…" Max glanced at Lexi for help.

"Hopefully, we will eventually," she said, "but that's not what we wanted to tell you tonight."

Caden's questioning gaze darted between them.

"We got you this," Max said, handing Caden the gift bag they'd put together the night before after he was asleep.

"It's not my birthday or Christmas," he said suspiciously.

"Open it," Max said, reaching for Lexi's hand under the table.

Caden pulled the tissue paper out of the bag and then the T-shirt they'd bought him that said Big Brother and the year the baby was due. His mouth fell open. "You're having a *baby*?"

"Yeah, buddy, we are, and we're so excited to make you a big brother, because you'll be the best one ever."

"A baby," Caden said as tears filled his eyes. "I'm going to be a big brother."

"That's right. Are you excited?"

"Yeah. Of course I am. Is it a boy or a girl?"

"We don't know," Lexi said. "We've decided to let it be a surprise."

"What do you hope for?" Max asked him. "A baby brother or sister?"

"I'm fine with either," Caden said as he put on the shirt. "Can I wear it to school tomorrow?"

"Sure," Max said, pleased with how happy his son seemed about the news.

Lexi gave his hand a squeeze and smiled at him.

"So why aren't you guys getting married? You're having a baby, Lexi is here all the time anyway, and she helps me with math."

Max glanced at her. They hadn't talked much about that as they prepared for the baby and faced the hurdle of breaking the baby news to Caden. "I don't know why we aren't getting married yet. We haven't really gotten there."

"Well, you should," Caden said, folding his arms. "Why don't you ask her, Dad?"

"Like, um, now?"

Caden gave him a challenging look. "Now would be good."

"It's okay," Lexi said with a nervous giggle. "You don't have to, Max."

"Yes, he does. You're having a baby. He loves you. I love you. You should get married."

Lexi stared at Caden. "You… you love me?"

Caden shrugged. "Don't make a big deal out of it."

"It's a very big deal," Lexi said tearfully as she leaned in to hug and kiss Caden, who tolerated her affection admirably. "And guess what?"

"What?"

"I love you, too."

Caden grinned at her.

"Hang on just a second," Max said as he got up and left the room.

"WHERE'D HE GO?" CADEN ASKED LEXI. "THINGS WERE JUST getting interesting."

Lexi laughed as her heart pounded with excitement and anticipation. Was this really happening?

"When will the baby come?" Caden asked her.

"In the fall."

"That's a long time from now."

"We've got a lot to do before then. It'll be here before we know it."

Max returned to the room, looking as undone as she felt. He moved his chair out of the way and then dropped to his knees before her. "Cade, come here, will you?" Max held out a hand to his son.

When Caden stood next to his dad, Max put an arm around him and then looked up at Lexi with his heart in his eyes. "My son and I were doing fine for years, but since you came back into my life and into his, we've discovered there's a lot of ways to improve on 'fine.' You bring the light and the laughter and the love. So much love." Max seemed to falter for a second before he found his composure again. "In all the years we were apart, I was looking for you, for what I have with you, and it took seeing you again to realize there's only one you, and no one else will ever do. Will you marry me?"

"And me?" Caden added, making them laugh through tears.

"Yes," Lexi said, reaching for them. "I'll marry you both."

They hugged for the longest time as tears spilled down her cheeks. This was really happening. She was going to marry Max Abbott—and his beautiful son. Dreams did come true. She was living proof of that.

"I forgot the best part," Max said, pulling back to reach for her left hand.

Lexi held her breath as he slid a diamond solitaire onto her ring finger. "It was my grandmother's engagement ring. Gramps gave it to me to give to you when the time was right."

"Oh, Max, it's beautiful! I'll treasure it always because it was hers."

"Why do girls cry when they're happy?" Caden asked, making them laugh.

Max used a napkin to wipe away her tears and then kissed her.

"We cry when we're happy because our hearts are so full, they overflow with tears," Lexi said.

"That's weird. Can I go watch TV?"

"After you clear the table."

Caden made fast work of clearing the table, while Max and Lexi lingered, still in happy shock over how this evening had unfolded.

"So," Max said to her after Caden had left the room, "that happened."

Lexi held up her hand for another look at the gorgeous ring. "It sure did."

"Are you happy, love?"

"You really have to ask? I've never been so happy. Not only do I get you, but I get your wonderful, adorable son and a new baby to love and your big family and this town I love so much. I spent a decade in and out of the hospital dreaming of the life I have now. Yes, Max, I'm happy. Are you?"

"God, yes. I never knew this kind of happy was possible. It's even better than it was the first time around."

"Because we know now how precious it is."

"Yes, we do. When do you want to get married?"

"Can we wait until after the baby so I'm not pregnant in the pictures?"

He gave her hand a gentle tug, brought her onto his lap and wrapped his arms around her. "Whatever you want, sweetheart."

"I have everything I've ever wanted—and then some."

"Me, too," Max said, kissing her. "Me, too."

LATER THAT NIGHT, MAX TUCKED CADEN INTO BED. "THANKS FOR your support earlier. It meant a lot to me and Lexi."

"You wouldn't be engaged if it wasn't for me," Caden said with a grin.

"That's true. Thanks for giving me the push."

Caden shrugged. "It's what you wanted. I just helped you get it."

"You know that if you weren't happy about Lexi and the baby, I couldn't be either."

"I know. Grammy told me that you couldn't be happy unless I was."

Max tipped his head as he gazed at Caden. "She said that?"

"Uh-huh. She said you really loved Lexi and that it was important to you that I do, too, or you wouldn't be happy. I want you to be happy."

"Grammy is very wise."

"She's the best grammy."

"She sure is." Max bent to kiss his forehead. "Get some sleep, pal. I love you."

"Hey, Dad?"

"Yeah?"

"Will you love the baby more than you love me?"

Max shook his head. "I'll love the baby differently than I love you. You and me... We'll always be special friends because of the seven years we were a team. Nothing and no one could ever change the bond we have. You know that, right?"

He nodded.

"I'll love the baby so, so much, but you and me..." Max held up his hand for a fist bump. "Best friends forever."

Caden smiled and returned the fist bump. "Best friends forever."

"Night, buddy. Sleep tight."

"Night, Dad."

CHAPTER TWENTY-EIGHT

"To love abundantly is to live abundantly, and to love forever is to live forever." —Henry Drummond

*M*ax joined Lexi in the living room, where she was curled up on the sofa under a blanket, e-reader in hand. He sat next to her and reached for her free hand, linking their fingers. "We need to call the parents and tell them our news."

"You go first," she said, handing him the phone from the end table.

Max took the phone and dialed the number at the barn.

"Hi, honey," his mom said. "How was the stew?" She'd shared her recipe with them.

"Excellent."

"Good."

"So, we told Caden about the baby over dinner."

"How'd that go?"

"Really well. He's excited, doesn't care if it's a boy or a girl, and the fall is too long to wait."

"That's great," Molly said with a chuckle. "He'll be the best big brother ever. He has so much experience with his younger cousins."

"Yes, he will. He wanted to know when we were getting married."

"What'd you tell him?"

"That we hadn't really got there yet, and he said why not, and one thing led to another, and now Lex and I are engaged."

"Oh, Max," Molly said on a long exhale. "That's wonderful news! He and Lexi are engaged! Dad and Gramps are thrilled, too. Congratulations, Max. We couldn't be happier for you guys —and for us."

"I heard you might've helped things along for us."

"How so?"

"You talked to Caden about me and Lexi?"

Lexi gave him a questioning look.

"We talked ages ago, the day you guys got home from Texas."

"I think that made a very big difference for us, Mom, so thanks for doing that."

"All I wanted was for you to have a real chance with Lexi, because I knew she was the one you wanted. I was sensing some pushback from Caden, so I thought it might help if he and I talked about it."

"It helped a lot." Max had another thought all of a sudden. "The day we got back from Texas... That was why he stayed with Lexi while I went to return the truck. Because you'd talked to him."

Lexi placed a hand on her heart, letting him know what she thought of what his mother had done to help them.

"Yes, I suppose that might've been why."

"I get it now, and I'm very thankful for that and ten million other things since the day I was born and especially since the day he was born. I never would've survived single parenthood without you and Dad and the rest of the family."

"Every one of those days has been a joy to me and us, Max. Every one of them."

"Well, thanks. For everything."

"You got it. When can I look forward to a wedding?"

"Probably later next fall, after the baby. Lexi doesn't want to be pregnant in the wedding pictures."

"Can't say I blame her. Tell her we said congratulations."

"Thank you, Molly," Lexi said.

"Love you, Lex. Thanks for making my boys so happy."

"It's my pleasure."

"We're going to call her parents now."

"They'll be over the moon."

"See you tomorrow."

"See you then, son. Love you all."

"Love you, too."

MOLLY PUT DOWN THE PHONE AND DID A HAPPY DANCE ACROSS the family room where her husband and father were trying to watch *Jeopardy!* Who cared about the Daily Double when Max Abbott was *engaged*?

"This right here is what victory looks like, boys! Ten kids, married, engaged or happily cohabitating."

"And you were responsible for exactly one of them," Linc said.

"Is that what you think?" Molly asked, brow raised.

"What's that supposed to mean?"

"Do you honestly think you two were the ones making all this happen?"

"We were," Elmer said indignantly.

"No, you were not."

"I brought Cameron here to build the website, and she met Will," Linc said.

"Six months before she came, I talked to Patrick about how we should get her and Will together. We came up with the idea of her coming up to pitch a website to you."

"You did not!" Linc said.

"Did so! And I told Patrick that he ought to meet our Mary Larkin when he came for the wedding, and we all know how that worked out. Not to mention me suggesting Colton and Lucy come to dinner with us after the website presentation because I saw a spark of something when they met in the conference room that day."

"Well, I sure as hell know that you didn't buy the diner to keep Megan in town," Elmer said.

"No, but I told Brett about the job in France to clear the way for Megan to take over the diner and suggested that she ask Hunter for help with the accounting."

"You're diabolical," Elmer said.

"You have no idea," Molly said with a smug grin.

"What about Lucas and Dani?" Linc asked. "That happened because I brought Amanda here, and that caused a rift with him and Landon."

"The night Lucas met Dani, he called and asked me to vouch for him with her. I gave him such a glowing review that she couldn't help but fall in love with him."

"Did you also push Charley off a mountain so that Tyler would have to come to her rescue?"

"Nope, but when Vivienne Westbrook called me in England to tell me what'd happened and that Tyler had stepped up for Charley, I extended our trip by four days to give them more time together."

Linc's mouth opened in shock. "You... You were so mad when you got home and found out what the kids had kept from you!"

"I was *thrilled*. I thought Tyler was the perfect man for our Charley for years before they got together. Vivienne and I had talked many times about how we might get them together."

"Can you believe this?" Linc asked Elmer.

Elmer eyed his daughter with amusement and pride. "She's her mother's daughter."

"What does that mean?" Linc asked.

"Why do you think I didn't kill you that first week you came home to Butler holding my Molly's hand like you had some right to? Because my Sarah knew true love when she saw it and told me in no uncertain terms to butt out and leave you two kids alone."

"Aw, I never knew that," Molly said, smiling at the memory of her sweet mother. "She was the best."

"She sure was," Elmer said.

"What about Gavin and Ella?" Linc asked. "And Hannah and Nolan? I messed with Hannah's car myself, so I know you didn't do that."

"I'll give you that one, but I was the one who told Nolan to keep asking everyone about her so it would get back to her that he was checking on her all the time. I told him I felt like that was having an impact on her and eventually it would matter when he finally got around to asking her out."

"This is unbelievable," Linc said.

"You boys were so cute thinking you were the ones making it all happen, when the great and powerful Oz was working ten steps ahead of you," Molly said with another happy dance that had her hips swinging and her arms over her head. "As for Ella and Gavin, Amelia and I had been working on that one for *years*. Gavin wasn't ready yet, but once he was, well, let's just say Amelia and I made sure things worked out for them."

Linc sat back in his recliner, clearly stunned.

"What about Wade and Mia?" Elmer asked.

"That one was a genuine shock to me," Molly conceded. "But the minute I saw how crazy he was about her, I was all in."

"Was that before or after you expressed grave concerns about our son marrying a woman we'd never met?" Linc asked.

"After." Molly smiled at her husband. "But not long after. I dropped off their wedding night dinner, don't forget."

"I brought Amanda here," Linc said, "so there's no way you can take credit for that."

"I *kept* Amanda here when she was thinking about leaving town after the fire."

Linc raised a brow, conveying skepticism.

"Ask her about the talk we had and how she told me she was thinking about going home to her mom and getting out of Landon's way. I told her that was the last thing Landon would want her to do and look at them now." After a beat, she said, "Face it, boys. You're nowhere near as clever as I am."

Molly leaned in, going for the kill. "And while we're at it, you should know that I encouraged Ray to ask out my sister and suggested to Grayson that he ought to talk to Emma at Hunter and Megan's wedding. I was busy that night with Ray and Grayson and then with Chloe showing up to relinquish custody of Caden."

"I can't believe this," Lincoln said to Elmer. "How'd she get this by us?"

"It's like she said, my friend," Elmer said with a grin, "we're just not as clever as she is."

"Speak for yourself," Lincoln said with a scowl for his father-in-law.

"You boys were so cute thinking you were responsible for all the kids finding their forever loves." Molly patted Linc on the head. "So cute."

"I'll give you cute," he said in a low growl.

"Max is engaged! All our kids have found their happily ever afters. Most of Hannah's have, too. Wasn't that your goal?"

"It was, but we wanted to be the ones who did it," Linc said.

"Who cares who did it? It's done. That's what matters. Right?"

"Of course," Linc said, still sounding miffed.

"I just wanted everyone to be as happy as we are," Molly said, kissing his cheek. "You can't fault me for that, can you?"

"Never, love," he said, softening a bit.

"I'm sorry to rain on your parade."

"You're not sorry. Is she, Elmer?"

"Not even kinda."

"You're supposed to be on my side, Daddy."

"I am, most of the time, but this time, I'm with Linc."

"Thank you, Elmer."

"Max is *engaged!*" Molly said, still in amazement. "We've got another wedding to plan!"

A FEW MILES FROM THE BARN, MAX HELD HIS NEW FIANCÉE IN BED and whispered with her in the dark about plans and dreams and babies.

"Are you happy?" he asked her.

"So happy," she said with a giddy-sounding laugh. "I feel so lucky to get to spend my life with you and Caden."

"I'm so glad you guys love each other."

"He's been wonderful to me. So sweet and welcoming."

"We have my mom to thank for that."

"She really stepped up for us."

"She sure did, but then again, she always does."

"I'm so lucky to have such a wonderful mother-in-law."

"My sisters-in-law love her."

"I can see why. She's the best. She was always so nice to me when we were first dating. I felt so at home at the barn any time I was there."

"That's how she is, and she made having ten kids look like no big deal."

"Ten kids. I just can't imagine that."

"How many do you want?"

"One more would work for me."

"That sounds good to me, too."

Lexi snuggled in closer to him. "It all sounds good to me."

"Why don't you stay tonight?"

Usually, she went home in the wee hours of the morning so Caden wouldn't catch them in bed together. Max hated sending her off alone into the cold darkness and made her text him when she got home.

"Are you sure?"

"I'm very sure that I want you here with me every night for the rest of my life. You're welcome to officially move in with us whenever you're ready to. I hope you know that."

"I do. Thank you for understanding that I wanted to live on my own for a while, even if I spend most of my time here with you guys."

"I understand that you're making up for a lot of lost time, and I'm happy to support that in any way I can. But I don't want you driving home in the middle of the night anymore. I hate that."

"I know you do, and I've told you not to worry. I learned to drive on these roads, and I'm perfectly fine."

He gave her shoulder a squeeze. "You're much safer here with me."

"And happier. You've ruined me for sleeping alone."

"Good, then my work here is finished."

Lexi lifted her head off his chest and kissed him as she gazed into his eyes. "Max Abbott, your work here is just beginning."

EPILOGUE

The following December...

*D*ear Cletus,
 Another year has passed us by, and things are still trucking along here in Butler. But I sure do miss arguing with you and Percy. It was so good to talk to you on the phone the other week, but as you said, I can't fit an update on my family into a twenty-minute call, so I'll give you the highlights here.

My grandson Wade and his wife, Mia, welcomed their third child, a boy named Crosby, in August. Then Charley and Tyler finally tied the knot in a low-key ceremony at their house with the girls serving as their attendants. Charley always said she never wanted to get married, but she changed her mind at some point. They're as happy as always, but even more so since the wedding, if you ask me.

Max and Lexi's daughter, Alexandra, was born in early September, and they were married in late October in a joyful ceremony held in the backyard at the barn. Caden served as his father's best man, with the entire family and extended family in attendance as the final Abbott took the plunge. Lexi's parents and grandparents are so glad to be back home in Butler. They couldn't contain their tears at the wedding.

What a truly wonderful day it was for all of us. Max was

glowing with happiness as he married his first and only love with his two beautiful kids by his side and in his arms. Caden has stepped into his role as big brother with great aplomb and affection for his baby sister. She will have a fierce protector in him as she grows up. Caden is seeing quite a lot of his mom and her new husband, Ben. They come to his baseball and soccer games and attended the Christmas show at school. He spends an occasional weekend with them. They're expecting their first baby in the spring, and Caden is excited about another baby sibling. He's adjusted well to having her back in his life. We're all happy for them.

Lexi is now halfway through her five-year wait to be declared cured of her cancer. We continue to pray every day for her continued recovery. If you ask me, that gal is the picture of robust health, and her days of fighting illness are long behind her now.

We took some amazing family photos at Max and Lexi's wedding, and I've enclosed three of them. The first is all the Abbotts. The second is all the Colemans. And the third is the entire crew. A friend of Izzy's helped her coordinate the group photos so Izzy could be in them, and they came out great. There I am, front and center in all of them, right where I want to be.

Ella and Gavin had their fourth child, a girl named Clara, in October, and my granddaughter Sarah got engaged to her boyfriend, Nathanial, in October. We like him a lot, and we're excited for them. Sarah, Jackson and Henry are all planning weddings for next year, which will be the last of them for a while.

The store had another banner year, topping last year's take by five million bucks. The kids have decided to start a foundation to share their good fortune with the community. They're focused on providing food, clothing, shelter and other essential items like money for utility bills to those in need. I give them credit for putting up a website that provides a simple way to make money available quickly to those in crisis. They've named it the Stillman-Abbott Family Foundation. I'm deeply honored to be included in the name and proud of all they've accomplished with my parents' humble little business. They would be so amazed and delighted!

In other news, our dear friend Bob Guthrie (Gavin's dad) had his memoir published this fall, and it's been very well received. The story of an army general who loses his precious son to war is a riveting and emotional read, and I highly recommend you get a copy of General. The Guthries recently welcomed their two hundredth guest to Guthrie House. The work they do there in Caleb's name has made such a difference to so many.

Speaking of books, our own Megan Abbott (Hunter's wife) has published the first in her Mountain Rescue Series, called Home to You, to great reviews and encouraging sales. She's decided to independently publish because, as she says, she doesn't have time to breathe with three kids, a diner to run and books to write. Deadlines would take all the fun out of it for her, so she'll publish the second book in the series when it's ready. We're so proud of her!

After the holidays, Linc and Molly are leaving me to my own devices for a whole month while they tour France and Italy with his brothers and sister and their spouses. They're so excited for the trip, and I'm planning a few keg parties while Mom and Dad are gone. Haha! In fact, they're shipping me off to Ray and Hannah's along with the dogs, so I won't have to take care of myself. It's funny how I did everything on my own for years after Sarah died, and now my Molly has turned me into a spoiled, kept man. I quite like that! Hannah has promised to continue the spoiling while I'm with them. In fact, I suggested she might try to outdo her sister, and her eyes lit up with glee when I said that.

Everyone here is healthy, happy, productive and looking ahead to another new year—number ninety-two for this old goat, but I'm still going strong. Even with all my grands happily settled, there's still a lot of work left to be done around here with all the great-grands, and I love every minute with them. I still do my rounds, stopping to see the local kids just about every day. They're always happy to see Grandpa-Great, as he usually comes bearing treats from the store. I even have something for

Fred and Dexter when I get to Hannah's, and of course I keep biscuits in the truck for all my fur pals! Life is good. I'm blessed beyond measure, and I know it.

I hope you and your family have a wonderful holiday season, and all the best to you and yours in the new year. Let's talk again on the phone real soon.

Your friend,
Elmer

~

WELL, THAT'S A WRAP ON THE DELIGHTFUL ABBOTT-COLEMAN-Stillman family, which has been a big part of my life for the last ten years. Every minute I spent in Butler was a joyful pleasure, and I so appreciate the support of the readers who embraced these characters, the moose, the dogs and all the craziness.

I was halfway through the writing of this book when it occurred to me that maybe Molly was more involved in the matchmaking shenanigans than we thought, so that was fun to write! I also LOVED writing Max and Lexi's second-chance romance and how thankful they were to have found each other twice in a lifetime.

I'm not making any promises, but I hope to someday revisit Butler for a catch-up.

Please join The Long and Winding Road Reader Group at *www.facebook.com/groups/thelongandwindingroadreaders/* to talk about Max and Lexi's story with spoilers allowed.

As I say a fond farewell to this series, I want to thank the Orton family and the staff of the Vermont Country Store for their hospitality over the years. It's amazing what came of me seeing a report on NBC News about the store and its third-generation proprietors. I enjoyed exploring the stores Weston and Rockingham and creating my own fictional version of their incredible stores.

Thank you, as always, to the incredible team that supports me behind the scenes: Julie Cupp, Lisa Cafferty, Jean Mello, Nikki Haley and Ashley Lopez. A shout out to Dan, Emily and

Jake for author support services and Gwen Neff for continuity help. Many thanks to my editors Linda Ingmanson and Joyce Lamb, as well as my front-line beta readers Anne Woodall, Kara Conrad and Tracey Suppo.

Thank you to the Vermont Series beta readers: Jennifer Anderson, Marchia Jones, Deb Tilden, Katy Nielsen, Alice Shea and Doreen Pagliaro.

And to the readers who've embraced my tiny mountain town, a moose named Fred and a family of kids raised in a barn, thank you for coming on this ride with me. I loved every minute I spent in this world with these beloved characters.

Much love,

Marie

ALSO BY MARIE FORCE

Contemporary Romances Available from Marie Force

The Green Mountain Series

Book 1: All You Need Is Love *(Will & Cameron)*

Book 2: I Want to Hold Your Hand *(Nolan & Hannah)*

Book 3: I Saw Her Standing There *(Colton & Lucy)*

Book 4: And I Love Her *(Hunter & Megan)*

Novella: You'll Be Mine *(Will & Cam's Wedding)*

Book 5: It's Only Love *(Gavin & Ella)*

Book 6: Ain't She Sweet *(Tyler & Charlotte)*

The Butler, Vermont Series

(Continuation of Green Mountain)

Book 1: Every Little Thing *(Grayson & Emma)*

Book 2: Can't Buy Me Love *(Mary & Patrick)*

Book 3: Here Comes the Sun *(Wade & Mia)*

Book 4: Till There Was You *(Lucas & Dani)*

Book 5: All My Loving *(Landon & Amanda)*

Book 6: Let It Be *(Lincoln & Molly)*

Book 7: Come Together *(Noah & Brianna)*

Book 8: Here, There & Everywhere *(Izzy & Cabot)*

Book 9: The Long and Winding Road *(Max & Lexi)*

The Wild Widows Series—a Fatal Series Spin-Off

Book 1: Someone Like You

Book 2: Someone to Hold

Book 21: Trouble After Dark *(Deacon & Julia)*

Book 22: Rescue After Dark *(Mason & Jordan)*

Book 23: Blackout After Dark *(Full Cast)*

Book 24: Temptation After Dark *(Gigi & Cooper)*

Book 25: Resilience After Dark *(Jace & Cindy)*

Book 26: Hurricane After Dark *(Full Cast, coming 2023)*

The Quantum Series

Book 1: Virtuous *(Flynn & Natalie)*

Book 2: Valorous *(Flynn & Natalie)*

Book 3: Victorious *(Flynn & Natalie)*

Book 4: Rapturous *(Addie & Hayden)*

Book 5: Ravenous *(Jasper & Ellie)*

Book 6: Delirious *(Kristian & Aileen)*

Book 7: Outrageous *(Emmett & Leah)*

Book 8: Famous *(Marlowe & Sebastian)*

The Treading Water Series

Book 1: Treading Water

Book 2: Marking Time

Book 3: Starting Over

Book 4: Coming Home

Book 5: Finding Forever

Single Titles

Five Years Gone

One Year Home

Sex Machine

Sex God

Georgia on My Mind

True North

The Fall

The Wreck

Love at First Flight

Everyone Loves a Hero

Line of Scrimmage

Romantic Suspense Novels Available from Marie Force

The Fatal Series

One Night With You, *A Fatal Series Prequel Novella*

Book 1: Fatal Affair

Book 2: Fatal Justice

Book 3: Fatal Consequences

Book 3.5: Fatal Destiny, *the Wedding Novella*

Book 4: Fatal Flaw

Book 5: Fatal Deception

Book 6: Fatal Mistake

Book 7: Fatal Jeopardy

Book 8: Fatal Scandal

Book 9: Fatal Frenzy

Book 10: Fatal Identity

Book 11: Fatal Threat

Book 12: Fatal Chaos

Book 13: Fatal Invasion

Book 14: Fatal Reckoning

Book 15: Fatal Accusation

Book 16: Fatal Fraud

Sam and Nick's Story Continues....

Book 1: State of Affairs

Book 2: State of Grace

Book 3: State of the Union

Book 4: State of Shock

Historical Romance Available from Marie Force

The Gilded Series

Book 1: Duchess by Deception

Book 2: Deceived by Desire

ABOUT THE AUTHOR

Marie Force is the *New York Times* bestselling author of contemporary romance, romantic suspense and erotic romance. Her series include Fatal, First Family, Gansett Island, Butler Vermont, Quantum, Treading Water, Miami Nights and Wild Widows.

Her books have sold more than 12 million copies worldwide, have been translated into more than a dozen languages and have appeared on the *New York Times* bestseller list more than 30 times. She is also a *USA Today* and #1 *Wall Street Journal* bestseller, as well as a Spiegel bestseller in Germany.

Her goals in life are simple—to finish raising two happy, healthy, productive young adults, to keep writing books for as long as she possibly can and to never be on a flight that makes the news.

Join Marie's mailing list on her website at *marieforce.com* for news about new books and upcoming appearances in your area. Follow her on Facebook at *www.Facebook.com/MarieForceAuthor*, Instagram at *www.instagram.com/marieforceauthor/* and TikTok at *https://www.tiktok.com/@marieforceauthor?*. Contact Marie at *marie@marieforce.com*.

Made in the USA
Middletown, DE
14 January 2023

22136034R00175